KV-389-505

A DESIRABLE RESIDENCE

Darrington, a small country village, is not destined to remain so; development consortia rumble nearer. The Grots are leaving London, buying in, taking over.

Ella Caine, almost divorced, has a lover to add sparkle to her otherwise pointless days. He is Philip Russell, failure in farming and in life. The Graysons are delightfully unsuited to running the village shop, and the couple who own the Black Swan public house unashamedly gay. Tom Antony, villager, sees and knows all, says little.

A DESIRABLE RESIDENCE

A DESIRABLE RESIDENCE

by
Sheila Cole

Dales Large Print Books
Long Preston, North Yorkshire,
England.

British Library Cataloguing in Publication Data.

C001971778

Cole, Sheila
   A desirable residence.

   A catalogue record for this book is
   available from the British Library

   ISBN 1-85389-426-5 pbk

First published in Great Britain by Robert Hale Ltd., 1990

Published in Large Print 1993 by arrangement with Robert
Hale Ltd.

Printed and bound in Great Britain by
T.J. Press (Padstow) Ltd., Cornwall, PL28 8RW.

ONE

The headline shouting up from this week's rag was different, Ella Caine noted. 'LOCAL LANDOWNERS OFFERED MILLIONS TO SELL.' No question mark this time. Fact, not speculation—that's if you can believe what newspapers print. Other attention grabbers had been less positive. 'THE THREE D's TO BECOME DARRINGTON NEW TOWN?' 'FIVE HUNDRED EXECUTIVE-TYPE HOUSES TO BE BUILT?' Yes to both, so it now seemed. People she knew and probably liked must be squirming under the burden of their guilty secret, rehearsing their excuses for when the crunch came. Conservation and principles are all very well but, let's face it, money is magic. And so it begins.

The kitchen in which Ella and the newspaper sat was well appointed and sunny, a comfortable family room importuning the family to linger. Only there was no family, just Ella, and the two small terrier dogs squabbling peevishly over a crust of toast.

For the umpteenth time she wondered why she had been fool enough to take on such a disagreeable double act. She rolled the newspaper and whacked two black noses before marching the offenders out of the kitchen and up the stairs. Door open, door shut and repeat the exercise. In separate bedrooms, just as she and David had ended up sleeping. Until he left and she stayed on.

There was a pier-glass opposite the bathroom and she examined herself as though assessing a person newly introduced. No country bumpkin she. Belted tailored navy slacks and cream wool blouse tucked in. Navy waistcoat (soft suede), navy scarf (carefully casual). And all for taking the dogs out, or dashing to the shop, or calling on Jenni or Fran...no, not Fran, not unless she really had to. And under the outer elegance, what? Hips trim as a boy's, small waist, breasts full and firm as an adolescent's. Mid forties now and looking at least ten years younger. Hardly a line to the smooth olive skin that would tan an attractive brown come the better weather. No wrinkles around the wide brown eyes, no droop to the firm mouth, no grey in the dark curls hugging the neat head. All very satisfactory. Appearances count, or so her mother had said. Repeatedly. They do, Mother, they do, but doesn't what's inside count for something too?

So. Back to the sunny kitchen and the headline and another cup of coffee. Nine-thirty, plenty of time before...before what? Before a dash to the shop or visiting Jenni or counting the tulips or taking the dogs out again. Too much time, although she was loath to admit it. A job would help, though not financially. David was more than generous (he could afford to be) and whatever she earned would probably go straight back in tax. Forget about jobs, think about what to do. Write to the boys? Yes, good idea. Write to the boys, regale them with village gossip (only there wasn't much), update them on the exact state of the garden (as if they cared), describe the weather, exhort cleanliness, sobriety and caution and send her love, masses of it. Did they ever *read* her letters? she wondered. She doubted whether she, in their shoes, would be so inclined.

With pad in front of her, she took up pen and drew a large circle, and then another a fraction smaller inside the first. Not a perfect circle because Darrington wasn't, and the Street she had just drawn, the only main road, meandered stream-like around the shallow bowl of field and woodland known as the Dip. She decorated the Dip, drew in trees and the pond that offered good coarse fishing, and then she moved her pen to the top of the page. How often had she done this? Dozens of times. Friends, acquaintances, tradesmen, all seeking directions to Highcroft Cottage. Her detailed maps must be world-famous by now. Right. This is the main road from Brunton, she would say, drawing it (or from Reading or Aldershot, the M3 or the M4). If you're coming this way you'll pass through Down Darrington two miles before our left-hand turning. And if you find yourself in Upper Darrington you've gone over three miles too far. OK? Watch for the sign, watch for the turning and once you've turned, watch out for the mini-roundabout ahead. Yes, frightfully sophisticated for such a small backwater, but necessary. You can't go *through* Darrington, only around it, and traffic used to come to blows until the council saw sense. (Quite a lot of traffic actually, mornings and evenings. We're commuter territory now. Sad, isn't it?) Turn right at the roundabout and you're into the village proper. Left? Left is Grotland and you don't go there unless you're a Grot. I'll explain all that later. So. Right at the roundabout, past the Foresters' Arms on your left, then the shop on your right—amazing bow windows, very distinctive. The church and the school next, both on your left, and opposite them track up to Dowsett's Farm. There's a board that says so. Village hall right, then the Black Swan the same side and a house on its own just before a field. Briar Cottage. And then it's our lane—you can't miss it. There's a no-through-road sign and another saying HIGHCROFT FARM AND HIGHCROFT COTTAGE only. You can see the farm roof through the trees, slates falling off all over the place. We're the white house half way up. Highcroft Cottage.

She printed 'DARRINGTON' at the top of her map, at which point the upstairs dogs erupted into a frenzy of hysterical barking. She waited until she heard the plop of letters onto the hall carpet, then went to retrieve. Late today—and shut up, you two! Nothing of interest, nothing to stir. Bills, circulars, her monthly gardening magazine. Nothing from the boys, not that there ever was. Nothing from David, ditto.

11

She went back to the table and her map. Not one of her best, she decided. She had been careless; she would improve. Not only that, she would breathe life into the village. Because if Darrington was destined for destruction by smooth-talking filthy rich development consortia, it deserved remembering as it had been. And still was remembered, but only to an extent.

Back to the mini roundabout and the Street leading right. Draw in the stone cottages, those elbowing the Foresters' on either side and those opposite. Antonys and Hubbards. Hubbards and Antonys. Mention one family first, offend the other. Two clans either side of Darrington Street, still active in distrust and dislike, one for the other. No rock-hurling these days but the Montague and Capulet element remains. Intermarriage is a criminal offence punishable by banishment. One unfortunate couple ended up in Brunton, and no crime on earth warrants such an unforgiving life sentence. And the Foresters' itself, tightly pinioned by the Antonys. Square, homely, a little shabby but inviting. Harry Junior running it these days and much more efficiently than Harry Senior ever did. But not so much fun now behind the stout oak door. No carpet slippers, no odd socks, no vest inches below the yellow shirt-sleeves. No one to tell you to frig off. Harry Senior went to his grave in Darrington churchyard still nursing his grudge against the wartime government, still claiming they diddled him out of thousands for the potatoes he grew, digging for Victory. Was he still writing letters wherever he was, lobbying support from presidents, royalty, the Pope even? A nutter, Darrington had called him, but it missed him. No faults with Harry Junior—decent, honest, hard-working—but not the same.

The shop now. It was hard to draw bow windows on a small inked square but Ella tried. The shop, and that meant Adam and Eve, and God knows how they found the guts to marry thirty-two years ago, knowing full well the gamut of ridicule to come. Fig leaves, serpents, apples—there wasn't one feeble joke that hadn't been made at their expense. But marry they did and thank the Lord for that. Gentle wise Adam, straight as a die. Formerly Foreign Office, on the staff of one particular governor for over twelve years. Just kept on following him around the world. Flamboyant, irreverent, vulgar

Eve. Eve Grayson MA. One-time gossip columnist, accurate and acidic; one-time diplomatic wife with a difference. And now village postmistress. The role fitted her as comfortably as raw steak would a Vegan take-away. The Graysons, rock-solid. Despite the odds, a misalliance that had worked a treat. She wrote in their names.

And as we've remembered Harry Senior with affection, let's remember Annie Chalker —with pity. The cottage opposite the shop, that's where Annie lived. A boorish balding schoolmaster inhabits there now; blah-blah wife, two revolting children. Poor Annie. Widowed, pale, limp, lifeless. But compulsively motivated. Annie Chalker threw bottles at full moon and Eve was her only guardian angel. No harm in the woman, the quacks said—wouldn't hurt a fly. Bit of a nuisance, bottle-throwing; makes a noise, makes a mess, but no danger to anyone. A danger to herself, Eve had insisted, and Eve had been right. Annie Chalker cut her wrists with one of her broken bottles one moonlit night. She's in the churchyard too, not far from Harry Senior. But not so Carrie Tring. She's in Parkside along with four of

14

her seven children. Not surprising really. The name Hubbard predominates over Carrie's family tree. Scrubbing out bus shelters, polishing the windows—that was Carrie's compulsion. Or cleaning up road signs with Brillo pads. How strange, the authorities judging Carrie in need of care and protection and leaving lonely Annie to decide her own fate. How many other monumental cock-ups are made every minute of every single day?

So that disposed of nostalgia, Ella thought, moving her pen down the Street. Nostalgia in Darrington proper, that is. What next? The church and the school. No need to linger on either. The church is little more than a Christian monument now, doors open one Sunday in three and the vicar scurrying from one Darrington to another like an anxious black beetle. No organ practice, no bells, no confetti for the kids to scrabble amongst and carry away in grimy fists. If the church disintegrates, what is there left that is solid and safe? If God turns His back on you, do you still give Him your vote?

The churchyard remains open to the public. There are more than a few family plots with space to fill. In death as in life, the Hubbards and Antonys are strictly segregated, their flattened headstones at opposite ends. Another change for the worse—no patterns and shadows to please the eye. And where, as a consequence, has Maggie Hubbard gone? Maggie Hubbard, plump, pleasant, late forties. A lady of generous pleasure, once wont to sell her wares around the church. No intimacy now, no privacy, everything flat: so where the hell has Maggie gone? Still at it by all accounts, but where?

The school. It warranted little mention but she dutifully wrote 'school'. No more than a dozen pupils and scheduled for closure a few months back. And then suddenly...She shivered a little as the import struck home. The headlines *were* true and someone somewhere knew a lot more than he or she was saying.

Familiar ground opposite. Her pen shook as she traced the track up to Dowsett's Farm and wrote the names. Philip and Fran Russell, Dan, Liz and Emma. Dan? That rang a bell somewhere but she couldn't remember why. Such a shame the house is so ugly, sitting into the hill and relatively high up. Red brick and bits added, willy-nilly.

Fourteen years? Yes, it must be. Fourteen years since the Russells bought Dowsett's. Fran was so pretty then, a golden slip of a girl; and Philip golden too and horribly handsome, full of dreams and aspirations. But, as we all know, Philip is also a rotten farmer. Nothing goes right for him. Can't make up his mind and can't make things work. Arable, dairy, sheep, beef, he's tried the lot. Lord, the dramas we've all lived through: sheep on safari, grain stores collapsing, tractors toppling off hillsides. And now it's dairy again with a bit of arable thrown in. Will it work? No. But now that Tom Antony's looking after the fencing we may see an end to the popular sport of early morning heifer-chasing. Tom. She had forgotten him, how unforgiveable. Tom Antony, *real* Darrington, more real by far than Maggie Hubbard for all her games in the grass. Ella Caine took her pen back to the stone cottages beside the Foresters' and wrote two names: Tom Antony and Doris.

And now let's get Dowsett's over and done with. Let's get rid of the guilt and the lust, at least for the time being. Guilt because she and Fran had once been the closest of friends, allies, confidantes, and no longer could be. And why? Because Ella Caine and Philip Russell were lovers of nearly two years' standing and that was where the lust came in. Unashamed animal lust, but now beginning to wane. How would she regard her energetic mate when it had gone? Not too well, she thought, possibly with active dislike.

The telephone rang and she was glad. But not when she answered it.

'Is that the fish shop?' a woman's voice demanded.

'No, it is not.'

Now that she was up and about she ought to do something other. But what? The dogs were scratching from above, and she relented and let them out. Into the garden for five minutes, she said, but with me, so put all thoughts of the Great Escape out of your horrid heads. Her voice sounded strange in her ears and it occurred to her that, apart from their earlier scoldings and her terse telephone response a few minutes since, no other words had passed her lips that day. And it was now...ten-thirty. Only an hour gone since she had last checked. Plenty of time before a dash to the shop or visiting Jenni or...Sod it, I'm not going through all *that* again.

The garden was pretty, it soothed, but it was not enough. The unfinished map drew her back, demanding completion on the day when the writing on the wall had been read and fully understood. She wrote 'village hall' over a solid inked square and remembered the fun it had once been. Jumbles and dances to raise funds for whatever; whist drives and wedding receptions; and amateur dramatics that had them all stuffing hankies in their mouths. Not any more. Outside bookings in the main and coach-loads of foreigners laughing and screeching into the early hours. And scorching the Street with hotter tyres than any Grot's, clocking out and clocking in.

The Swan next. The Black Swan, free house and gold-mine in one. All credit due to Giles and Toby and the unique Henry. Two gays and a straight—an unlikely combination but, by golly, it works. Restaurant always full, booked for weeks ahead. Good bar food, polished tables, fresh flowers. No wonder the Swan's reputation is

19

spreading fast over southern England. Giles, the man about the house, an absolute charmer. How many girls must wish him more available? Dear old Toby, correction dear *young* Toby, sensitive and vulnerable, blushing and twitching when he's upset. Which he often is. And Henry, quite indescribable. A chef any top-rate restaurant or hotel would eagerly employ, but only if he were permanently gagged.

And now the Templetons and Briar Cottage, the last house before the lane up to Highcroft. She wrote the names. Stephen and Jenni Templeton plus three (the children were too young to be significant). The Templetons. Here was trouble; if not in fact, definitely in the making. Stephen, officer and sometimes gentleman but with some sort of madness within. How those blue eyes blazed and burned when the mood took. Stephen with the high-pitched zany laugh, knocking Jenni about, smashing furniture, terrifying the kids. And lovely Jenni almost egging him on. Jenni, sensuous and openly inviting, sinking pints down at the Foresters', singing—if you can call it that—so loud she has to be evicted. And the next day, there they are, both in full combat gear, both in heavy-duty boots, stomping the Street arm-in-arm and laughing like kids playing some dressing-up game.

Almost the end now. She was not going into Grotland, that would be too painful. That would mean Nostalgia with a very capital N. All those lovely old houses tucked away behind trees, all the memories of names and faces. The Swaythlings, the Dykes, the Harringtons, all gone. Gentle folk, a title or two, a few colonels and wing-commanders. Friendly, no show, ready to turn their hands to anything that kept Darrington together as a community. Inflation and the cost of living finished them off. Their money ran out and they moved away. Or they died. And that's when the rush started. It was Fran who christened them Grots, the barristers and bakers, consultants and Stock-Exchange types who took over. They don't belong—they never will but they think they do. Money. They've so much they don't know what to do with it. And so many plums in their flabby-lipped mouths we need a resident interpreter. Now here's a thought. How will the Grots react to the developers? Money fighting money. Should be interesting, that's if you live somewhere distant from Darrington.

So what are we left with? The lane, the cottage and Highcroft Farm. Hardly a house-by-house search of the village but all that was needed. Highcroft Cottage. She wrote David and Ella Caine, John and Andrew, and then she crossed out all names save her own. Ella Caine, living in solitary splendour in a house miles too big for her, a super house that she and David had created from a neglected cottage. Three thousand, that's what they paid Ruth Downing back in '66. Lord alone knows what the place must be worth now, the way prices are rocketing. David. In Oxford now, living with Helen, planning to cement the relationship once his divorce was final. John in the Navy, Andrew at University. Both home every few months or so and a special effort at Christmas. But not really *wanting* to be there; itching always to get back to their own lives. Why? Didn't they like Darrington, didn't they like their mother? Stop it! You're at it again. Analysing, dissecting, probing, and all you end up with is a huge emptiness that hurts.

Highcroft Farm. Apart from the rats, uninhabited for fourteen years. She wasn't sure why the farm featured on her map. Except, perhaps, because someone—she couldn't remember who—had mentioned it was on the market. If so, what sort of idiot would want to buy? Dreadful dilapidated place, the house in a worse state of repair than the tumbled stables and barns. Ruth Downing, the last to live there, had slipped on the stairs in '70 and Sammy, the son, found her three days later. Dead. And six years before that, old Reuben (so she had been told) blew his head off cleaning his gun. Accidental death, the coroner said. And that (again as she had been told) caused the biggest stir Darrington has ever known. Reuben Downing careless with a gun? Not him. Checked everything four, five times did Reuben. Locks and bolts at night, change from a pound, dates on the calendar even. Village legend has it that Highcroft is cursed, a gypsy's curse. If so, if you believe such rubbish, that could account for son Sammy being crushed by a pile of scrap metal a few months back. And Sammy's death could account for Highcroft being on the market. If the rumour was true.

23

Oh Lord, what was she in for? Being realistic, all Highcroft needs is money and there's plenty of that around. Forget how it is, project how it could be. Wonderfully positioned, secluded, at least an acre of land remaining. She was already reading the estate agent's blurb. A very desirable residence.

Done. Finished. Frame it, shall I? Or put it away and forget about Darrington in every possible tense? She chose the latter and opened a dresser drawer and then, as her morning's work disappeared from sight, she remembered. Dan Russell. The bell that had rung earlier had been in celebration of his birthday. She had a card but nothing to go with it. Too late for Brunton. Birthday gifts are for the morning, not mid-afternoon. The shop was her only hope. What a blessing she had remembered in time and another similar that the day had finally found purpose.

A further thought occurred as she went to the car. There was no need to work for gain, she could do so on a voluntary basis. But wouldn't that put her in line with the bored unfulfilled women she tended to despise? Exactly.

24

TWO

She was turning out of the lane and into the street when Toby cut across her bows. Very pink-faced and close to tears by the look of him. She wound down her window.

'Good morning. Lovely day, isn't it? The spring has definitely sprung.'

He came back reluctantly. No doubt about it, there were tears in the brown eyes, tears magnified by his owlish glasses. 'Good morning, Ella. I'm sorry, I didn't see you. Yes, it's a heart-lifting day.'

So why does yours appear to be down in your boots? 'Anything wrong?' she asked. 'You seem a little—discommoded.'

'Do I? I can't think why. I'm in a rush, of course. Giles will be thinking I've left the country.' He trembled a smile. 'I really must dash. See you soon, Ella. Take care.'

Well, well. Trouble at t'Swan? She doubted it. Just Toby, magnifying something out of all proportion. She wondered what, but only until she saw Jenni Templeton coming towards her on the other side of the street. Energetic three-year-olds pulling and pushing, the pram in the middle, Jenni had the look of a dreamer. Judging by the discolouration under one eye and the bruised lips, the dream had been a bad one. Ella stamped hard on the brake pedal.

'Wrong side of the road,' she shouted even before she was out of the car. 'You should be facing the oncoming traffic and you should damn well know that by now, especially with kids.'

From Jenni a smile of sorts. 'I forgot.'

'What happened?' Ella demanded, inspecting the damaged face.

'Stephen happened, what else? He was in a foul mood this morning. You should see the kitchen. It's Connie's day off so I've just left everything to marinate.' A wide smile this time though it must have hurt like hell. 'The joke is we're dining the Major and Missus tonight. How will Captain Templeton explain his wife's unusual appearance? Better still, how will he explain the state of the kitchen? I shall make sure they friggin' well see it.'

Ella frowned towards the twins, now

26

happily assessing the quality of mud in the ditch.

'Don't worry about them, they've heard much worse.'

'Look, I can't stop now, I simply must make the shop. Shall I come down this afternoon and help you clear up?'

'I'm not clearing up. I told you.'

'I'll come anyway.'

She pulled into the shop forecourt just as Tom Antony wobbled his bicycle to an unsteady halt and almost fell off. 'Heavens, Mr Antony, did I do that? Are you all right?'

Straight as a ramrod, at seventy-five Tom Antony was still a fine figure of a man: thick white hair, lean lined face, far-seeing blue eyes. He shook his head sternly at the anxious Ella. 'Now, Mis' Caine, you be careful now. Good men like me's hard to come by these days.'

Doris Antony, far too young and personable to be a widow of over ten years, came to the shop door and smiled at her father-in-law. 'Hello, Dad.'

''Lo Doris. What's it today then?'

'Shepherd's Pie. That suit you?'

'That suits me fine.' He went into the shop. 'Morning, Mis' Grayson, morning,

27

Mr Grayson. Nice drop of sun but it won't last. Leave those bikinis in mothballs, I should.' And he winked at Ella.

'Half of the usual, Tom?'

'That's right, Mis' Grayson, half of the usual.' He paid for the tobacco with care verging on reverence. Pausing in the open doorway, he sniffed the air. 'Wind's veering east. Changes coming with it.'

'Changes for the better?'

'From an east wind?' His smile was wry. 'Nothing good ever came from the east 'cept that blessed star. No, change'll be for the worse.'

'I love that man,' Eve chortled after he had gone. 'Imagine the joy he'd bring to the weather forecasts.' Certain that she would not offend this particular customer she barked, 'Make it snappy, madam. What do you want?'

'I don't know.'

'Great. Super.' An exaggerated sigh. 'It's been a helluva morning, why change the trend?' She furrowed her broad brow and gnawed at dry skin on an index finger. Appreciable warmth to the sun yet she had dressed herself in two thick sweaters and monstrous checked trousers. Unattractive even as a child, the years had not been kind to Eve Grayson. They had neither softened nor refined. At fifty-eight, she could justifiably be described as ugly: coarse skin, broken veins, snub nose, black piggy eyes and yellow teeth. Strong black hair, liberally shot with grey, that defied discipline, man-size hands and feet, body bulges in all the wrong places, it was impossible to find one redeeming feature. Until you knew her. Until her enormous personality burned out all memory of physical defect. You either loved or loathed Eve Grayson and whichever way, you dwelt on what she said and did. Not how she looked. 'You're looking smart,' she said. 'Have you come to the right place? Think, woman, think. What do you want?'

'I just remembered it's Dan Russell's birthday,' Ella said. 'What on earth can I get him?'

'From here? How about a non-stick frying pan? Ella, we just don't cater for sixteen-year-olds, not boys.'

'Lord, is he that old?'

'Money is always acceptable,' Adam said mildly. He was watching them both affectionately. Strange that such a thin grey stooped man should exude such warmth. Sparse grey hair, bushy grey eyebrows, eyes grey behind rimless spectacles. Skin too, grey. An unhealthy pallor, the colour of pain. Such a silly tumble off such a dear old horse millions of years ago (so it seemed). And now the limp, the stick and the constant nagging reminder that too often became acute. But no complaints, no grumbles. Eve grumbled enough for both of them; it was one of her ways of letting off steam.

'But money's so unimaginative,' Ella argued.

'Rubbish.' Eve was positive. 'The imagination works overtime in the spending. Got a card? Slip something in it. Pity, you've just missed Fran.'

'I'm glad.'

Eve arched her heavy black eyebrows and Ella tripped over her tongue to explain.

'I mean to say, it's hardly the done thing, is it? Good thing I caught you, here's Dan's birthday card, that's saved me a trip.' Does that sound plausible? Please, dear God, rid me of the guilt. 'Why has it been such a bad morning?'

'Fran got up a Grot's nose though that's not all bad. Provided the silly bitch returns. Grot, not Fran. Mother Hubbard brought her obscene tree-trunks in for inspection and...'

'You upset Toby?'

'How do you know?'

'I saw him about ten minutes ago. Close to tears.'

'Oh hell!' Having drawn blood from one finger, Eve proceeded to mutilate the another. 'He must have been dawdling for hours. He left here ages ago. Yes, Adam, I *will* ring. I said I would which means I will.'

Toby had already been distressed when he foolishly sought Eve's advice that morning. Eve had things on her mind other than blighted begonias and she had told him so in no uncertain terms. Hurt to the very quick, Toby had departed in a hurry and Adam had seen fit to interfere.

'You were very unkind to him.' The admonishment had been mild, so Eve informed Ella, but Adam had meant what he said.

'He's besotted by his bloody begonias. *I* don't know whether they've contracted hardpad, dry rot or galloping consumption. If he mentions them again I swear I shall go for him with the bacon knife.' Unrepentant, Eve had trumpeted her intention across the

31

empty shop. Empty save for one crisply laundered customer fingering the escargot tins. Out in the back, Doris Antony giggled over the orders she was making up.

'Nevertheless you were unkind. You know how sensitive Toby is. You also know that he thinks you're a direct descendant of the Throwers.'

'For God's sake, why?'

'Because you run the gardening side.'

'I do not. That Nazi at the nurseries runs it. He tells me exactly what to order and how much to charge. All I do is water when the wretched things start wilting.'

Adam had tried very hard to look stern. He lowered his eyebrows to almost spectacles level and narrowed his grey eyes. His effort failed abysmally. He knew this extraordinary woman too well, knew the physiological make-up of her heart: a thin shell of granite and within, a transparent veneer of acerbity protecting a nugget of pure gold.

'You're right, damn you, I was unkind.' Her words supported his analysis. 'I'll ring him in a minute and apologize. I'll even ask Himmler to pop in and prescribe the next time he delivers. That suit you?'

'Good girl.'

32

'Huh!'

At this point in the related tale, a steady stream of shoppers had been seen trudging purposefully towards the emporium, baskets and purses at the ready. Fran Russell among them. Something, Eve now told Ella emphatically, will have to be done about that woman. If she gets any fatter she'll burst. It's such a shame when you remember how she was. Her feet never seemed to touch the ground. Now she bounces like a round rubber ball. *You're* her chum, haven't you said anything? And Ella, hoping no reasons would be required, had to admit that she had not.

'Then you must,' Eve insisted, 'for her own good.'

'It's difficult,' Ella argued. 'It could be called interfering. She knows she's fat—isn't it rather up to her to do something about it?'

'But she obviously isn't. Doing something. Doesn't Philip let rip at her? It wouldn't surprise me to learn he had a bit on the side. Making love to Fran must necessitate meticulous forward planning. How do you gain purchase on something so spherical?'

Philip's bit on the side sought an

immediate change of subject. 'So what's the latest bulletin on Mother Hubbard's legs? Did she tell you.'

'My dear girl, do you honestly believe I allowed her the opportunity? As soon as the elephant legs hove into view I hollered for Doris. May Day, I bellowed. Old Mother Hubbard's under full steam and her disgusting afflictions are freshly bandaged. I will not listen to detailed descriptions of purple veins and rotting flesh, not unless I am forcibly gagged and bound. Doris, being the splendid person she is, rallied to my aid. Giggling. What is there about me that causes Doris to giggle? And Fran it was who suffered the repercussions. I was hovering and heard.'

The recapitulation continued. Fran Russell, searching the shelves for icing sugar with which to garnish Dan's sixteenth birthday cake, had bumped into the Grot beside the freezers. 'Hello,' she said, forced to be sociable. 'Super day, isn't it?'

The other woman had something on her mind. 'What a ghastly person. She's so rude.'

'Who?'

'That big messy woman with the loud mouth.'

'You mean Eve? I disagree entirely. She's wonderful and warm-hearted and we all adore her.' Furious at the outsider, she had forced a sweet smile. 'If you don't like us here you can always go up or down.'

'I beg your pardon?'

'The other Darringtons. They're frightfully sophisticated. There's even a betting shop in one of them.' She examined the newcomer carefully without appearing so to do. How many hours had it taken to achieve the ultimate in casual? The linen safari suit was immaculate, the soft shoes Italian leather, the knotted silk scarf positioned exactly and unobtrusively pinned. Her hair spoiled the effect. It was too smooth and lacquered, and the rings, a half dozen at least, were positively vulgar. Real people wear rings only on special occasions. Repenting a little, Fran assumed interest. 'You're new here, aren't you?'

'We moved in last week. The Harrington house. Do you know it?'

'Very well, and the Harringtons. Super people, salt of the earth. It's so sad, Darrington is losing all the well-beloveds.' God I'm being bitchy. Eve will be proud of me. Out of a corner of an eye she could see the sitting-room curtains twitching with

35

delight. She waggled a plump finger in their direction.

'My name is Alicia Hargreaves.' A smooth sparkling hand was graciously extended.

'Fran Russell and I won't shake. I'm covered with cake mixture.'

'Dowsett's Farm?'

'That's right.'

The thoughts of Mrs Hargreaves were so clear a blind man could have read them. Local farmer, really quite acceptable and one simply *must* make an effort to mix. 'Would you and your husband care to join us for drinks? This Sunday around...'

'Sunday is out, but thanks.'

'How about—'

'Shall we leave it for now? You must be up to your eyes in unpacking.' She had made her escape so nimbly she surprised herself. Eve drew her swiftly inside the sitting-room and closed the door. 'Who is she? Any good?'

'About the same as the others. They've bought the Harrington house.'

'The Harringtons, God bless them.' Eve raised an imaginary glass. 'Yards of mourning at the masthead, muffled drums and reversed boots. They will be missed.'

Quite a morning, Ella thought, I'm rather sorry I missed it. And the Harringtons are already missed; I missed them dreadfully when I was wasting time with my map. No, not wasting it. Filling it, passing it. Oh hell, is there any difference?

'I'll chase after Fran with Dan's card,' she said. 'Not that I'll catch her.'

'You might. She doesn't bounce fast. Do me a most tremendous favour thereafter, will you, Ella? Drop a token of abject contrition into the Swan. Bloody begonias, no less. I'm sure I have a pot out in the back and yes, Adam, I *will* ring. The minute Madam has departed, I will coo and grovel till the cows come home.' Urging Ella out of the door she remembered something. 'What's wrong with Jenni? She looked battered when she passed.'

'Exactly that, and bruised.'

'Bloody man. Anything I can do?'

'I don't think so. I'm going there this afternoon.'

'Well done. Make sure you keep in touch.' The thick lips parted in a huge yellow grin. 'Birthdays, batterings and bloody begonias. Not many of us left but we manage to keep the old pot boiling.'

37

THREE

At the end of it, looking back, Ella Caine reflected that it had been a rotten day. Even the sun had gone by mid-afternoon. It must have heard Tom Antony's prediction. And now, ten of the evening, wind howling and rain lashing, she wished very much that it was bedtime, that she could sleep and afterwards start again. Or that there was someone to talk to. A sympathetic stranger preferably, one who could sit and silently listen. No comment needed. Neither criticism nor condemnation required. I can provide the summing up, just sit there and listen to me.

How could she have forgotten? How the hell had she managed, almost deliberately, to forget? It wasn't as though her diary was spilling over at the edges, there was simply no excuse. Yet forget she had and it wasn't until she called Fran back from the rear door at Dowsett's that she remembered.

'For Dan, with our—my love,' she had said.

'Ella, how kind. You are good, you never forget.'

Don't say that. I do. I have done so twice already today. Forgotten. First your son and then your husband.

'Will you come in? Philip should be around and we can drink a toast to the birthday boy.'

'I'd love to, Fran, but I can't. I've a peace offering to deliver for Eve, then out with the dogs, and putting Jenni together again is next on the agenda. Did you see her?'

'Jenni? Yes. She looked awful. What happened?'

'Guess.'

'Stephen again? That man should be locked up.'

'I know.' Christ, what a feeble, banal exchange of words. We used to strike sparks off each other. Now listen, Fran. Listen carefully and be so kind as to relay precisely, not just the gist. 'I said I'd pop down about two but only for an hour. I can't spend the entire afternoon with her, far too much to do.' Got that? One hour only, two to three, and then I shall be home again. Philip, if you tell him and he twigs, can tie a knot in his passion

39

and adjust his timing.

Fran's sapphire blue eyes, large and luminous until camouflaged in flesh, showed sympathy rather than understanding. Just as well. Message received and understood would have tapped out disaster.

Down at the Swan, the atmosphere had been light and comfortable. Hooray. Just what she needed to get back on an even keel. Toby had regained his good humour and composure immediately after Eve telephoned her apologies. He was skipping jauntily between the tables in the lounge bar, a smile here, a welcoming nod there. His light brown hair, too soft and fine to stay in place, beat time on his forehead. Behind the bar, Giles watched him affectionately and with relief. Such a dear fellow, but *so* difficult when off balance.

Ella was welcomed warmly. Not too many customers as yet but every restaurant table fully laid in expectation.

'For me?' Toby gasped as though she had presented him with the crown jewels.

'With love from Eve.'

'She rang a few minutes ago. Terribly apologetic and contrite and she's going to ask her nurseryman to call here and look at my poor petals.' Not quite feminine, the voice, but getting there. 'Isn't that kind? And now this. She really is a darling woman, always thinking of others.'

'That,' Giles said, 'was not your opinion a half-hour ago.'

'I was a little distressed then.'

'What will you drink, Ella?' Giles asked.

'I don't think I should, thank you. I've rather a full—'

'Oh but you must,' Toby insisted, 'mustn't she, Giles? A drink with us both to christen this beautiful plant. Look how glossy and healthy the sweet thing is, just like my poor invalids should be. Excuse me for a moment, Ella. I must put it somewhere safe.'

Ella accepted a gin and tonic. It bit cleanly into any lingering inner churnings and she was glad she had been persuaded. She watched Giles putting the finishing touches to his faultless public presentation. Giles, so different from his partner. Tall, manly and extremely handsome. A Nöel Coward with thick wavy hair and a deep voice that thrilled. Artistic dark eyebrows, elegant hands and impeccable dress sense. A charmer, a lady's man if ever one was—if

41

only the casting director had been kinder. So near and yet so very very far.

Raised voices carried from behind the swing doors into the kitchen. A woman, shrill and upset, a man laying down the law.

'Excuse me, Ella,' Giles said, frowning, 'a minor altercation and absolutely forbidden.'

Henry's fault, she was afterwards told. Who else? It was always Henry's fault. The verdict was indulgent, as though excusing a naughty child who was infinitely precious. Henry, Giles said, had upset Tracy, but not intentionally. Yes, well, it *might* have been intentional but Tracy was quite devoid of all humour. And Toby, who had hurried back to hear all, agreed. Tracy was not a good waitress but she was adequate and willing. One of these days, Giles said, Henry will go too far and we shall find ourselves in the consommé. But he laughed as he said so and Toby did too. So what had happened? Tracy had complained that there must be better ways of earning a living and Henry had said there were. Only, he had added, even thinking of England might become boring after a while. Tracy had not understood and had asked Henry to

42

explain. He had been happy to oblige, remarking also that if she was interested enough, cousin Maggie could doubtless pass on a few tips. (A *distant* cousin, Giles said, but they are related.) So Tracy was now locked in the staff lavatory, refusing to come out, and Henry, a pale and poor imitation of Rhett Butler, was maintaining he didn't give a damn.

'Oh dear,' Toby said, giggling, 'Henry is awful, isn't he?'

The kitchen doors opened and Maggie Hubbard's distant cousin swept out with a pile of plates, head high, a crimson spot on each sallow cheek. A plain dowdy girl under normal circumstances, anger became her. A face appeared between the two doors, a doughy greasily sweating face with a grizzled crew-cut on top. And around the face a distinct haze of cigarette smoke. Fleshy lips parted and a yellowed tongue shot out, fast as a snake, and pointed at the retreating back. And then, just as swiftly, at the bar. Toby turned his back and Giles bit his lip.

'Oh dear,' Toby said again, 'do you think anyone saw?'

'Apart from us, no one was meant to,' Giles said. 'I'll speak to him.' He explained

43

to Ella. 'The cigarette, not the—gesture.' As it turned out, he did not. His attention was drawn elsewhere and, in that instant, all laughter died. 'Do we know that couple by the door?' he asked.

Toby looked. Two men, one thick-set and into his forties, the other young and fair, almost beautiful. He saw the younger smile, but not at him, and a knife went through his heart. 'I don't think so. Should we?' He managed a tone of disinterest.

'I've no idea, that's why I asked you. I thought earlier that they seemed familiar. Especially the boy.'

Aware that he was under discussion, the boy in question smiled like an angel and saluted with his glass. Toby was quite excluded, totally ignored. Giles, perspiration light on his brow and upper lip, returned the compliment courteously.

Toby wanted to die. 'They look common,' he spat, 'especially the boy.' He leant over the bar for the reservations book. 'Who have we tonight? Horrors, the Templetons. Are they on their own? No, thank God, a table for four. With luck they might behave themselves.'

It was then that Ella left. She was intruding and she knew it. She wished she had gone before the fun changed to yet another battle of the sexes.

At two precisely she stopped the car outside Briar Cottage. Stupid to use it, it being only a five-minute walk, but the dogs became hysterical if they saw her setting out without them.

Jenni opened the door. 'Lazy blighter,' she accused. 'It's only five minutes, less if you cut across the field. Or are you going on somewhere?'

'I'm not,' Ella admitted. 'It's the boys—dogs, I mean. They hate being left but they hate the car even more. I couldn't bring them because you don't like them.'

'I do not. Aggressive ill-tempered brutes.'

Ella turned cool. 'One speaks as one finds.'

'Quite so, and I find them aggressive and ill-tempered.' Jenni laughed, a head-back rafter-ringing gurgle. 'This is ridiculous. Come in, you fool. Let's agree to differ, shall we? I see little good in your dogs, you see none in Stephen.'

'Not true. He's not my type admittedly, but I've nothing against him apart from the way he treats you.' The cottage seemed strangely silent. 'Where are the children?'

'Miriam's asleep, the twins are out with Connie. Yes, I know I said. She had a tiff with her boyfriend and came back. Super job. No baby-sitter problems for tonight.'

'What about the kitchen?'

'As was, is now and forever shall be. Want to see?'

The kitchen was an extraordinary mess, table, worktops all clean and shining wet, the floor a disgusting soup. Cornflakes, eggs, bread, milk, broken china, soap powder, a legless chair. Despite constant drainage under the back door, Ella estimated the water level to be at least two inches.

'Good God. What did he do?'

'He hit me, then he started smashing things on the floor and afterwards he turned the hosepipe on the whole caboodle. A clean sweep, you might say.'

'Come on. We can clear it in half an hour.'

'No.'

'Jenni, come on. Forget exhibiting to the Major. You simply cannot live like this. Think of the kids.'

Jenni Templeton, twenty-seven. Despite swellings and bruises, a lovely creature. Long hair, shining brown, falling in strong natural waves. Large eyes to match, a full

46

sensuous mouth and a page three figure. Born Eileen Mary Donovan in a dreary Birmingham suburb, Jenni spent most of her childhood hating: her parents, for being so blatantly Catholic and Irish; her seven brothers and sisters for existing; her drab and overcrowded home. And she hated her names, all three of them. She left school at sixteen. Another hate but, naturally bright, she had learned a lot. What next? The lyrics said it all for her—when you feel your song is orchestrated wrong, why should you prolong your stay? She needed to plan and prepare. She worked in shops and bars and at night she went back to school and learned shorthand and typing. She read avidly. Magazines mostly, the right ones. She became expert, in theory, in social skills and graces, and she knew she could be the perfect wife and mother. She worked even harder at losing her Irish-Brum accent. She took her transistor radio to an abandoned garden shed on a local allotment and tuned in to plays and debates and discussions. And she practised. She had become a loner; she had no friends. Her glorious young body cried out for physical fulfilment but she eschewed sex. It was not that she placed any value on chastity, she simply did not have time. At twenty, she was ready. A born actress and one who might have been great, she preferred to play on the human stage. She enlisted in the WRAC. An army officer would suit her very well. 'Jenni', she decided, was a snappy name and Jenni she became, except on official documents. With her looks and personality, her abilities and upper-class accent, she landed the job of secretary to the CO at Catterick. Free at last to indulge her repressed sexual appetite, she let rip. Officers in the main but an occasional senior NCO as long as the coupling was discreet. At twenty-two she met Stephen Templeton and married him six weeks later. Eileen Mary Donovan was dead and Jenni Templeton arose from the crematory ashes.

No one knew of Jenni's background, not even Ella, and she was the closest to a friend the young woman had. No one knew what to think of the Templetons either. They were, in the main, larger-than-life characters acting out some outlandish play. Despite the often extreme irritation caused, Ella was fond of Jenni and determined to guide and protect her. Caring, not interfering, she told herself. Whatever the definition, she was batting her head against a brick wall.

The denuded kitchen clean and tidy, they sat afterwards in the pleasant sitting-room and drank coffee that had somehow survived the onslaught. Miriam chirruped upstairs and Jenni left her to do so.

'How old is she now?' Ella asked, smiling at the happy noises.

'Eleven months. She's a sweetheart.'

'The day may come,' Ella said, guiding the conversation back to the main issue, 'when Stephen lashes out at the kids. Have you thought of that?'

'Of course. But he wouldn't.'

'How can you be sure?'

'I know Stephen. It's me he hates when he flips. I also know that he won't smash any of these.' There were some good paintings on the white walls, delicate china on shelves. 'Templeton plunder, therefore precious.'

'If you know him so well, tell me why he flips.'

'God, Ella, we've been over this a thousand times. I don't know. His promotion —or lack of it rather—has a lot to do with it. He's been Captain since forever and we're both heartily sick of it. That's why we're entertaining Major Tom tonight. Good food, lots of booze and even more bum-licking.'

'We should have left the kitchen. It was your ace card.'

Jenni laughed, but shortly. 'I would have cleared it up on my own eventually. I just don't like being bullied into things, not even by you.'

'Jenni, I don't believe for one moment it's being passed over that does it. I think there's something wrong inside his head. I also think that Stephen is dangerous and that you should leave him.'

'Fine marriage counsellor you are.'

'I don't profess to be one—I simply want to help you. But not today obviously. You're all prickly and defensive and I'm wasting my time.' She rose to leave. 'What about your face? The bruise is darkening.'

'I know. I'll slap stage make-up on it. My mouth's much better, I've been bombarding it with ice cubes. Hell, I don't care. If anything is said I'll spin the usual crap about walking into a door.'

I should have stayed away, Ella thought as she drove home. I broke the rules, Jenni's rules. Only stick your nose in when asked. How long before Philip turns up?

OK, so it's waning a bit, but I could do with him right now. I'm churning again, just thinking about the warmth and weight and the smell of him. Compensation for being snubbed, is that what I'm after? I don't know. To be honest, I don't know anything. Not any more.

Philip did not turn up at all and somehow the afternoon passed. And the early evening. It was near eight when he telephoned. From a call box, the wretched pips destroying all intimacy, emphasizing the clandestine nature of their conversation. Or rather, Philip's monologue of complaint.

Why hadn't she let him know *properly*? Yes, Fran *had* said, but only a mention, nothing specific. And was Jenni Templeton so much more important than he? Honestly, he was beginning to feel a failure in every possible respect. Dan's birthday, for instance. He had wanted to give him so much more than a couple of tenners, surreptitiously slipped. Oh yes, the lad had been well pleased but that was beside the point. Sixteen's an important age, it's nearly there. He should have had a new bike or stereo deck, but anything costing more than tuppence was out of the question. Another letter from the bank this morning, lurking among the birthday cards. A foul rotten beastly letter. Yes, OK, they had the facts right, but did they have to be quite so...threatening? And the headline in the paper, had she seen that? Which landowners had been offered millions? That's what he wanted to know. As a landowner himself, as Chairman of the 'Hands off Darrington' group, as sole distributor of car stickers urging 'Fight the Developers', he had a right to know. Had she looked at the map? Did she realize how close they were to annihilation? All the farm boundaries run alongside each other. Lump all the land together and what have you got? One mighty big farm or, as Fran pointed out, one mighty big chunk of development potential. And to really put the lid on things, he had missed out on being with her. Yes, understood, not deliberate but it had seemed so at the time. Had she any idea of how much he *needed* her? She was his safety valve, his brighter side of the moon. Honestly and truly, it may sound crap, but he didn't think he could *exist* without her.

'Philip,' she said, gently but firmly, 'shut up a minute.' The pips had gone a million times, he must have spent a fortune. She could see him, ramming the coins home, bottom lip petulant, a thwarted child. 'Shut up and listen to me. *I've* had a bad day as well and missed you. I still do. But, Philip dear, you must not depend on me so. I'm not your wife. I'm your lover and that's as far as it goes.'

Off he went again, on and on and on. She was glad when his money ran out. Do you know what I wish? she asked the silent invisible listener she had conjured up. I wish tonight that I was anyone other than myself.

* * * *

An ill-considered wish, Ella Caine, and were it to come true, one you would regret. Become someone else and you immediately take on their particular worries and problems. Much better to stick with your own.

Tom Antony, for instance, with Doris at the Foresters', waiting his turn at the shove-ha'penny board. Tom read an article on chemical pesticides before he came out and now knows why the cabbage

Doris cooked up with his chop tasted so awful. Tom is not concentrating on the game nor is he much aware of the jolly company around him. He is praying hard that his allotted life-span will not be extended and he will be allowed to die of natural causes. And the other pub, the Swan, how goes it there? Giles is in fine form, so is Henry, but Toby is down. Again. The day has been a see-sawing experience ending with his spirits at rock bottom. That wretched creature, younger and so much more attractive than himself, has reappeared. The worm has returned and is even now ogling Giles with limpid blue eyes.

The Templetons, dining Major and Missus, are having a ball. At least, Stephen is. Wild laugh subdued, blue eyes clear of all save solicitous interest and attention, Stephen is doing an excellent job. And Jenni? How is she ending the day that began so painfully? Another triumph, another superb performance and the curtain not yet rung down. She laughs, she sparkles, she is the perfect dinner companion. But her thoughts are wandering. She is wondering, as she often has of late, whether she hitched her carefully constructed wagon to the wrong star.

Up at Dowsett's, young Dan is well content with the day that has run, his father is not. Fran has opted out. She is fatly asleep in her chair, acres of flesh rhythmically surging, biscuit crumbs moist on her pink mouth. Philip is concentrating on hating her. A bad day for Philip. Realization of the debt-ridden hole he has dug for himself; deprivation of the carnal satisfaction that would have eased the impact. He is also trying to come to terms with the new label attached to his life. Philip Russell: failure, adulterer and—traitor. The millions offered, he must find out who and how much. And then he must possess his unhappy soul in patience and wait for the knock on his own door.

The Graysons. The pivot around which the day has turned. Of all the people so far encountered, they must surely be at peace with the world. They are sitting now in companionable silence. The fire purrs low key and whisky glows amber in their glasses under the soft light of a single table lamp. They have talked the hind legs off the evening, shot off at tangents, dug up the past: national anthems played over the wartime wireless, antimacassars, Adam's time in subs, the Foreign Office. They have bemoaned the untidy clutter in their large beamed sitting-room, a room made beautiful by jade and ivory and dark old furniture. A room disguised by cartons and crisp packets, itinerant tins and bottles and packets of seeds. They will clear it, but not tonight. One piece of furniture alone has defeated the invaders. A small table stands under a window. On it, a silver-framed photograph of a handsome laughing boy with dark curls, and a bowl of early roses. Nothing else. Those who know Eve never comment on the photograph, those who do not never see it. Edward, the boy was called. He drowned only days after his mother marched him into the studio and pulled faces at him from behind the camera to make him laugh. No tears for Eve since Edward died. Nothing since has been worthy of such personal tribute.

Adam and Eve Grayson, at peace with the world? Shall we see?

'Ella rang,' Eve said. 'She says she wasted her time with Jenni this afternoon.'

'No comfort needed?'

'Apparently not. She worries me.'

'Jenni? She worries us all.'

'No, Ella. She's much too busy doing nothing. I think we should help.'

'In what way?'

'A small dinner-party, Saturday perhaps, just to make her feel she still belongs. No need for a spare man, number two son is home for the weekend, so she says. Why does a woman on her own present a threat, a single man a distinct advantage? Yes, a dinner-party, very informal. I'm too lazy and too tired for any frills. Ella and Andrew, the Russells and—the Templetons. Eight. A good number.'

Adam opened wide eyes. 'The Templetons? Do we have to? Jenni's overpowering and—'

'Stephen will behave impeccably, I promise you. And I want to observe him, try to find out what makes him tick so unevenly.'

'In the rare event that you precede me into the life hereafter I shall inscribe on your tombstone—"Eve Grayson, a Glutton for Punishment".'

'Then don't bury me in Darrington's miserable, flat past. No filthy foot shall sully such poetry.' She looked at the clock. Ten-thirty. 'Taken your tablets?' He nodded. 'But they're not working yet, are they? My poor darling. Mother Hubbard makes me want to vomit, moaning and groaning. She doesn't know the meaning of pain. Adam, you don't mind about the dinner-party, do you?'

'Not at all, my love.'

'I'd like to get inside them all. There's much more than the fronts they present. Take Philip, for instance. He's such a thoroughly nice bloke but he makes me feel—uneasy. And Fran. Is she fat because she's unhappy or unhappy because she's fat? Jenni Templeton's a gold-digger at heart, I'm sure of it, and I've a strong gut feeling she's sleeping around.'

'That feeling could be slander if voiced.' Adam pulled at his long nose, a thoughtful habit and quite endearing when compared with Eve's frequent compulsion to consume herself. 'What grounds have you?'

'I hear things. You must too unless you stuff your ears with cotton wool. We're the only market-place in Darrington. Cars parked discreetly when Stephen's away, figures disappearing towards the Dip, two shadows behind bedroom curtains when there should only be one. Add fact to gossip and you come up with a gut feeling.'

'What fact?'

'Jenni's pure animal. Don't tell me you haven't realized that. She has to be near, has to touch. Her flirting and flaunting isn't normal, it's foreplay, an open invitation. I expect she and Stephen have a rumbustious sex life, but that's not enough for Jenni. I *may* be wrong but when am I ever?' No answer to that. 'She seemed such an innocent when they came here but she's changed and will change even more, mark my words.'

'I have marked them.' His smile had grown sleepy. The tablets were beginning to do their job. 'Is all this investigation grist for the Great Novel?'

'That won't get written. I'm fifty-eight and running out of original thought.' She was on her bare feet now, pounding the carpet like a ponderous panther. She passed a mirror and glowered at her image. 'I hate myself. I must be the ugliest woman in the world. Look at me, if you dare.' She turned back to him. 'You're almost asleep. Come on, lover. Let's hit the hay.'

Adam was drifting sweetly when he felt Eve slip away from him and out of their bed. His face twisted but the pain was in his heart.

Downstairs again, she was a grotesque figure. Face white and shining with night cream, pins in her thick hair. Beside the table with the photograph and roses she spoke softly. 'A rotten day, Edward. Not much fun in it, no kindness either. My fault. Daddy's tired, his back hurts more than his leg now. Sleep well, my dearest love. Remember I love you.'

Why do you do this, Eve? Adam agonized. Two tears ran from behind his closed lids and he brushed them away. He was our son, not yours alone. Why cannot you share your grief with me?

★ ★ ★ ★

Well, Ella Caine? Still want to change places with someone else?

FOUR

The rumours about Highcroft started a few days before Ella saw the car. Some whispers said developers, others said Grots. Not one was remotely near the truth.

'I have it on good authority that Highcroft has been sold,' Fran spoke over the telephone.

'Whose good authority?'

'Harry Junior. He hears most things at the Foresters'.'

'But he's only a publican, he isn't God. I don't believe it, Fran. There've been no comings and goings, no viewers, no sleek estate agents. I went up this morning and there isn't a for sale board to be seen.'

She made a point of allowing the dogs their favourite walk just to set her mind at rest. Up the lane, through Highcroft yard and onto Philip's land. They were ecstatic. The mouldy straw littering the tumbling stables was the happiest of hunting grounds, as was the house if one of the doors had blown open. Ella had been inside the farmhouse once only, when she and David had collected the keys of the cottage from Ruth Downing. She had hated it then, wondering where dark passages led, and sickened by the stench of boiled swede and rancid fat. After fourteen years' decay, she hated it even more. Nothing would induce her to enter, nor could she believe that anyone in their right mind would consider living there. Every window broken, gaping holes in the roof, peeling grey outer walls and rats as big as badgers. No. Only when she saw demolition men moving in would she believe that Highcroft had been sold.

She came upon Tom Antony replacing fence posts in the last field before she cut down to the street. 'Morning, Tom.' Mr Antony in public, Tom in their intimate moments. The dogs greeted him like a long-lost friend. 'You must be the only man in Darrington they like.'

'Cupboard love, Mis' Caine.' He touched his cap to her. ''Lo Bill, 'lo Ben. Sit then.' Immediate obedience was rewarded by broken biscuit pieces from a capacious pocket. 'See what I mean? Cupboard love.'

'Have you heard the rumours about Highcroft? Who would want to live there, it's a horrid place.

'Some folks more money than sense.'

What did that mean? The rumour was true or he was philosophizing?

'When we first moved here, someone told us there was a curse on the place.'

'That right?'

'Is there?'

'There may be. On the other hand, there might not.'

Infuriating man. 'What sort of curse?'

'Don't rightly know. Gypsy's curse, so I heard. But that were a long time back.'

Aware that she would learn nothing further, Ella called the dogs to heel. But Tom had questions of his own. 'Mis' Caine, who'm that wummin that crosses the Dip morning and night? Nose in the air and two Labradors, both black?'

'That's Mrs Crown, Tom. The Honourable Alexandra Crown. She's staying with the Courtneys at the Manor.'

'Bet she sings well.'

'Why do you say that?'

'She'm got legs like lark's.'

I will save that gem for the Grayson's dinner-party, Ella thought. It's bound to be a show stopper.

Naked under her dressing-gown, she was waiting for Philip when she heard the car. Go away, whoever you are, she pleaded. The car did not stop. It rattled up the lane past her garden and she caught a glimpse through the hedge of a single occupant. Through belches of exhaust smoke, she saw the rear number plate. P registration. Not a Grot, not a developer. Then who?

A short-cut enthusiast perhaps, hoping to reach Upper Darrington through Indian territory? Idiot if so, in view of the no-through-sign.

The dogs barked and she opened the back door to Philip. 'A car went up to Highcroft about five minutes ago.'

'Good grief! Have you written to *The Times?*'

'Did you see it?'

'Quite probably, but it made no lasting impression.'

'It would have done if you lived here,' she assured darkly.

He leant against the door, blue eyes caressing and teasing her. A smile lifted his full lips, strengthened them, made them at one with his splendid physique. Lazily, as though playing to an audience of hungry eyes, he took off his jacket. His shirt was open to the waist and his sleeves rolled high. Fine golden hair gleamed on his smooth skin and she thought, you fool. After all these months, you don't have to undress to turn me on. I know how you look and how you feel. I don't need to see you, only remember. The car and its implications disappeared far beyond import. She felt nothing other than the sweet flow of juices and a longing to touch and be touched, to unite.

'I'm not coming near you,' she said steadily. 'We won't make the bedroom if I do.'

'It wouldn't be the first time. What's wrong with the table, or the floor?'

'Uncomfortable,' she said. 'Neither earthy, nor primitive, just plain darn uncomfortable.'

'What do you want, Ella?' It was a game they often played. Build up with words. No endearments, no mention of love. Just words, flicking through the electric air. Words, stripping them naked, gilding their limbs with sweat even though they stood yards apart.

'I want you.' She was a young tree, pliant and bending to his will. She was an arched statue, breasts proud and pushing her robe, legs parted to ease the agony of desire. She was motionless. 'I want you inside me.'

'Move!' he commanded huskily, and she went.

Afterwards, gentle in his arms, she worried further at the day's main event. 'For a horrible moment I thought the car might be Fran. The inevitable has to happen some time.'

65

'Not if we continue to be careful. Fran's taken Lizzie to the dentist. I told you so over the phone.'

'I know. But the best-laid plans of mice and men, et cetera. It's bound to happen one day.'

'I don't agree. I don't think we're important enough to bother the Fates.' He stroked the length of her body with a sensitive hand. 'You really are quite remarkable.'

'Why? Because I'm not wrinkled and haggard, or because of my scintillating mind?'

He laughed his light laugh. Incongruous really, almost as though someone else was in the room watching them, someone else was amused. 'It's your body I'm after, woman. That and that alone. I adore every inch of it. And it's all mine, isn't it?'

She shivered sensual agreement and stopped his hand over a breast, holding it still. 'No more. There isn't time.'

'I know that.' Abruptly he slid from the bed. 'There never is, damn it.' He glanced at the bedside clock. 'You're right. I must go.'

'Me, too. The fatted calf is still in the fridge and Andrew's coming tonight.'

66

Number two son, Eve called him. 'My escort for tomorrow night,' she added.

'The Garden of Eden?' Had she heard, Eve would have killed him. 'I'm glad. I won't feel jealous.'

'Don't do anything silly, will you, Philip? Don't call me darling. Don't touch me at all.'

He sat on the edge of the bed. 'Why are you suddenly so cautious?' The disappointment of the other day still rankled. 'Are you beginning to think that we have run our course, should finish things?'

'God, no.' She went into his arms, moulding her damp flesh against his, kissing his neck and shoulders, loving him almost. Of a sudden he was desperately important. 'That damned car. I don't feel private any more.'

The unidentified car had lost significance by Saturday. Just someone nosing around. No through roads draw some drivers like magnets. And Andrew was home, not exactly ecstatic to be there but happy enough to be waited upon and fussed over. It was good to hear footsteps other than her own.

She dressed with care for the Graysons's

dinner-party. More of a family get-together really, but still requiring that extra show of confidence. No husband to support, corroborate, sometimes correct. 'Isn't that so...?' 'When *was* that, darling...?' 'They were *such* fun, weren't they...?' No face so familiar as to be almost boring. Or actually so. The choice was yours, Ella Caine, so shut up moaning. She wore red because she looked good in it and because she felt the colour appropriate. A scarlet woman. If only they all knew.

The Templetons were the last to arrive which was predictable. Eve was not perturbed. Everything was ready and the Burgundy beef would not harm. She examined her other guests, assessing their hunger. Fran seemed relaxed, no starvation symptoms but doubtless she had devoured chocolate bars before leaving home. Young Andrew alone appeared unhappy, emptying the nut dishes as fast as she refilled them.

'I do believe you've grown some,' she said to him. 'You're almost up to the ceiling. When's it going to stop?'

'Don't boys keep growing until twenty-one-ish?' Ella answered for him in the irritating way mothers often do.

She wears well, Eve thought. And she's made an effort tonight. That's nice. She, Eve, had not. Black trousers, black sweater, Scholls and a daub of lipstick. She had found the lipstick in a trouser pocket and it seemed a waste not to use it.

'Here they are,' Adam said. There were footsteps outside the french windows. Andrew Caine's eyes kindled with hope.

'Hel-lo!' Jenni was on form. A figure-hugging dress, long hair loose, lips painted a provocative red. She danced the room, a kiss and a comment for everyone. 'Eve, darling! Sorry we're a tiny bit late...Ella, you look super, absolutely super. I hope I look as good as you do when I'm your age...And who is this handsome young man? Andrew! We must get together later.' A long, lingering kiss on the mouth followed by a lewd wink. Andrew's colour matched his mother's frock and everyone else, apart from Stephen, looked and felt uncomfortable. 'How well you look, Fran. That frock really suits you.' Fran was wearing a navy blue tent, the neck high to her several chins. She would have hit Jenni with the peg mallet, had she brought it. 'Philip, you are just too gorgeous to be true. *Un peu bronzé, oui?* It

69

suits...Adam, my positively favourite man. When I leave Stephen I shall come for you so be prepared.'

Ginned up and impossible already, Eve thought. I'll box her ears if she doesn't ease up. 'Did you call in at the Swan on your way?' she asked sweetly.

'No.' Stephen was positive. 'Eve, Adam, I—we—really are most frightfully sorry. Quite inexcusable, late on parade. We had baby-sitter problems.'

'Connie went bolshie on us,' Jenni elaborated. 'Said we hadn't told her and she had a date. So we broke a house rule and she's entertaining the dreaded Kevin *chez nous*. God knows what they'll get up to.'

'No more than any of us did at that age.' Mild Adam, gentle Adam, always placating.

'Since we appear to have developed a French connection, *à table, tous!*' Eve gave the s of *'tous'* the sibilance of a serpent. She slapped prawn-heaped avocados on the table. 'Stephen, Jenni, bring your drinks.'

'You're cross,' Jenni said.

'Only because you're behaving badly, like some third-rate movie queen.'

Jenni laughed, an infectious gurgle, and

70

the world forgave her. 'What a blow to my ego. I thought I was in line for an Oscar.'

In the lighter atmosphere, Ella related her small tale of Tom Antony and the lark's legs. It was well received.

'He told me something even funnier this morning,' Philip said.

'*Told* you? Actually imparted information?'

'He does sometimes. It seems he was near the Harrington house in the early hours. I didn't ask why. The dogs started barking and the master of the house came down and let them out. They made a beeline for the shrubbery and the next thing was two semi-nude figures disappearing fast over the horizon. Maggie Hubbard and client, *in flagrante delicto*.'

'My God,' Eve said, 'house prices will plummet. Can't you see next week's front page? Grotland revealed as Darrington red light district.'

'Alicia Hargreaves,' Fran was delighted; 'I wonder if she was wearing her rings when she waved them imperiously away.'

'I can't get over Tom actually volunteering anything,' Ella said. 'I never extract direct answers. The supposed curse on Highcroft, for instance. He knows but he won't tell.'

'I know that legend,' Adam said. Suitable surprise, unashamed interest. Even Andrew took time to look up from his second helping. 'It happened years ago, the very early sixties. Highcroft was doing well in a haphazard sort of way. Poultry, pigs, a few head of beef. There was even a small riding stables, no more than four horses and a half-dozen ponies, but very popular. A bit of this and a bit of that, Harry said.

'Then Reuben Downing decided that afternoon teas in the garden could be a money spinner. Yes, there was a garden then, very traditional and pretty according to Harry. Ruth put her foot down, said she was worn out with work as it was and would take on nothing more. Reuben was mean when it came to hiring help but he was sold on the idea of home-made scones and cakes under the chestnut. So he brought in a distant cousin of his, one by the name of Isobel. Bella.' Adam paused to smile. 'Harry waxed quite lyrical when he spoke of her. Evil old hag, he said, Romany as far back as Canute. The village boys christened her Belladonna and she frightened the life out of them all. Bella was not a success. She was dirty in appearance and habit.

Customers began finding—things—in their cake, grimy marks on the cups, and they stayed away. So Reuben told Bella she must pack her bags and go. She did so eventually, but not before she had cursed every inch of Highcroft and all who sailed in her. And it was then, Harry said, that things started to go wrong. Horses lame, cattle dying, barn fires, the odd broken leg. In 1964, Reuben had the—accident—with his gun.'

'And Ruth fell down the stairs fairly soon after we moved in,' Ella said. 'That must have been 'seventy.'

' 'Seventy it was. Sammy, the son, took fright and ran. He had already started his own business, never wanted anything to do with Highcroft. He sold off the land to you, Philip, and doubtless injected the money into his firm. Harry said he was doing very nicely, thank you—second-hand cars, scrap metal, junk dealing—and then *he* died last year.'

'It was in the paper,' Philip remembered; 'crushed and suffocated. Lord, it *is* all a bit weird.'

'If,' Eve said, clearing the plates to the kitchen, 'you believe that sort of thing. I don't.'

Adam went with her.

'So what *is* happening to Highcroft?' Ella called through. 'Have you learnt anything on that score?'

Out of sight of their guests, Adam winked at his wife. You do know, she deduced, but you've only just heard. I'll allow you that. 'Later, as a digestive,' she murmured into the mousse.

★ ★ ★ ★

The brown Rover, P registration, that had so disturbed Ella, drove past the shop around nine-thirty the same evening. Still light but darkening. The Graysons' dining-room curtains remained open and candle flames admired their reflections in glass and silver. 'Nobs noshing,' the driver said aloud and sardonically. He could have added, good luck to them, but he was not a man who wished anyone well.

Along the street, past the church and the school, past the track up to Dowsett's. Never should have sold the land, Dad, never should have done it. Worth a fortune now by all accounts. Past the Black Swan, pulsating with lights and life. Call in for a quick one? Some other time when things were sorted. Past Briar Cottage. Something going on there by the sound of it. Loud music, no lights and lots of laughing. On further, then slow. A grinding gear change and right into the lane. HIGHCROFT FARM AND HIGHCROFT COTTAGE ONLY. Quite right too. Pity about the cottage but no point wishing. He was eighteen years too late.

Highcroft Cottage. No sign of life. Porch light on and garage empty. Nice-looking place, done a good job there and, come June, the garden pretty as a picture. What's *she* like? he wondered. Going to mind her own business and let me get on with mine? Best she does. Inside the house dogs barked and he saw dim shapes leaping at upstairs windows. Terriers. He hated small dogs: into everything, snapping and snarling at your ankles. Keep 'em away, missus, he warned, or they'll feel my boot.

Highcroft Farm. His. Gate to the yard broken, propped like a drunk against the wall. Mend that first, put up a sign. Keep out. No. Folk would wonder why and questions were the last thing he wanted. The car headlights showed him the stable block, shabby silhouettes against a pale sky.

75

Where's the bloody moon? Late rising, just when he needed her. He lit and pumped a hurricane lamp and went to inspect. Soon fix these. Get the boys in to help. Ned and Lofty and Fat Charlie. Something shifted, then ran from under the stinking straw. Rats. He shuddered. Hated rats, always had done. Mebbe those terriers down the lane should be encouraged.

No sign of Maggie Hubbard. Got that one wrong down at the Foresters'. Not that he minded if she was using the place. Come to some arrangement most like, charge her rent, bring her customers. The house perhaps? He turned his lantern on it. Jesus, what a mess. Need more than the boys to fix that. Roof, windows, gutters, drains most like, and God knows what it's like inside. A paying-out job, this one. No matter, there was money coming in fast.

Right, then. Let's take a look. Let's see the stairs Ruthie fell down and the tack-room where Reub splattered his brains. The peeling door creaked open to a fingertip. Inside was black as hell and he drew back, shivered even. Should have waited till daylight, should have brought one of the boys. He searched for and found a stout stick. Rats. No more than big mice when you think about it. Come on, Jack lad, in you go. Man of property now. Let's have a look at what's rightfully yours.

Dark inside the house. Dark in the kitchen where Ruthie had grumbled over the old range. Dank too, where rain had seeped over the years, stagnating in filthy puddles on the stone floor. Beetles and spiders ran from his light, scurried into cobwebbed corners and rotten skirtings.

The front room, smaller than he remembered. Jam-packed at Christmas, fifteen or more. God knows where they all sat. His memory was vague on that one though he could still see the tree in the corner by the fireplace and smell the old goose and taters and the bit of old sheet boiling around the pudding.

Upstairs? No, leave it. Rotten floorboards most like, rotten rafters and ceilings ready to fall. And rats. He could hear them, scampering and squeaking. Fear and disgust knotted tight yet he must see the room. His room. 'Yo, yo, yo!' he shouted, banging and thumping and knocking plaster from the walls. Silence. Safe for the moment. Up you go, Jack.

Three and a bit bedrooms, he remembered, and the bit had been his. But only for holidays, and once he was big enough, fourteen, fifteen, holidays had been in the yard. It was the yard then, learning the trade. Learning to botch and patch, sweet-talk and cheat. But still his room until Bella came and she lasted no more than a month or two.

The door was sound enough and squeaked open. Room? Cupboard more like. How had he moved in it? Bed along one wall, white-painted chest of drawers, curtain across the corner with a rod for his clothes, and a chair. And a po under the bed. Red cushions on the window-seat and a hook in the beam for the lamp. Seven, mebbe, eight, he'd been when the electricity came. Last outpost in Darrington without electric, Highcroft. 'Twas only Ruthie packing her bags and trudging the lane that made Reub see sense. Mean old sod, Grandad, mean as they make 'em. Window-seat gone along with the cushions but the hook still fixed in the beam. He raised his lamp high and stared at it, a long-lost legacy. The only part of his childhood that remained and mattered.

No window-seat so onto your knees, Jack. Like you knelt on those cushions all those years back. Now then, what do you see? Not a desolate yard with the moon making monstrous shadows. You see sunshine and yellow chicken fluffs and water from the pump running clear. You see horses, four of them. Two chestnuts, a black and grey. Flash and Royal, Star and Peter. Why Peter? Daft name for a horse. Why the hell Peter? And ponies on the other side, your favourite, Nellie. Dogs yapping, cats sleeping, the old white cockerel yelling his head off. Sunshine and smells. Sweet hay and pig swill, garden mint and manure. How long ago? Near on thirty years yet as clear as yesterday.

Down again, no call to linger. Mind those stairs, Ruthie's downfall. Mind that handrail, strong as matchsticks by now. Mind...a slip, a tumble, an almighty crash. Friggin' hell! Lamp all right? Get off my back, Bella you old cow. Done nothing to you, none of us did, you black bitch you. Belladonna, belladonna, mount your broomstick and get gonna.

Nothing broken, no harm done. Stupid to panic. Stupid to think of her. Dead by now, all her dark looks and mumblings with her.

When Ella came back from the cloakroom she found Eve slumped on the sofa, a careless comfortable black heap. A glass of wine was on the floor beside her. The other guests were out in the kitchen, washing, wiping, stacking away. Adam, too, filtering the coffee. Nice party, nice people. They could all come again.

Sent from the room in disgrace, that had been Ella's punishment for breaking a commandment dictated by convention. Thou shalt not make a public fool of thyself. No, not fair, not dismissed. Given the opportunity to retire and quietly compose herself, to clean her mascara and tighten her lips.

'Sorry,' she whispered to Eve, bending to kiss her cheek.

'Don't be. We all snap at times.'

'But not usually in company.' Ella went through to join the other whistling workers. Brave of her, Eve thought, to go so brightly into their embarrassment and I bet she wishes she could grind Jenni along with the coffee beans.

Quite innocently, Andrew had started the action. Full to bursting point, he began

80

to fidget. Eve had been sympathetic. 'We will gladly excuse you, Andrew, if you so wish. Run along, why don't you?'

'Honestly?' Relief shone plain. 'Thanks awfully, and the meal was super.' He turned to Ella. 'May I take the car? I fancy a run into Brunton.'

'No, dear, it's not a good idea. I don't like you driving at night, especially when you've been drinking.'

'I haven't!' He was incredulous.

'A very small Scotch and a glass of wine,' Adam confirmed.

'Don't be mean, Ella.' Fran this time. 'Surely you can remember how boring your elders and betters become? Let him go. We'll give you a lift home.'

'He's using us, he always does. Eve for the meal, me for the car.'

'He's no different from any other youngster.' It was the first time that evening Philip had spoken directly to Ella. He did so now with gentle insistence.

'The answer is still no.'

'It doesn't matter.' Andrew was very pink. 'I'll go to the pub.' He glowered at his mother. 'Dad rang this evening. They had a row and she's been uptight ever since.'

81

'We did not have a row.' The denial was a near shout. Furious, Ella scrabbled through her handbag and flung the car keys at her son. 'Here! Drive carefully. It's *my* car, remember.'

Andrew gone, she had apologized. 'It was a disagreement, not a row.'

'About what?' They had a right to be interested, they had all known and liked David Caine.

'David wants to marry—her—after the divorce.'

'That's not unreasonable. Has she a name?' Eve's enquiry was polite.

'A name? Yes, of course, Helen.'

'Have you met Helen?'

'No. The boys have.'

'And?'

'They liked her. Said she was good fun and obviously fond of David.'

'So what's the problem? You surely can't object to his remarrying.'

'I don't, not at all. I hope they make it work. It's just—he wants to sell the cottage, says he needs his share of the money to start again.'

Silence while the news was digested and then Fran, slowly: 'That's not unreasonable either. Sad but necessary. Have you thought where you would go?'

'Go?' Anger flared again. 'I'm not going anywhere. I'm not selling. It's my *home*, our home. I love the place. I couldn't bear to leave the garden and the boys would be desolated.'

'By boys, I presume you mean the human variety as opposed to canine?' Jenni had been quiet too long, she needed to spark.

'The boys are grown up now,' Fran said gently. 'They've left home. They'll visit, of course, but they won't really care where as long as you are there.'

'I am not selling.' She was close to tears.

'I think you're bloody selfish.' Jenni again in ringing imperious tones.

'And *I* think,' Eve said, 'that we should drop the subject and have coffee. Ella, go and powder your nose. Everyone else, clear the table and do the dishes, if you please. Adam, coffee.' Like lambs they had all obeyed.

And now they were all trooping back, virtuous children eager for praise. 'I cannot remember,' Eve said, 'when I enjoyed a dinner-party more. Excellent food, stimulating company. Who gave it, do you know? I must thank them.' Adam limped in with the coffee tray and she received it graciously. 'Thank you, my man. Do, please, everyone sit down.'

Stephen Templeton sat in Adam's chair. Leather, high-backed and hard. 'Not that one,' Philip said, 'that's Adam's. For his back, you know.'

'Good Lord, I'm so sorry.' The culprit leapt as though scalded. 'Please sit down, sir. I really do apologize.' Solicitously he enquired, 'An old war wound?'

'Nothing so heroic.' Did Templeton really not know? 'I fell off a horse.'

'Not *hunting*, I hope.' Malicious Jenni, stirring again. 'Fran wouldn't approve, would you, darling?' Fran's views on blood sports were well known.

'A hack actually,' Eve said. 'Adam sits lousy in the saddle and Jenni, I shall slap you hard if you don't hold your meddlesome tongue.'

Eve looked at her husband. Now? she asked with her eyes. Behind his glasses, his twinkled back at her. Why not? 'Adam has some news that should interest you all, especially Ella. Go on, Adam, I'm bursting to know.'

'Well, now,' Adam sipped his coffee,

enjoying the attention, the riveted eyes, 'contrary to supposition, Highcroft has not been sold. It has been inherited. I met the new owner early this evening.'

As in all the best cliff-hangers, the episode ended there. Dan Russell telephoned from the farm to say that Lizzie's tooth was playing up and she wanted her mother. Immediately purposeful, Fran's plump legs trundled her, Dalek-wise, towards the door. Philip said he would come back and by the time he did so, the Templetons had gone. Toby had rung from the Swan. A customer had reported sounds of riotous goings-on from Briar Cottage.

'Stephen wanted to stay,' Eve said, 'but Jenni was adamant.' No men as such left, she could have added, and the randy lady raring to hit the bed springs. 'We're doing an Agatha Christie. Now we are four.'

'On tonight's showing, I don't see Stephen as the villain of the piece.' Philip could afford to be magnanimous, he was well pleased with the turn the evening had taken. Fran out of the way, young Andrew in Brunton and Ella his for a delicious half hour. His senses tingled with anticipation.

'He's not bad looking, is he?' Eve

said—'in a very military way. Losing his hair, and complexion too ruddy, but otherwise quite acceptable. I wanted to examine his eyes, try to see behind them, but they were never still long enough. I vote with Philip. I could find little fault in the man, not tonight.'

'Agreed,' Ella said, 'but that was tonight. Tomorrow could be very different.' She raised imploring hands to Adam. 'Please. Please tell us now. I'm the most affected. Who is he? What's he like?'

'*He?* How can you be sure?' Adam relented. 'All right, no more teasing. He is Jack Downing, Sammy's son. What's he like?' He considered. 'Let's say I can't see him socializing with Alicia Hargreaves.'

'A point in his favour. Or is it? What does he look like?'

'Not tall, stocky, a lot of black hair, swarthy skin. To sum up, a Downing.'

'Oh dear. Married?'

'Not at the moment. I believe there's an ex-wife and a couple of kids somewhere... Ella, I couldn't pry.'

'Of course you couldn't. Did you actually speak to him? Did he outline his plans for Highcroft?'

'Harry introduced us. He was polite

enough, said no doubt we'd be seeing more of him—at the shop, that is. One thing I liked. His expression is naturally surly but when he smiles, it's like the sun breaking through. He said he wants to restore Highcroft and live there as soon as possible.'

'That,' Philip said, 'will take a lot of money. Does he have it?'

'Not by the look of him or his car but he carried a fat wadge of notes. I understood that he opted for Highcroft as his share of Sammy's estate. The business went to the mother and sisters. Jack still runs it, though, and obviously takes a cut.'

'Congratulations, Hercule,' Eve said. 'You did well. No other snippets before we speed our parting guests?'

'Harry doesn't like him. No one at the Foresters' does.'

'I don't think I shall like him either,' Ella said as Philip drove her home.

'Don't prejudge. You probably won't see much of him and anyway, it will be months before he moves in.'

'There's a light up there now.' They had turned into the lane. 'Look, you can see it through the trees, weaving around like a will-o'-the'wisp.' She spoke softly. 'He's up there.'

'Why are you whispering, you idiot?' He stopped in front of the cottage. Andrew not back yet. Good. 'You didn't enjoy the evening, did you?'

'No. I made a fool of myself.'

'Are you going to hold out against David?'

'As long as I can. Jenni's right, I am selfish and I don't care.' She moved his hand from her breast. 'No, Philip. Don't rouse me just to leave me high and dry. You can't come in. Go home and make love to Fran.'

Disappointment showed in his petulant lower lip. 'Is that what you think I do?'

'It's what I hope you do. She'll be suspecting something otherwise.'

'And you don't mind?'

She laughed shortly. 'For God's sake, she is your wife.' She opened the door. 'I'm sorry. I'm being beastly, but I have to make my peace with Andrew and I have to think.'

He could have come in, she thought as she sat waiting for the return of son and car. We could have had a few pulse-racing minutes together. We may even have achieved more. Hot for each other, wasn't that the vulgar expression? No need for preliminaries, just a searingly sweet coming together. But not tonight. Tonight she needed kindness and understanding, someone wise to listen and advise. And not someone silent and invisible as had been her penchant the other evening. Her pleasantly monotonous routine had received some severe jolts and she needed to talk through the implications. Another Downing for a neighbour, but not for long if her husband had his way. Adam would have filled the chair opposite well, but not Philip. Adam was her friend. Philip was her lover and she valued him as such. But tonight she needed a friend.

FIVE

Sunday was a bad day for Ella. She was still embarrassed by her showing at the Graysons and Andrew, when she told him, did little to reassure. In every respect she was wrong and Dad was right. Won't you miss it if we do sell, she had asked, don't you like living here? Yes, he would miss the cottage, but not passionately, and he had no intention whatsoever of spending the rest of his life in Darrington.

What happened along the way, she wondered, looking out onto the lawn and seeing a strapping youth of nineteen shrink to a two-year-old toddler. I don't understand either of them any more, nor what they're doing with their lives. Computers. How can you enthuse about something so soulless? She remembered first hearing about 'silicone' chips and thinking them edible and adulterated. Fish and artificially inflated chips. What a joke that had been. David had dined out on her ignorance for months. And John choosing the Navy, that had been another blow. Not that she had anything against the Senior Service. No Drakes or Raleighs in either family but the incentive had somehow been there. A fine career, 'they' said, and doubtless 'they' were right, but she saw so little of him now. There was no continuity, no day-to-day small-talk. Admit it, Ella Caine: a large part of you wishes you had been born a Hubbard or an Antony.

Her elder son rang after lunch and dealt the final blow. Six months in the

Falklands. 'But why, darling? The war's been over two years.' He neither bothered nor tried to explain, said simply he would have leave before sailing and love to everyone, Andy included.

She drove Andrew to Brunton in time for the two-thirty stopping train to London. 'All right for money?'

'Well...'

'I've only ten, no, fifteen on me.'

'Thanks, Mum. Thanks for the weekend. Super time.' A lie, a hug and a kiss and he was gone.

She returned home to find a battered blue Ford van parked outside her house. A long streamer of pink festive ribbon spiralled from under one rusty door. It must have come gift-wrapped. A man and a woman, long hair, dirty jeans, were leaning over the gate. 'Please move your van,' she called through the open window. 'I want to drive into my garage.'

Slowly, insolently, they turned. The man came towards her. 'Nice place. Yours?'

'I have just said so. Please move your van.'

'Lived here long?'

Furious, she switched off the engine, pushed the woman out of her way and marched up to the front door. Dogs out first. Their acrobatics at separate bedroom windows were quite alarming. Then what? Phone Philip? Phone the police? She heard the van start and watched it lurch away.

She sweated long and hard over the garden that afternoon. Between weeding and clipping, she counted the cars going up to Highcroft. They all sounded the same, rattling, screeching boneshakers, so after an initial assessment she kept on weeding. And counting. Fifteen. I counted them all up and, if I stay here long enough, I shall count them all down. Why the Falklands, John? Is danger there still? She went inside to telephone Eve.

'Calm down.' The advice was sympathetic but strong. 'It's probably a house-warming of sorts...Yes, I know it's Sunday...Our pleasure, my dear. We loved having you both.'

So that was Sunday. A rotten day. Monday was peaceful so she turned her thoughts to David and his quite acceptable suggestion. She decided to write to him, a reasonable detailed letter stating her case. By Tuesday morning she had rallied all her arguments and sat down at the kitchen table to work on the first draft. 'My dear David.' Too personal, too possessive. 'Dear David, I'm sorry I reacted so badly to your idea about selling the cottage but it came as a bitter blow.' The telephone rang. Damn.

'Guess where I'm going,' Fran said. 'Morning coffee with Alicia Hargreaves. Aren't you impressed?'

'Tremendously so, and surprised. You aren't switching allegiance by any chance?'

'Don't be so daft. She sounded so desperate, I felt sorry for her. Want to come?'

'I can't recall being invited.'

'She said bring a friend. Do come. It should be a laugh.'

'I can't. I'm busy.'

'Doing what?'

'Trying to write to David.'

'Ah. That *is* important.' No sarcasm intended. 'Shall I call in on my way back?'

'Do.' If I'm struggling to make sense I shall hate you, but do.

'Dear David, I'm not pulling out all the sentimental stops but please remember the cottage has been my home for nearly eighteen years. Your home too, the four walls between which our sons grew up.'

Slush. Crap. And can you be *between* four walls? Surely not. 'Dear David, I'd buy you out if I could but Daddy's money wouldn't stretch that far, not the way house prices are currently rocketing.' No. That would only strengthen *his* argument. More than enough for both of us, he would say. And quite right too, only I don't want to sell. 'If I found a decent job—I probably could, even at my vast age—I might be able to raise a mortgage and buy you out. And/or, when the divorce is final, I could put a stop on your maintenance. That way, *you* could afford a mortgage. Woolly and wild, hypocritical, no positive substance. Minutes before Fran arrived she wrote simply 'Sorry I reacted so badly. Please give me time to think. Andrew is fine. University appears to suit him. John is going to the Falklands for six months and I am not happy. Please find a moment to reassure. Bill and Ben send licks.' She crossed that out, started again. Bill and Ben sent licks to no one, least of all David. There had been mutual antipathy between them. She ended 'love, Ella' and stuck the letter in a drawer. No harm in love. She did love him, but distantly, if only for the years they had shared. She was sure Helen would not object.

Fran seemed in a paradoxical mood; bubbly, yet subdued by inner thought.

'How was it?' Ella asked.

'As I predicted, a laugh. You should have come.'

'Were you the only guest?'

'Heavens, no. There were millions more, all Grots. I cannot tell you how ghastly they are *en masse*. Still,' she brightened, 'there was a scrumptious chocolate cake.' She looked around the kitchen. 'Anything to eat?'

'No. You may not be able to see them but there are padlocks on all the cupboard doors. How about a gin?'

'You're on. Did you do the letter?'

'Sort of. Everything I intended saying looked rubbish on paper so I simply asked for time to think.'

'That's reasonable.' Approval shot off at a sudden tangent. 'Philip's having an affair.'

Somehow Ella did not spill her drink, somehow she sculpted her expression to one of genuine surprise. 'Are you sure? Who with?'

'Don't ask me that and no, I'm not

absolutely sure. It's just a gut feeling that's been growing over the months. He doesn't come home smelling of scent or covered in lipstick. He's away from the house no more than he ever was. He *seems* the same old Philip, but he isn't, not with me.'

'I haven't noticed any difference in him,' Ella said bravely, hating herself, hating Fran for activating such self-disgust.

'I don't suppose you have, you're just a friend. God, Ella, I don't mean "just" in a derogatory way. As a friend you're probably closer to him than I am. We're not any more. Friends, I mean. We don't talk, we don't communicate.' She sighed. 'Maybe it's because I'm so repulsive to look at—and that's another thing.'

'What is?' I cannot remember a time I have loathed more.

'My being fat. He doesn't care. I don't think he even sees me. When I first started putting on weight he was on at me the whole time. Try this diet, try that, see the doctor, stop eating, *why* do you stuff yourself, is something wrong? All he does now is grumble mildly if my munching disturbs his thoughts.'

She was plumped on her chair. Not many years ago one would have said perched. Like a bird she had been, a golden bird. Now she was like...? There was no apt comparison. She was simply Fran gone wrong, Fran with rolls of ugly flesh, Fran fat. Her hair was still a lustrous gold, her eyes sapphire-blue and bright. The spirit was willing enough but the flesh was too much. The golden bird was grounded. A block and tackle and it might get airborne, but only might.

On firmer ground, Ella said, 'You simply must do something about your weight. It's not just your appearance, it's your health. You'll have a coronary if you don't slim down.'

'So long as it's all over quickly, I really don't care.'

'That's stupid and selfish and I'm ashamed of you.'

'I don't think much of me either. Perhaps that's the trouble, perhaps that's why Philip has found someone else.'

'You cannot be sure.'

'Not yet but I'll find out. She's probably some tart in Brunton being paid for her services. Or Maggie Hubbard? No, that's too close to home. You know the saying, don't shit on your own nest. I'll find out and when I do I'll ask her what she sees in

97

him. He looks good enough but he certainly isn't a thrill a minute in bed. Never was. One thing's for certain, he won't leave me. I'll take him for every penny if he does.' She smiled bleakly. 'Every penny, that's pretty accurate. Pounds wouldn't feature at all. My father must be twisting and turning in his grave. He was a farmer, you know that, don't you? He had bad years too, all farmers do, but there were dozens of good ones to compensate. I don't think Philip's ever had a good year. Just mediocre, poor or downright rotten. That's probably why I'm so narked about his having another woman. If he's such a loser, how did he manage to score in that respect? She really must be a tramp.'

Ella threw up into the sink after Fran had gone. Afterwards she screamed silently. She must see Philip soon.

But Philip was out and about, playing detective. In his guise as land preserver, he was finding excuses to call on all his neighbouring farmers. Just passing, Wilf, thought I'd drop in and have a chat. Your barley looks good, Bert, best I've seen, what's the secret? Lots of chitchat. Prices up, prices down. Chaps from the animal feed companies boring your ears with advice. Articles in the *Farmer's Weekly*, adverts for tractors and trailers. New markets for free-range eggs, closed shops for beef. He heard it all. But the carefully introduced new topic of development and related approaches drew blank after blank. Stony silence, shuttered eyes, swings in conversation. Only one man, Eric Norton at Down Darrington, admitted that the consortium had called.

'Very persuasive they were,' he said, 'not that I needed persuading. I'll be honest, Philip, I'll sell if they ask me again. Farming's on the way out unless you specialize on a big scale. The EEC's clobbered us good and proper. And at my time of life' (he was near sixty) 'I'd be glad of a chance of security. Suppose you think I'm the rotten apple in the barrel?'

'I'm disappointed, Eric, and sad, but I won't condemn.' How much, man? Tell me how much. 'But you're the thin edge of the wedge. Imagine what would happen to the Darringtons if we all opted for security? Can you visualize the size of the development?'

'Aye, I can, and I'm sorry. Someone else can preach principles: I'll take the money.' He spat accurately into the eye of a daisy.

'Not that it'll happen yet. There's more than enough like you'll hold out against temptation.' You're wrong, Eric, you are wrong. 'And those chaps have big ideas. They don't just want my three hundred acres, they want the lot. Otherwise it isn't,' he spoke carefully, 'a viable proposition.'

'As a matter of interest, how much did they offer?'

'Three.'

'Three—what?'

'Million, what else? Don't deal in pennies, those chaps.'

Back in the car, Philip rested a reeling head against the steering wheel. Three million. What couldn't he do with a mere fraction of the ridiculous amount? Good schools for the kids, a new car, a proper house with a proper garden. And money left over to invest in the future, a future in which he could look the wretched bank manager squarely in the eye. Patience. Wait. They'll crumble one by one. There surely is nothing money can't buy.

While Philip questioned, Ella agitated. Much as she needed to see him, there was no way she could track him down. Not now. Not with Fran's bitter words still ringing in her ears. It was ridiculous, really, the way guilt had her cornered. Turn back the clock to the time before involvement and she would have gone looking for him. Or rung the farm, asked Fran to give him a message. The washing-machine's on the blink, please may I borrow your husband? Those days were over. Even if they ended the affair—and end it must—it would take years before she felt comfortable again.

As far as the other village problems were concerned, Jenni seemed all right and Toby did not. Ella and Eve had put their heads together one afternoon and decided that Toby was—a problem. Or that he had one. But Jenni, Eve confirmed by telephone, was very definitely all right.

'There was a big party in Grotland at the weekend. Celebration of the opening of yet another heated swimming pool. The Courtneys and the Hon Alex were invited and, being the splendid people they are, they went along. It was all very circumspect—DJs and a string quartet playing Gershwin. Caroline thinks the intention was that, later in the evening, some of the younger set would change into swimsuits and christen the pool. Around eight-thirty the Templetons presented themselves. In bathrobes. "Hello," Stephen said to the bewildered host. "We understand you're having a party." "That is so," was the reply. "So we've come," Jenni said. Give the man his due, he was apparently very polite but very firm. No invitation, no party. "Not to worry," Stephen said cheerily, "we'll just cut back across your garden if you don't mind." And so they did, stopping at the pool—floodlit, of course—to drop their robes and dive, naked, into the unsullied blue. Two lengths and out they came. "Thanks awfully," Jenni called to the open-mouthed audience, "lovely pool. The temperature's just right." On with the robes and off they went, laughing all the way.'

'Was Caroline shocked?' Ella asked.

'Not at all. Thought it an absolute hoot.'

'Good for her. Yes, a lovely story and I'm delighted to hear it. It lets me off the hook. Not that I anticipate being called on again to render services. I'm sure she resents me for trying to help after the last bit of fun and games.'

But Toby was a different story. It was apparent that he was not happy. Despite the nurseryman's advice, his begonias continued blighted. And that boy Keith was around every day now, lunch-times and evenings. Smirking and twirling and making enormous eyes at Giles. Horrid boy. He wished he could find a legitimate excuse to send him packing. He wished also that the new owner of Highcroft would stay away from the Swan. Rough man, dark like a gypsy and no manners at all. Never a civil word out of him since he started patronizing the house. No conversation, no inkling of his plans or intentions. Pint of the best, but no please, never a thank you. Giles says he will find his own level soon and stick to the Foresters' and Giles is always right. Oh dear, oh dear, why does love hurt so much?

Take the other day when he had tried so hard to summon the courage to ask outright. Giles had looked so debonair. Pale grey trousers with a crease that could cut, navy blazer, a crimson carnation that final distinctive touch. You're wilting again, Tobes, he had said; buck up, dear boy. And he had squeezed poor Toby's shoulder affectionately with an immaculately manicured hand. And what had Toby done then? Dropped his head so that his silly hair flopped, pushed at his glasses and admitted that he felt depressed.

But not why. He dare not ask, not when he dreaded the answer. Reassure me, he begged silently, tell me I am still the most important part of your life. And Giles had understood, at least Toby *thought* he had. You must not jump to conclusions, Giles had said, and looked very stern. Did that mean he wasn't attracted? Was it a positive no? He wished he, Toby, wasn't such a pathetic fool at times, and he wished he really knew. About Giles and that wretched Keith.

If Toby was jumping to conclusions, the postman was not. He was not even tentatively forming them. He continued to ram letters addressed to J.M Downing through Ella's letter-box. A natural mistake to begin with, she thought, but by now he must surely realize that Highcroft Farm was occupied. Not in an orthodox way, but occupied, and never more so than at weekends.

By Sunday she was sick to death of the untidy pile. Telling the man in the red van had no apparent effect; re-posting would only mean a speedy return. She steeled herself into walking up to Highcroft. The terrible convoy had already gone up. If she did not see Jack Downing immediately she

104

would dump his mail by the gate with a large stone on top.

The yard at Highcroft resembled a second-hand car mart. Bangers of all shapes and sizes cluttered it, some with engines still hicupping. Jack Downing was distant, in deep conversation with a group of unsavoury-looking men. Long hair and tangled beads predominated. The air was heavy with exhaust fumes, the aroma of unwashed bodies and the drone of flies. And something else. Ella did not recognize the almost sweet, cloying smell. There was a deal of smoking going on, compulsive almost, but cigarettes don't stink of—what?

She stood at the gate feeling an inadequate idiot. A tall thin man with pale watery eyes strolled idly towards her. Hair a reasonable length and himself fairly clean, he seemed harmless. 'Yes?' he asked. A flat dreary voice.

'I'm Ella Caine from the cottage down the lane. I'm afraid the postman is behind the times. These are Mr Downing's.' She handed over the letters.

'Oh? Thanks.' Jack Downing, she saw, was looking over enquiringly. 'Lady here's brought your post, Jack.' A curt acknow-ledgement from the dark-skinned owner of

Highcroft, nothing more. It might have been thanks but it was more like dismissal. 'I'm Lofty,' the tall man said.

'Hello, Lofty.' A difficult pause, then: 'What a lot of cars,' Ella said lamely.

'Yeah. Friends of Jack's. His place, his friends. You'll get used to 'em. Be here, regular as clockwork, you'll see.'

Don't go on. Please. Do not confirm my worst nightmare. 'Is Mr Downing making any headway with the house? There must be a great deal to do.'

'Water's connected, electricty'll come soon as the wiring's done. Phone on next week.' She raised her eyebrows. 'Yes, 'tis quick but Jack slammed in for it soon as Sammy died.' He yawned, showing broken teeth. 'Bringing in horses, Jack is. Stables'll be first. Already mucked out, see?' She looked at the heaving, fly-swarming mound then looked away. 'Won't know the old place soon. You'll see.'

She went home, as depressed as Toby and as close to tears. She could avoid Highcroft, that was no problem, but not the stream of weekend visitors. Regular as clockwork, the man had said. Her only hope was that the clock and the cars would break down.

She finally came upon Philip by chance. On impulse, she took the dogs one afternoon through Topfield Copse. The weather was in a perverse mood, teasing the countryside with blue sky and hot sun one minute, withdrawing all favours and threatening rain the next. Primroses and bluebells gone but everywhere a tangle of sweet green. Campions and windflowers in the grass, blackberries in flower. Already? Blackberries are almost autumn and beyond. What is it they say? After Hallowe'en, the fruit belongs to the devil. That puts us neatly into November. Why don't I plan my Christmas shopping?

She heard voices she recognized and followed them. The dogs were there before her, adoring Tom Antony, treating Philip to a show of curled lips and disdain.

'Funny old day,' she called, braving the brambles. 'Can't make up its mind one way or the other.'

They talked weather, they talked about Jack Downing and Highcroft, and Ella found courage to speak to Philip direct. 'Walk back with me a short way, will you? I've had the most extraordinary letter from John.'

Out of sight, out of earshot of Tom, she turned on him savagely. 'Where the hell have you been? I need desperately to talk to you.'

'About the letter?'

'There is no letter. It's something much, much worse.' Tripping over words in her haste, she related all Fran had said. Except, of course, the crushing condemnation of his husbandry. 'You see? It's got to stop, Philip, we have to put an end to—us.'

'I don't see why,' he said slowly. 'She obviously doesn't think it's you.'

'But she thinks it's someone and that's almost as bad. Besides, if she's as good as her word, it will only be a matter of time before she finds out. God, I feel so guilty.'

'Don't.' He caught one of her hands and kissed it. And then, 'Was she really upset?'

'Of course she was. Wouldn't you be if you thought she—?'

'Perhaps.' Considered thought. 'Probably. Yes, I would be.'

'Men,' she jeered. 'What's sauce for the goose is exclusive. Ganders toe the line, or else.' She pulled her hand away. 'This overweight business and your not being interested, I don't know what to say. If you start commenting now, she'll know I told you. If you don't, she'll keep on believing she's right. Which she is.'

'You could have told me, as a friend.'

'But I'm not just your friend, am I? And I'm not a liar either, or an actress like Jenni. I can't go on pretending. It was bad enough when she suspected nothing. Now I feel I'm carrying a sandwich board—I am sleeping with my best friend's husband.'

Beside them was a narrow strip of grass slotted between trees and bushes. He took her arm and drew her towards it. 'Remember the first time? This very place. Who seduced who?'

'It just happened,' she murmured, relaxing under his hands, feeling the tension ease with his kisses. 'Philip, this is the height of madness. We should be saying goodbye.'

'We will after we have loved each other.'

He explored her body with confident hands, undoing buttons, searching for her skin. And still he kissed her. A warm moist tongue teased an ear, then beat against her throat as though there too it would find entry. She arched herself into him, her thighs hard onto his. Rhythmically and compulsively she moved against him and then she moaned as her own hands flew to release his sex. Her moan was both ecstasy and despair.

'Don't worry, darling,' he said, 'it's all in your mind. We're safe here, no one will see us.'

Tom Antony saw, just as he had seen from the very beginning. Silly young things, playing with fire. Liked them both, 'specially Mis' Caine. Liked Mis' Russell too. Someone'll end up being hurt. Be sure your sin will find you out.

SIX

'Why don't you trot up and see him instead of banging on about it?' It was Eve dishing out the advice. Ella had called in at the shop around five-fifteen and been persuaded to stay on for an early-evening drink.

'What do I say if I do? Your weekend visitors are driving me mad?'

'No, dear, be more subtle. Introduce yourself, ask how the work's going. Stress how peaceful Darrington is, how happy

110

you've always been here. You might get around him if you play your cards right.'

'I doubt it but maybe I'll try.'

'Any news from David?' Eve was bored with Highcroft.

'None. Not even a phone call to tell me not to worry about John.'

'I don't know why you are. Worrying, that is. It's not as if he's going anywhere near the mines those wretched Spaniards left behind.'

'Argentinians,' Adam corrected mildly.

'Oh, yes. Wrong war.'

'Do you know what Jenni said when I told her?' Ella flushed pink as she remembered. 'She said, how super, Stephen *loved* the Falklands. And when I asked how anyone could enjoy killing she went all superior and said, darling, you shouldn't join the armed services if you're not prepared to kill. And that made me feel even worse because, in a way, she's right.'

'There's a difference between enjoying and being prepared,' Eve said. 'Your John is not Stephen Templeton.'

Adam was thoughtful, fingering his long nose. 'An interesting comparison. John's a gentle soul but he would do his duty. My feeling is that Templeton would do more than his and love every minute.'

On Eve's advice and against her own inclinations, Ella walked up to Highcroft the same evening. 'No rummaging and we can't cut through the yard the way we used to,' she warned the dogs, wondering why she bothered. As always, they would go their own sweet way. They did. They shot under the gate. Jack Downing, tinkering with an old generator destined to illuminate a shabby caravan, looked up.

If the yard was a mess before, Ella thought, at least it was one created by nature and time. Now that man had moved in it was almost beyond fair description. Two dead cars had been pushed into a corner. The engine of a third seeped oil. Masonry, plasterboard, chunks of stone floor from perfunctory explorations had been dumped along the back wall of the house. Oil drums, wheelbarrows, cable and hosepipes seemed everywhere and, even with a clean wind, still from the east, the place stank. Jack Downing had clobbered the weeds with diesel and the stench lay heavy over the cracked paving-stones. Someone had been creosoting the stables and killing the sweet air at one and the same time. But the worst offender of all was the enormous mound of rotten straw under a rotating black umbrella of flies. It stank of maggots, vermin and decay. Thank God I'm not next to him, Ella thought; thank God I'm seeing this purely through choice.

'Hello!' she called from the gate, feeling an idiot. 'May I come in?'

'Might as well. Your dogs didn't bother to ask.'

'I'm sorry about them,' she said when she was nearer. 'They've had full run of your yard for six years since they were pups. It's hard to explain that they're trespassing now.'

''Twas private property then as 'tis now.'

'I know. I apologize.' And that's your lot, you nasty creature. I will not prostrate myself. 'I'm Ella Caine from the cottage.'

He nodded. 'I know.' Her proffered hand was ignored. 'Come to complain, have you?'

'I came to be neighbourly, to wish you well at Highcroft, but since you've raised the subject, yes, I do find the weekend traffic in the lane a bit much.'

'My lane. You only have right of way as

113

far as your place. My friends. Sorry, Ella, if you don't like it you'll have to do the other.'

'I can see that now,' she said, angry at his insolence, angry that he was succeeding in upsetting her. She wished fervently that she had never come. It was Bill who created the necessary diversion. He had been into everything, sniffing and snorting, short tail beating the air with delight. Only the mountain of dank straw remained unexplored. Energy in every muscle, he leapt at it, snuffling and yapping and tearing it apart.

'Bill! Come out!' He'll need a bath when we get home, they both will. Jeyes' Fluid, Dettol, the lot. 'It's rats he's after,' she apologized. 'Well, mainly rats. He's awfully good at finding things, he should have been a sniffer dog. Bill! Leave! He really does hate rats, I think there must be one—Oh God, he's caught it.'

But it was not a rat Bill brought proudly to lay at Ella's feet. She picked up a package wrapped in polythene, something that felt like a chocolate bar but much heavier. 'What on earth is this?'

It was in her hands no more than a second. 'Well, now,' Jack Downing said, examining Bill's find. 'Here's that little parcel of Ned's he was going on about all day Sunday. He'll be pleased as Punch, thought he'd lost it for good. Lord knows what's in it but 'tis important to Ned, that's for sure.' He put the package in his pocket. 'Good dog,' Jack applauded Bill, but from a distance. 'Big bone for you from Ned I'll be bound.'

'I'm glad he's done something useful for once.' Ella felt inexplicably puzzled. The atmosphere had changed, lifted. Jack Downing was actually smiling. It was, as Adam had said, like the sun breaking through.

'Well, now,' he said, 'since you made a friendly visit, want to look around?'

'No, thanks. You must be in an awful muddle. Just tell me what you're planning.'

'Putting the house to rights, that's the main job. Wiring, proper bathroom, fitted kitchen. Want it like it was only better. And horses. Must have horses. Four, like when I was a nipper.'

'You lived here as a child?' She was genuinely suprised. There had been no one other than Ruth in the house when she and David had moved to Darrington.

'Holidays mostly, sometimes weekends.

115

See that little window over the tack-room? That were mine.' He smiled again and, despite everything, she felt herself warming towards him. 'See the bars? Old Reub fixed those so I couldn't climb out. Always doing it, I was. Five, six-year-old. Out of the window, slide down the tack-room roof, shin down drainpipe and away. Day or night, whenever the fancy took me. Old Reub put a stop to that.'

Ella walked home thoughtfully. She was glad she had been to Highcroft, glad she had seen both sides to Jack Downing. But she was not happy. Something was wrong. Not just Highcroft itself; a feeling, a chill breath of bad things to come. Philip, had he said anything to allay Fran's suspicions? Was he even remotely concerned?

He was, but in his own way. It had taken Philip a few days to work out how to deal with Fran. Unlike Ella, he felt no guilt, only a sense of irritation. Silly woman, what did she mean he was different towards her? They still chatted about the kids, exchanged village gossip. They worried together about money and the farm and the nasty letters from the bank. They even made love every week or ten days, and that after eighteen years

116

of marriage. Not a bad average. True, he kept a lot to himself but that was to spare her. True also that he was having an affair with Ella Caine.

Not really an affair as such. No wining and dining, no secret weekends together, no flowers or presents or letters swearing undying love. And no demands. Just a glorious coupling of two superb bodies. Carnal lust. Uncomplicated sex without promise or commitment. Ella. Such a mixed-up bag of tricks. Quick to sense a wrong, eager to right it but quite unable to put her own house in order. Lord, he was fond of her, but that only. So why should Fran grumble that she was missing out? An affair, yes, but not a *love* affair. Love was an enormous word, love was for—who? The children? Yes, but who else? Not Ella, not Fran, not anyone. I've been deprived, he thought, unaccountably angry. I've missed out on the big one just as I've bungled everything else.

While Ella wondered and worried, Philip went into the attack. 'I think we should call another group meeting.' He and Fran had settled in the kitchen. The sitting-room was too much effort away. 'I've been sniffing around and there's no doubt approaches

117

have been made. No admissions apart from Eric Norton but a distinct impression of unease.'

'OK, Call one.' Fran couldn't be bothered to open her eyes.

'You actually heard what I said?' Here was the opportunity. Turn the tables on her. 'You might show more enthusiasm.'

The blue eyes opened wide. 'What do you want, a peal of bells or twenty-one guns? I heard everything you said. It's worrying and I agree we should call a meeting.'

'Should we go public, do you think, or is it too soon? Committee only?' His tenor voice climbed higher up the scale. 'Come on, Fran, wake up! Help me.'

'For Christ's sake!' She sat bolt upright. 'What's got into you? You've never needed help before, not with the consortium caper. OK. I'll help. Committee only. When and where? Soon and here. Give me some dates. Give me the list as well and I'll ring around in the morning. Satisfied?'

'No, I'm not. That was all too glib and you've probably forgotten the import already. Why don't you involve yourself more? You greet everyone, serve the coffee and biscuits, then disappear upstairs.'

'I am not on the committee.'

'I know that but you could stay and listen. Or you could prime me with your ideas and let me be your voice. Don't you care about Darrington?'

'Of course I care, you stupid oaf.' She looked at him curiously. 'You're not sickening for something are you?'

'No, I am not. But I am sickened. What's happened to you over the years? You never have anything different to say. What's happened to us? I'm fed up with carrying a sleeping partner.'

'That's because there is nothing different to say, and if I sleep, it's because I'm tired. Tired, inside and out.'

'And you know why you're tired, don't you?' God, it was easy to be angry once you built up steam. 'You're too bloody fat, that's why.'

'So you've noticed, have you?' She was fighting back tears. 'I thought I had become invisible.'

'Not much chance, the size you are. Of course I've noticed. A blind man couldn't miss you. But you never listened to me years ago so why should you now? If you're hell-bent on self-destruction, that's fine by me, but try to remember occasionally that

119

you have three children.' He was not prepared for Fran's comeback.

'Ella told you, didn't she? She told you I was upset because you never notice me. That's why you're bullying in such a beastly manner. It can't be coincidence.'

'What the hell are you on about?' Think, man, think quickly. Deny seeing Ella? No. No lies. They trip you later. Attack again. 'Have you been discussing our marriage with outsiders? All right, don't say it, I know she's a close friend but that's still no excuse. You women are all the same, have to stand on a rostrum and air your grievances in public.' Lord, Ella would be proud of him when he told her. And she would see clearly that there was nothing to worry about, that they could continue enjoying each other without a care in the world. 'Leave it for now, Fran. We'll talk things over sensibly another time.' A sigh, an expression of monumental fatigue. 'I've had more than enough for one day.'

He listened to her quiet weeping for the time it took to drink a large slow Scotch. Then he went to her, loving and tender, begging her forgiveness. The only thought that occurred as he drifted towards sleep was that Ella must mean an awful lot.

The energy expended on the pantomime had quite exhausted him.

David Caine telephoned his wife around ten on a Friday evening. Sorry about not contacting you sooner. Yes, I know you wrote but I've been busy. No, not an excuse, genuinely busy. About John, do stop worrying. Routine exercises, no more danger than if they were working out of Portsmouth. About the house, I'm still keen to sell but I understand your reluctance. Why don't you let me know when John has leave and I'll come down for the week-end? How does that suit? We can have a family pow-wow.

It suited Ella very well. If Andrew came home too, which he would, they would be a unit again. Tenuously held together and easily dismantled but a unit nevertheless. The phone rang again. This time Harry Junior from the Foresters'. 'Sorry to bother you so late, Mrs Caine, and I'll quite understand if it's inconvenient, but could you come down? Mrs Templeton's had more than enough and she's causing a rumpus. Yes, singing. Terrible, it is. It's near closing time and I don't want to lose my licence.'

'I'll come,' Ella said. 'Has she the car?'

'It's not likely. She's wearing a pair of the Captain's army boots. Said she was yomping.'

'Oh God. Thanks, Harry. I'm on my way.'

She could hear Jenni even before she parked the car. The tune was unrecognizable but the words familiar.

'Just a lit-tle bit of heav-en fell from out the sky one day
And it set-tled in the ocean in a spot not far away...'

Ella opened the Foresters' door in time for the punchline. 'A-and when they had it fin-ished sure they called it Ir-e-land.' Applause mixed with derision. Shouts of 'Shut up, Jenni' and 'Give us a break. Go home.' 'By Kil-lar-ne-e-ey's lakes and fells,' Jenni carolled, flat as a pancake. It was obviously an Irish evening; Eileen Mary Donovan resurrected. Harry Junior covered his ears and Ella pushed her way forward.

'Be quiet, Jenni! Do you hear me? Stop that awful noise this instant.'

'Ella! Darling! Super to see you. Have a pew, have a drink. Look, everyone, my

122

friend Ella's come to sing along with Jen. What'll it be, Ella? I know.' A deep breath. 'Oh Dan-ny boy, the pipes the pipes are ca-al-ling...'

'No, they are not,' Ella said firmly. 'The pipes have gone to bed and that's where you're going. Come on.'

'I can't. I haven't finished my drink.' A brimming pint was beside her elbow. 'I'm not leaving my lovely drink so pooh to you, Ella Caine.'

'Have one yourself, Mrs Caine?' Harry Junior invited. He looked strained. 'I don't mind her staying so long as she doesn't sing.'

'All right Harry. A half please.' To Jenni she said, 'Finish your drink but no more singing. Understood?'

'*Jawohl, mein Herr.*'

'On the house,' Harry said, drawing Ella's beer. 'Thanks for coming.' He grinned. 'Whatever does she look like?'

'Different.' Ella turned away to hide her own smile. Jenni, perched high on a bar stool, was wearing a figure-hugging sweater cut almost as low as her navel and a matching blue short skirt. Very sexy. The incongruity began with Stephen's red beret pulled low over her eyes and ended with

123

his loosely laced boots at the tip of her long elegant legs.

'I,' Mrs Templeton announced in strident tones, 'am going to the bog.'

'Try it a bit louder,' Ella suggested, 'I don't think everyone heard.'

'Didn't they? I AM GOING...'

'Shut up, you fool. Can you manage? Want me to come?'

'Don't be bloody ridiculous. Just point me in the right direction.'

Jenni gone with surprising dignity, Ella took time to look around. Hubbards and Antonys split as usual, seated along opposite walls. Old Mother H, fat white legs, and her brood. Maggie even, upright for once. Tom Antony, and Doris, pink and giggly from the floor show. Jonno Antony, disgustingly handsome, more like a film star than the village bobby. His poor wife must suffer agonies the minute he leaves her sight. What fun the Foresters' was, not snooty like the Swan. When David came, and the boys, they must all come down here for a pie and a pint. Her assessment took her to the corner by the fireplace. Jack Downing, no less. She raised her glass and he acknowledged it with a curt nod.

124

'That man,' Jenni's clear tones carried far as she returned to base, 'was very rude to me earlier.' She scowled in Jack Downing's direction. 'Do you know what he said when I told him I was yomping? He said the Paras didn't yomp, it was the Marines. How does *he* know? He wasn't there.'

'Irritating to be contradicted, Jenni, but not all that rude. Come on. Let's get you home.'

But Jenni had more to say. She pulled away from Ella on the way out and swayed beside Jack. Unsteady she might be but her enunciation remained perfect. 'My husband,' she said, 'was recommended for a medal during the Falklands campaign.'

'Didn't get it though, did he?' It wasn't the words that were so insolent, it was the tone.

'There were too many heroic deeds and too few medals. Captain Templeton is a fine soldier.'

'That why he's still Captain?'

'Rank is irrelevant. At least he was there. What did *you* do in the war, Daddy?'

'Out,' Ella commanded, 'before you start another one.'

It was Jack Downing who fired the

125

parting shot. 'No takers tonight, then?' he shouted after them. 'Must be the boots put 'em off.'

In the car, Ella said, 'What on earth did he mean by that?'

'I've simply no idea,' Jenni said, and then, 'I can't make up my mind.'

'About what?'

'Which to do first when we get home—be sick, or have a bath.'

The choice was taken from her. Still encumbered by Stephen's heavy boots, she made the cloakroom just in time. It was left to Ella to check with Connie that no dramas had occurred and to look in on the sleeping children.

'I don't think I'll bother with a bath.'

'Well reasoned. Wash your face, clean your teeth and I'll tuck you in. And take those silly boots off before you break your neck.'

Sweet and sleepy, Jenni obeyed.

'By the way, where's Stephen?'

'Duty officer. Not home until tomorrow night.' A seraphic smile. 'I enjoyed this evening. Such fun. Don't go yet, Ella, I want to talk.'

'Sleep would be wiser. All right, five minutes. Talk away.'

'You know you're always on at me to leave Stephen...'

'Not true,' Ella interrupted, 'not always. Only when he's violent. For your sake, and the children's. I quite like Stephen at other times.'

'I do too. He's super in bed, did I ever tell you? But I have decided. Yes, after much thought, I have decided.'

'Decided what?'

'If he doesn't get promotion this time, I shall leave him.'

'But you can't, not just for that.'

'I can. My own sake, you said. I've always wanted to be the colonel's lady. If Stephen can't do that for me I'll find someone else who can.'

'That,' Ella said, 'is the most selfish amoral reasoning I have ever heard.'

'I knew you'd understand.' Jenni snuggled down sleepily. 'You're always so good to me, Ella. I'm glad we went out tonight. We had a lovely time, didn't we? And I was very good.'

'I'm not sure about that one. You were noisy, you were rude—'

'I was very good.' Mrs Templeton raised herself on the pillows and folded her hands complacently over the bed cover.

Not pretty hands, stumpy with square nails, her worst feature. 'I didn't seduce anybody. I could have done. I often do.'

'Really?' Ella smiled, indulging the fantasies of a sleeping child.

'Yes, really.' It wasn't just the beer talking, it was Jenni needing a confessor. 'I've had more men than Maggie Hubbard.' A probable exaggeration but the comparison was acute. 'When Stephen's away, of course. I don't want him to know.'

'I don't expect you do,' Ella said, reeling a little at the revelations. 'But why, Jenni? You just said Stephen was good in bed.'

'He is, he's tireless and full of new ideas. But he isn't enough. I have a lot of time to make up.' The large brown eyes grew dreamy, the full lips curved in a reminiscent smile. 'My childhood was deprived, Ella, my youth too. My parents were desperately poor. Well bred, but poor. They sacrificed themselves so that Mildred—my sister—and I could have a fine education, and then, worn out by worry and work they died. Within six months of each other. Sad, isn't it, but rather beautiful?'

She was revelling in her lies but cross that she had christened her mythical sister

128

Mildred. What a ghastly name. And if Ella remembered, she was stuck with it. And if she said anything to Stephen, there would be questions. Stephen's briefing had been much nearer the truth. Shit.

'I'm telling you this, Ella, because you're my dearest friend and I love you. Even Stephen doesn't know the *real* truth.' That should do it. 'I was only sixteen when Father and Mother passed on. They had given me a good education but nothing else with which to combat the world. I worked long hours—I had to. First in a library, then as a nanny, as a governess of sorts even. I had no time for boyfriends, no energy for recreation after my endless toil. And now I have. Do you understand? Please say you do.'

'I think so.' Amused confusion, confused amusement—one definitive word, that's what Ella needed. There was truth somewhere amidst the rubbish she had heard but she was damned if she knew where. 'Be careful, Jenni. Make sure Stephen doesn't find out about your—conquests. But then, if you're leaving him, it doesn't matter too much, does it?'

'You can be horrid, Ella Caine.' The spell was broken. 'I didn't say I would,

I only said if. And I'll tell you another thing. Once I make up my mind there's no changing it. You didn't know *that*, did you? They wrote a song about me: "Jenny Made Her Mind Up". My mother used to sing it. You should know it, you're the same generation. It goes—'

'Please, no,' Ella implored. 'I think I remember the one you mean.'

Driving home she knew that she did. In particular, she remembered the last stanza. 'Jenny made her mind up at seventy-five, she would be the oldest woman alive. But Fate and Destiny played her tricks and Jenny kicked the bucket at seventy-six.' Worth reminding such a ruthlessly determined young woman? She thought not.

Bill went missing on a Thursday morning. The terriers had dug under the wire netting on the garden side of the hedge in the early hours and headed for freedom. They had done this before but Ella did not worry unduly. She rehearsed the scolding they would get and waited. Around midday, Ben returned. Alone. 'Where,' Ella demanded, 'is your brother?'

She walked for miles that afternoon, searching every inch of familiar ground, calling until she was hoarse. Ben, already exhausted from an eventful morning, began to flag and droop and Ella finally took pity on him and carried him home. Her telephone book beside her, she rang around everyone she knew.

'He'll turn up,' Eve said. 'He always has done before.'

'Correction. *They* always have done before. It's a double act, remember?'

'How's Ben taking it?'

'Quite desolated. Very sad.' Which was far from true. Ben had fallen asleep looking extremely smug. 'How well you deserve the name of Caine,' she had said to him. 'I hope your potage chokes you,' Days later, it occurred to her that the real mess had been her confusion of biblical brothers.

Friday morning and the wanderer had still not returned. Ella rang the police. A disinterested voice asked for a description and in the afternoon, Jonno Antony called on her.

'Sorry to hear one of your dogs is missing, Mrs Caine. Like to tell me about it?' She told him and he asked for a photograph. 'Try not to worry. I expect he'll turn up.'

'That's what everyone says, Jonno, but

I'm beginning to have my doubts. He's not after a bitch, they've both been neutered. Could he have been run over?'

'Might have, but most folk report dogs run over. Or someone finds them at the roadside and rings in.'

'If it was Saturday or Sunday I'd search the lane with a fine toothcomb,' she said darkly.

'Why's that, then?'

'Haven't you noticed them? They must come through the village one way or the other and probably past the Foresters' because it's quicker. Awful old cars and vans and all bound for Highcroft. It's like the hippie descent on Stonehenge for the summer solstice. You *must* have seen them.'

'Can't say I have, though I've heard mention. If I'm not working weekends I usually take the wife out—Brunton Saturday, her mother's the Sunday.' He reopened his notebook. 'Nuisance, are they?'

'More than that, they're a nightmare. But there's nothing I can do about it. Mr Downing says they're all friends of his and that the lane belongs to him anyway.'

'Not too sure on that one,' Jonno said.

'Jack Downing'll say anything but his prayers. But you're right, there's nothing can be done to stop them. Casually he asked, 'Taken their numbers at all?'

'No. Should I have done?'

'No reason you should, just wondered.' He stood up. 'Well now, Mrs Caine, I'll be getting along. Bill, you say? Name on the disc?'

'No, just mine. Address and telephone number too, of course.'

'So a stranger wouldn't know his name, lure him away by calling him?'

'No chance at all. A stranger wouldn't get near him. They're both horribly independent and, I'm afraid, rather bad-tempered.'

'This one seems placid enough.' Jonno actually stroked Ben and Ben actually rolled on his back and smiled.

'I know. I'm thoroughly ashamed of him. I think he's pleased his brother's gone missing.'

At the gate, Jonno asked, 'Mrs Templeton all right, is she?' He laughed. 'A right one she is and no mistake. Bet she had a hangover after last Friday.'

'She did not. Bright as a button. There is no justice in life.' You too, Jonno?

133

Surely not. You're much too decent; but, as they say, the upstanding prick has no conscience.

'Very true, Mrs Caine, very true.' He adjusted his helmet over his black curls and flung a long lean leg over the bicycle saddle. 'I'll be in touch as soon as we hear anything.'

But what Jonno heard the same evening caused him to draw a large question mark under the notes he had made in the afternoon. Nor did he get in touch with Ella. His uncle had already done so. About the same time as Jonno was cycling home for his tea, Tom Antony found Bill. He was working the fences in the field beyond Topfield Copse when something in the bushes caught his keen eye. The glint of sun on something bright. Not a watch or coin as his imagination had hoped, but a metal disc attached to a dog's collar, and the collar around the neck of a very dead dog.

Thoughtfully, Tom went back to the fence for his spade. He dug a neat trench, removed Bill's collar and laid him in the fresh earth. He threw back the soil but, before stamping it flat, he cleaned the leather as best he could with the tea in

134

his thermos, then rubbed it thick with soil. Not a bad job; Jonno would be proud of him.

Ella knew, the minute Tom propped his bike against the hedge, that he had found Bill. She went to meet him swallowing a lump the size of an egg.

'He's dead, isn't he?'

''Fraid so, Mis' Caine. Right sorry I am too. Liked the little chap.'

'And he liked you. Tom, what happened?'

'After rabbits by the look of things. Ground caved in. Only his tail showing.'

'Was it quick, do you think? He didn't suffocate slowly, did he?'

'Quick as anything, Mis' Caine, quick as lightning. What with the weight and the suddenness, gone in a flash. No pain.' He reached into his pocket. 'I brought his collar.'

'Thank you. You are very very kind. You buried him properly, didn't you?'

'Decent and proper, Mis' Caine.'

'I won't ask where.' She took the collar. 'It's damp, wet even. Why, Tom?'

'Ground was wet. Probably why it caved, grown too heavy to hold up. Underground spring most like.'

'So now we are one,' Ella said sadly. Ben

135

was munching biscuit pieces from the other pocket. '*He* doesn't care, the wretch.'

'But you do. No doubt you'll shed a tear or two. Best you do, Mis' Caine. Clean the system ready to start afresh.'

Following Jonno's tyre-tracks almost to the inch, Tom cycled home slowly and thoughtfully. Who would want to do such a thing? Who would smash a small dog's skull like eggshell so that the blood and brains splattered his little body? One thing certain, there'd been truth among the lies he'd just told. One thing certain, the poor little buggar never knew what hit him.

SEVEN

The Hands Off Darrington committee took place at Dowsett's Farm on the third of July. It began some minutes after seven-thirty, because Harry Parr, Junior was late in arriving, and finished abruptly before business was ended. A telephone call from the Foresters' warned that someone was threatening to throw Jack Downing out on his arse.

In the chair: Philip Russell. Others present: Ella Caine, Caroline Courtney, Adam Grayson, Harry Parr (Junior). Invited to attend and contribute: Reg Powell, Planning Committee, Brunton District Council. Invited to listen but say nothing: Fran Russell because (the Chairman said) she was eager to learn more.

'Sorry to drag you here at such short notice,' Philip said; 'and special thanks to Reg Powell for finding the time to join us. I've been doing some snooping on your behalf...'

'Well,' Caroline Courtney said when the Chairman had done, 'I *am* surprised. I always thought Eric Norton a thoroughly decent chap.' Caroline was county through and through, and looked it. Limp cotton frock hideously patterned, lisle stockings, flat shoes. Tight curls around a craggy face, too many teeth and a voice to shatter glass.

'I think he still is,' Ella said—'decent. At least he was honest.'

'Had any approaches yourself, Philip?' Adam asked.

'Not one. I'm beginning to think my role in the plan is ancient as compared to modern.'

137

'Don't you believe it.' Reg Powell stood up. 'Where's the map?' The Ordnance Survey map was spread on the table. Reg pulled a slim roll of clear plastic from a cardboard tube, but clear at the edges only. When laid across the map, farms and fields disappeared under fine black drawings of houses and schools, houses and shopping precincts, houses and tennis courts. And houses.

'So they've submitted at last.' Philip looked closer. 'Good Lord, I'm going to be a public library.'

Silence afterwards. Silence and gloom as everyone, Fran included, looked and pondered.

'Are you supposed to be showing us this?' Adam asked the man from the council.

'No, I am not. Strictly confidential as yet so I'll be obliged if you pass on only a general impression. No detail.' Reg Powell was a very ordinary-looking man, instantly forgettable, but the bow he gave Caroline Courtney was worth of a peerage. 'Mrs Courtney can be very persuasive.'

'Hugh, really,' she said, although pleased. 'He did the digging and the general bullying. Don't worry, Mr Powell, your

138

knuckles won't be rapped so long as we all keep mum. And we will, won't we?'

'There are many more than five hundred houses here,' Ella said, trying to estimate and add the scores of new estates. 'And they're not executive-type. Far from it.'

'Who believes the papers?' Again, Reg Powell. 'More like five thousand, Mrs Caine.'

'Ella, please,' and then, brightly: 'Good for trade, Harry.'

'That's a joke.' Harry Junior was rubbing his balding pate with moist hands. 'How many pubs in among that lot? A dozen at least I should say. No, it'll be curtains for the Foresters', no mistake.'

'Only if it happens,' Adam said, pulling at his long nose. 'And perhaps not even then. They can't destroy the old Darrington as such, only build a new one around it.'

'But who will want to stay in the old one? Will you?'

'Probably not.' Adam turned keen eyes on Reg Powell. 'Will it happen?'

'Yes, it will happen. Not this year or next. It may take five, ten years but the developers will win in the end. Oh, we'll keep on turning the plans down for as long as we can but there's a limit to what the

Government calls negative thinking. Then there'll be public enquiries, then a legal battle. That will cost a pretty penny. You don't get a first class QC for peanuts and there's no doubt the consortium can afford the best. I'm sorry to bring you so little hope but, as my old mother used to say, it's all over bar the shouting.'

'I'll shout to the bitter end,' Fran said, speaking quite out of turn. She went to make the coffee.

'Money,' Mrs Courtney was thoughtful. 'Lots of lovely money. Mr Chairman, I move that this committee is not truly representative of Darrington. I move that it be expanded to include new blood.'

'New, but not blue?'

'Sad, isn't it?' Caroline still held the floor. 'Old Harrington would have gone for them with his shooting stick. My Hugh would have been livid, of course, outpaced for once, but the bloody gout's crippling him. Alexandra's pretty blue but no money and anyway, she's fairly feeble. No backbone. I'm afraid there is no alternative.' A bark of laughter. 'Where did I hear that, I wonder?' She looked around enquiringly. 'Who's going to be brave and venture into Grotland?'

'Fran will,' Philip said just as the coffee arrived.

'Fran will what?'

'Chat up Alicia Hargreaves. We need the Grots for their money only but, by Christ, we need them. Committee first, then unanimous and total support. Will you do it?'

'Why not?' She flushed with pleasure. 'I'll have a go.'

'I move,' Ella said, 'that Fran be co-opted onto the committee as well.'

'Seconded,' said Adam.

'All in favour? Great. Come on, Fran, join us at the table.' Philip felt quite jolly. It was all going well. Lots of positive thinking, action in the offing. Ten years was the outer limit, no doubt on that score. More like five. Could he last that long? Yes, with promises of better things to come. And come they would. It was there on the map, a public library. This week, next week, some time, the consortium would call.

'You know the chief culprit, don't you?' Reg Powell was leaving. 'I'm not sure of the constituency that voted him in but they ought to be eating their hearts out. Minister for the Environment, *he's* the nigger in the woodpile—not being racist, you understand.'

Caroline too was making a move. 'My dear man, I don't think you can blame him personally. He's only following orders from the top.'

The others sat for a while longer, toasting Fran's election and mulling the evening over in their wine. 'Who,' Ella asked, 'is Minister for the Environment?'

'I haven't the foggiest,' Fran said, 'but I hope he's suffering from rabies, diarrhoea and a streaming cold all at the same time.'

Ella and Adam left together. 'I wonder what Harry Senior would have made of all this,' Ella said.

'It probably wouldn't have registered, except in terms of new ground on which to air his grievances.' Adam smiled. 'I miss him still, don't you?'

'Tremendously. Apart from Tom, there aren't any real characters left.' He limped with her to her car. 'You're coming too, aren't you? I think you've done splendidly, walking here. No cause to overdo things.'

Adam sighed. 'It's supposed to be good for me. Gentle exercise. Why are things good for one usually unpleasant? Thank you, I will join you, but only if you allow me to buy you a drink at the Swan.'

'What about Eve?'

'She knows.'

'Ah! Is this Ella Caine therapy week?'

'Not at all. It's, and I quote, find out what the hell's up with Toby.'

Toby was suffering. He was also hiding something. Despite Eve's gentle—for her—probing that morning, he had revealed very little. Staff problems, he said. Tracy, the waitress, had left a few days previously and they were having trouble replacing her. Not that she had been much good. The girl who had taken over was, however, even worse. A Hubbard, and a very clumsy one. Giles said, and Giles was quite right, that they must advertise, there being no chance of finding an experienced silver waitress in Darrington. For the time being they must make do. And that was that. As Eve told Adam later, for once Toby was giving nothing away.

Had she followed him home, Eve would have seen Toby's worst fears realized. And Henry it was who precipitated the inevitable outcome.

Henry was already in a bad temper when the partners joined him in the kitchen.

'If you two old chestnuts would move your bums *I* might be able to get on with my work. Only might, mind you.' Sweat pouring, Henry made a great show of moving pots and pans from A to B, then back again. 'Honestly, boys, this galley's a nightmare, an absolute screaming horror movie. No room to swing your head, never mind a cat.'

'It's not as bad as all that.' Giles reproved in deep tones. 'You're simply—disorderly. I know the kitchen's not up to *QE Two* standards...'

'Nor Maxim's, nor the Café Royal.' (He had worked at neither establishment.) 'Those were the days if ever days were. Umpteen *commis* running helter-skelter, a couple of *sous-chefs*, kitchen boys, dishwashers and everything so shining you never needed a mirror to squeeze a pimple. Just looked at the bottom of one of the pans and—splat!'

'Please.' Giles shuddered. An artistic hand was raised to shield an artistic eyebrow. 'Spare us such details. I suppose one must be thankful you turned the pan over.'

'Not often, *Maître*, only if there was time.' Henry grinned showing a mouthful

144

of rather bad teeth. Good humour was on the return. An almighty crash from the restaurant and they all jumped. ''Allo, 'allo. Speedy Gonzales missed the table again with the tray? You can get rid of her since yesterday. Useless as you two in a brothel. There's more of my sauces gone down the sink than piss down the lavatory. Here!' He managed to pour two coffees with one hand while rolling pastry with the other. 'Take your drinks and disappear. I've problems enough without a couple of nancies breathing my share of air.'

They took their coffee to a polish-smudged table. 'Henry *is* awful,' Toby had giggled, not at all offended, 'but I do love him, don't you?'

'His humour is—unique.' Giles was thoughtful. 'He's right, that girl has to go. But what do we do in the interim?'

'We'll advertise as you suggested.'

'But it may take weeks before someone suitable pops through the door.' Giles sighed deeply and melodiously. 'If only we had time. *You* could train that wretched Hubbard creature, you could train anyone. You're so good in the dining-room—faultless service, everything precisely right.'

Toby blushed scarlet at the praise. 'I'll do it if you like. Until we find someone else, that is. But that will leave you short in here and behind the bar.'

'I have an idea. Tell me what you think. You know Keith, the young chap who comes in with Morris?'

'Yes.' Why was the day darkening? Why was the wind blowing chill?

'We were chatting the other night and it seems he's very experienced in our line. He's pleasant and well mannered and presents himself well. Why don't we ask him to help out? Only on a very temporary basis, of course.'

'Of course.' What on earth else could he say? 'Do what you think best, Giles. You always get your own way in the end.'

Tears behind the eyes and a feeling of impending doom, he had nevertheless managed to flounce through to the restaurant. There, voice shrill and hands shaking, he had asked Miss Hubbard to leave the premises. Immediately. His fine hair flopped and he pushed it back impatiently, his glasses steamed with pent-up emotion. He fidgeted with them, took them off, cleaned them on a napkin, fidgeted anew. With the maximum of noise he cleared the tables and relaid them, humming a gay ditty to allay any suspicions that he might remotely be upset—which, at ten minutes past nine the same evening, he still was. And not just remotely, extremely so.

'I don't think we need look any further,' Adam said softly to Ella.

They had found an unoccupied table in the lounge bar and were watching the drama. Toby doing restaurant duty, to and fro, from the kitchen. Enough said. Giles and the new boy cosily ensconced behind the bar. They seemed very happy together.

'Poor old Toby. He must be hurting like hell.'

'And they say women are bitchy,' Ella said.

'Women of both genders,' Adam summed up sadly.

Two days after the meeting at which the plan to change Darrington's face had been revealed, Fran telephoned Ella.

'She's coming here. I thought it only polite to return her hospitality and, besides, I'll be much more relaxed on my home ground.'

'Fair enough,' Ella agreed.

'So can you make it around ten-thirty this morning? Earlier if poss. I'd like to use you as my sounding board.'

'I thought you were going alone and bravely into the unknown? OK, I'll come.'

She took Ben with her. She had started taking him everywhere, even in the car. He was such a changed character, it was difficult to remember how monstrous he had been. How they both had been. Now he followed her like a lamb, hung on her every word and only barked when such arch enemies as the postman or milkman had the temerity to call.

'I would never have believed it,' Fran said, receiving an effusive greeting of licks and nudges. 'He's smashing now, isn't he?'

'Yes, and I feel awful about it. I mourn poor old Bill like anything but I have to admit that life with one dog is considerably easier than it was with two.'

Ella lowered herself carefully into an armchair. The occasion dictated decorum and they had both dressed carefully, she in brown and beige, accentuating the sheen in her dark hair, Fran in a soft sack of vertical stripes intended to lessen her stout impact.

Alicia Hargreaves arrived on the dot. She was cool and crisp in ice-blue. Frock, matching shoes and handbag, earrings and beads. Even her hair was skilfully coloured to tone.

'An interesting room,' she pronounced after greetings and introductions had been made. A fairly apt description. Some good pieces of furniture, a book-lined wall and a lot of jumble.

It was easy to interest her in their cause, easy to gain her enthusiastic support. 'We simply had no idea,' she said, dabbing her lips with a diminutive blue handkerchief. 'We had heard, of course, that development was possible, but not on such a large scale. Bertie—"may" husband—will be horrified when I tell him. Perhaps he could join your committee? He's terribly good at that sort of thing.'

A wallet was taken from the blue handbag and a twenty-pound note crisply extracted. 'Would you like a donation now?'

'Heavens, no,' Ella laughed, 'but if it comes to a court case, we'll all have to dip into our pockets.'

'Such a "nace" place, Darrington,' Mrs Hargreaves said as she was leaving. 'Bertie and I feel "quate" at home already.'

'You should have taken that twenty quid,' Fran scolded after they had done laughing. 'I'm short on the housekeeping this week.'

Philip, joining them for a quick noggin before lunch, could not have been more interested, approving or amused. A good morning's work, he assured, well done the pair of you. Yes, indeed, a good morning's work. He had finally been approached, finally acknowledged as an important link in the development chain. Best of all, he had been able to talk alone to the well-groomed emissary. All that was now needed was a brief, edited account.

The timing could not have been better. He had noted Alicia's sleek Mercedes, wished he could be a fly on the wall and decided to run into Brunton for the wire Tom needed for Lower Meadow. That is if the car started. It did not. He was tinkering when a shadow fell across the greased-up engine and there, dark suit, snowy shirt, polished shoes, was his guardian angel. 'Problems?' the stranger enquired pleasantly.

'A fly in the carburettor, I think.' Heart hammering, Philip asked. 'Can I help you?'

A slim card was proffered. Philip read without touching. 'Put it away,' he said.

'You don't wish to keep it?'

'Thanks, but no. I run the local anti-development group. You've walked straight into enemy HQ.'

'I know that, Mr Russell, but I would still like to talk to you. May we go inside?'

'Fraid not. There's a sub-committee meeting in progress. You'd probably be lynched.' He looked around cautiously for some form of transport. 'Did you walk?'

'Only from the main road. A pretty village.'

'We think so. Look, Mr...?'

'Smith.'

'Of course. It would have to be. Or Jones.'

A smile. 'No. It really is Smith.'

'You're wasting your time, Mr Smith. I'm not for sale.' Not yet but I will be. When everyone else capitulates I'll run up the white flag as well. Philip Russell was a hero, Darrington will say. He held out to the bitter end.

'Every man has his price, Mr Russell.'

'Is that right? Have you been jamming your foot in other doors?'

'You know I have. You made it your business to find out.'

'In my capacity as...'

'Yes, Mr Russell, we understand.' Another smile, broader this time. 'There's really no point in outlining our intentions, is there? You know them already. You have probably even seen our plans. I'll wish you good day. You know where to contact us if you change your mind.'

'As a matter of interest,' Philip asked casually, 'how much would you offer?'

Inside Mr Smith a green light winked mission accomplished. 'About one and a half, possibly a little more.'

'I see.' No, I do not. If Eric Norton's getting three, why am I down for a miserable one and a half? 'Quite a lot of money, Mr Smith.'

'I'm sure you would find it useful. Good morning, Mr Russell. Thank you for giving me your time.' And your agreement in principle. Greedy, aren't you, Mr Russell? You want more. You think if you continue to oppose us we'll slip you an extra million to co-operate. We won't do that, Mr Russell; we'll squeeze you out in the end and for much less. Stepping carefully around pot-holes, Mr Smith pondered the vagaries of human nature. With a place in such bad shape as Dowsett's, any reasonable financial offer should be more than acceptable. One and a half million pounds, the opportunity to get rid of a crumbling millstone, and yet he had seen disappointment in the farmer's eyes. An inability to comprehend the size of the sum? Perhaps. When you're juggling with two noughts an additional four might seem figments of the imagination, like flying saucers. Mr Smith knew better. He had yet to reach the dizzy heights but he was well used to dealing in them. Hundreds, what were they nowadays? No more than change in the pocket, and very small change at that.

'So,' Philip said cheerily, 'it's happened. I must have been last on the list.'

'It was probably only a token gesture,' Fran said. 'They must know they're beating their heads pointlessly.'

'What was he like, this Mr Smith?'

'Courteous, charming if you like. A smooth fast talker with all the blarney of a professional salesman.'

'Did he mention money at all?'

'I think he was going to but I cut him short.' Philip laughed expansively. Was it the timbre that made the sound so insincere? 'You never know, for a couple of million even *I* might have been tempted.'

The telephone was ringing when Ella reached home. She got to it just as the caller lost patience. Irritating. Five minutes later it rang again. 'Mrs Caine?' A voice she did not recognize.

'Yes.'

'Mrs Ella Caine of Highcroft Cottage, Darrington?'

'Yes.' Who on earth—?

'This is Detective Sergeant Jameson from the North Hampshire Drug Squad, Mrs Caine. Have you a moment to talk?'

Oh God, Andrew. What have you...? No, wrong county and anyway he's classed as an adult now, they wouldn't want me. 'Yes, Mr Jameson?'

'You have a new neighbour, Mrs Caine. I understand weekend traffic is...excessive, shall we say?'

'But you can't do anything about it, can you?'

'No. It must be very annoying. Mrs Caine, could we meet?'

'Well, yes, I suppose so. If you think—'

'I do. I would prefer not to visit you in your home, I may be recognized. Do you

154

come into Brunton at all?'

'Occasionally. I could make a special trip if need be.'

'Thank you. The station car-park tomorrow at eleven? What make of car do you drive, Mrs Caine, and the number, please?'

They agreed to meet the following day. He did not describe himself. No rolled umbrella, no pink carnation. He added that discretion would be advisable. She assured him that the secret was theirs alone.

Brunton was the sort of town anyone with taste disliked on sight. Intimate knowledge of the soulless streets and precincts did nothing to alter the opinion. Once a sleepy market town where only the mundane could be obtained, Brunton was now a sprawling, hideously designed, badly erected monstrosity offering the same facilities. The only pretty buildings, washed delicate pinks and greens, were sandwiched between brick and concrete. No longer shops with funny odds and ends, they housed insurance brokers, employment agencies and estate agents. Estate agents. They were sprouting like mushrooms on a moist August field. Fran, taking the girls on enforced trips to the dentist or school outfitters, made them play a game. 'Liz, you count the estate agents, Emma, the shoe shops. I, because I am grown up, will do the pubs.' The shoe shops won by a short head—twelve at the last Emma count.

Ella hated Brunton as much as most but she did not dislike the railway station unduly. It was dirty and depressing, spirals of litter chasing each other in an effort to amuse and, in winter, the coldest place on earth. But it was functional. It had a purpose. It took you away to London or airports or on visits to friends. It brought your loved ones back to you. As far as she was concerned, the station could stay.

Detective Sergeant Jameson, in plain clothes, was, Ella thought, a poor example of working incognito. He must surely attract a deal of attention. He was much too old for scruffy jeans, a faded denim jacket, cowboy boots and hair on the collar. What was it the French would call him? *Un vieux gamin?* But the French lent more elegance to their bid for eternal youth; a rose in the lapel, champagne in one hand and sad intensity of purpose. DS Jameson had none of these but his eyes were bright and intelligent and his handshake firm.

'Very good of you to come,' he said, once inside her car. 'No inconvenience, I hope?'

'None at all.'

'Call me Alex, will you? And you are—Ella, yes? It's easier in a working relationship.' Abruptly he turned the full power of his eyes on her face. 'What do you think about drugs, Ella?'

'You mean medical or—?'

'Don't be coy, dear, you're much too intelligent. You know the branch I'm in. I mean drugs as in heroin, cocaine, LSD, and that sweet little starter, cannabis.'

'I hate them all.'

'Excellent. Now we can really get going.'

He told a good tale, so much so that Ella stopped watching the incoming trains and wishing John or Andrew would come strolling to greet her. Jack Downing, he said, was into drugs in a pretty big way. Not just a user, a dealer. He had a terrace house in ˙Brunton, did she know that? Still living there for the time being which was understandable. Many a banging had they—the Drug Squad—given that old front door in the early hours. Never came

157

up with anything much, though. A few grammes of cannabis, enough to question, charge and ultimately fine, but not the big stuff, not the weekly pay-packet. The yard too, they'd been over that on numerous occasions. Ever searched a junk-yard, Ella? Don't try. It's a death-trap for man and dog. Look what happened to Sammy. Yes, he was in it too, taught young Jack the ropes from the word go. To sum up, we're watching Jack Downing as much as manpower will allow. Four of us, Ella, that's the grand total of the Squad, and although Jack's big, he's not the only offender.

A cigarette packet was offered. 'I don't,' Ella said.

'Sensible girl. Mind if I do? So where was I? Still in Brunton. Let's move on to Darrington, shall we? Highcroft Farm, sole owner one John Michael Downing. Isolated to an extent, in a hell of a mess and that's where we think the action is about to begin. No, hang on, Ella, I know what you're going to say. By action I mean Mr Big. Not a ginormous Mr Big but big enough, and bigger by far than Jack. Our particular Mr Big is probably London-based but he may shift himself if the wind blows hot or cold. He's probably fourth or fifth down the line but he's still important. For the toppest of top men you'd have to sift Parliament, the Church even, and that's not on, not unless evidence is irrefutable.' He grinned at her. 'What *were* you going to say?'

'Only that there must be a great deal of action, as you call it, at Highcroft at the weekends.'

'Small fry, Ella. We can pick them up any time and we do. Silly people with a habit but not villains as such. Jack the lad's a different story, he *is* a villain.'

He outlined what he wanted her to do. Watch the cavalcade for us over one weekend. Make, colour, registration numbers. Not good on make? Not to worry, colour and numbers will do fine. Let me have the list over the phone at Brunton Police Station, and here's the extension to ask for. We'll run a check to make sure there's no new blood. Then all you have to do is watch out for something different. Swisher and more expensive, not the usual Highcroft chummy. No, it doesn't mean sitting all day with your binoculars trained on the lane, it means going about your normal business but keeping your eyes and ears open. Will you do it?'

She said she would. He was out of the car before she remembered Bill and the package in the festering dung-heap. 'Mr Jameson—Alex! I've just thought of something.'

'Well, now,' he said after she had told him all, 'that's interesting. How heavy would you say?'

'I'm sorry, I've no idea. I'm not very good—'

'Same problem as cars, eh?' Another wide grin. 'Cannabis resin, I'll bet my boots on it. About that big?' His hands approximated the size. 'Two, two and a half thousand quid there.' Casually he said, 'Good on your little dog. We could use him.'

'Not possible, I'm afraid,' Ella said. 'He went down a rabbit hole last week and never came up.'

'Oh? Sorry to hear that, Ella. Thanks so much for your time and—keep in touch.'

That explains, he thought as he drove away, the report on the missing terrier that had somehow been diverted to his desk. Smart lad, PC Antony. Put two and two together and came up with the right answer. DS Jameson was fond of dogs, he had three of his own. I'll get you for that little fellow, John Michael Downing. It may take time but I'll get you in the end.

Ella called in at the shop on her way back home. Permission to do so had been granted, although not specifically.

'Strictly *entre nous*,' Eve told Adam later, 'and I mean strictly, Ella's spying for the local Drug Squad.'

'Is she now? I didn't realize she had been connected with the police.'

'She hasn't. It's all very unofficial, citizen co-operation or something like. It seems Jack Downing's a dealer.'

'I'm not surprised. I suppose that explains the friendly weekend visits?'

'It does indeed. But not a word to Bessie, not that you would, you old tortoise. I promised I would stress that secrecy is essential. The guy who briefed her, a detective sergeant with the Drug Squad, was apparently quite human. He said she would have to overspill to someone but to make sure she chose the right person.'

'She'll be all right, won't she?' Adam pulled at his long nose and frowned. 'There's nothing dangerous involved?'

'Lord, no. Observation in the main. It

161

will do her good. She hasn't enough to think about.'

A staccato of rain beat a tattoo.

'God, I hate this country. Vaguely warm one minute, back to the Arctic the next. How long do we have to stay here, Adam?'

'We'll go whenever you want. And wherever. Is it really becoming too much?'

'On nights like this, yes. I want to be hot again, dripping, miserably hot. I want to be plagued by mosquitoes, suffer damnation from prickly heat. I want to roll naked on cool marble floors, close the shutters at first light against the heat of the day. I want mangoes and guavas, humming-birds and hibiscus, rum punches and shellfish salads, and time. Blessed lingering time that slows to a gentle saunter. Time to talk, to think, remember. Adam, when can we go?'

'As I said, whenever you like.'

'We can't.' Eve scowled and gnawed with increasing appetite. 'We have to see Darrington through, don't we? Don't ask me through what, but through something. It would be tantamount to treachery if we left before...'

'Everyone else does?'

'Yes. Why are you always one step ahead

162

of me?' They sat silently, listening to the rain. 'Funny, isn't it, that Ella should tell us rather than Fran? Or even Philip?'

'Yes,' Adam said. 'Very funny.'

EIGHT

John Caine wrote to say he had three weeks' leave at the end of the month—wrote, not spoke, because he preferred not to listen to his mother's protests. He would be spending the beginning and the end with her, he said, but the middle had been allocated to Mary. Had he told her about Mary? A Wren from Nottingham. They had wangled leave together and he was going to spend some time at her home. They thought they might also pop over to the Continent for a few days.

Thoroughly fed up, Ella rang David. 'You'd better make his first weekend,' she said. 'Mary might have other ideas about his coming home for the last.'

'For God's sake, Ella, be realistic.' Her husband was unsympathetic. 'Three weeks in Darrington. He'd go out of his mind.'

'He managed to retain his sanity when he was younger.'

'But he's a grown man now with wider interests. I wonder what the girl's like. Be thankful he's coming home at all.'

'Out of duty, nothing more.'

'You could be right.'

His concurrence was not morale-boosting. 'Will Andrew be there?'

'If I can track him down. He's somewhere in the Lake District with a group of college friends.'

'Good for him. The birds have flown, eh?'

'Don't sound so bloody pleased.'

It was disconcerting to find that no one was on her side, that David's opinions were applauded. 'Let them go,' Eve advised; 'otherwise you'll lose them for ever.' 'What do you honestly expect?' Fran asked. 'They're not Darrington dumplings, they need more than Mum's apple pie.' Sympathetic to an extent, she added, 'Poor old you. It must get lonely on your own.'

'It doesn't,' Ella said truthfully. It wasn't loneliness that bugged, it was the feeling of not belonging.

She did her duty by DS Jameson the first

weekend after their clandestine meeting. The weather allowed her freedom of the garden and she noted all the registration numbers on a small pad of paper tucked into her gardening basket. 'Well done,' he said when she had read them out over the phone. 'Very familiar, all of them, but we'll double check. Now all you have to do is watch for the unusual.'

'I hope it doesn't occur this coming weekend. The family will all be home. My husband would certainly not approve.'

'I didn't realize you were married, Ella, I thought—'

'Separated,' she said, 'but still married.'

Philip arrived unexpectedly on the Friday morning. She was up to her eyes in baking and would not allow him to steer her upstairs. 'Don't be an idiot. There'll be burnt offerings all round if you do. Where, incidentally, are you supposed to be?' Since Fran's outburst, she had become cautious to the point of paranoia.

'In Brunton.'

'So it will look funny if you're seen driving from this direction?'

'I won't be seen. I'm not driving and anyway, that's where Fran is. Brunton.' He stepped back as she sped by with a steaming pie. 'You don't seem pleased to see me.'

'I am and I'm not. I thought the idea was to cool things?'

'Your idea, not mine.' He was aiming to break her resistance, to focus her attention on his unashamed need for her body. Not by touching her. He stripped her naked with his hungry eyes. 'Look at me, Ella.'

'Not unless you stop trying to get me into bed. I can't, there just isn't time. But I was going to break five minutes for coffee so sit down.' She ovened the next batch. 'Why didn't you let me know?'

'A mad impulse. I thought I would nourish your needs to prevent temptation over the weekend.'

'With David? You *are* mad?'

'You won't, will you, Ella? You won't get tiddly and sleep with him for old times' sake? All right, I know it's none of my business and I have Fran, but if you do, don't tell me. I should be horribly jealous.'

She became concerned. 'Philip dear, I think you're exaggerating what we have out of all proportion. No strings, remember? That was the agreement.'

'Tell me,' he said, 'if I were free, would

166

you marry me? Think about it.'

'I don't have to think. No, I would not. Would you ask me?'

'I might. Why wouldn't you?'

'Because I don't think we're suited except in bed, because if I made one mistake I could easily make another and because,' she flicked cake crumbs at him, 'I should hate to be a farmer's wife.'

'I may not always be a farmer.' He knew immediately that he had said almost too much. As though to cover his blunder, the cooker pinged enthusiastically and Ella leapt to open its door.

'Is Fran all right?' she asked as he was leaving. She had allowed him to kiss and fondle her but had managed to remain detached.

'Perfectly. If I didn't believe you implicitly I'd find it hard to accept that she suspects anything untoward in my life.'

Washing the crocks at the end of her stint, Ella pondered on how easy it had been to resist temptation. She was relieved that they had not made love, felt neither frustrated nor deprived. Why? Was it interest she was losing? No, that was too trivial an interpretation, the word was need. Her need for him was running downhill fast. There had been too little in her life when she fell under his spell, no problems to gnaw at, no decisions to make. Just mundane routine. Philip had filled a void with his animal appetite and his strong clean body. He had brought excitement, made her feel eighteen. Like a wartime romance, living only for the day and the hope of tomorrow, they had played beautiful games, been stimulated by their secret. Only the secret was now a burden and she felt sick with guilt. She wanted no more of it. She wanted to concentrate on other things. David, the house, John, the den of iniquity that was Highcroft. Marriage? To Philip? Never in the mind of man. What would they do, what would they say to each other when the magic of sex had burnt itself out? Nothing on both counts. Misery on both sides. When you are unhappy and alone, tomorrow is another day. When you are unhappy and married, tomorrow is the same day. Ella Caine knew all about that. So goodbye Philip, once she got the message across. And what did he mean, he might not always be a farmer? What else had he in mind? Wishful thinking, she decided, no more than that.

David drove down from Oxford on the Friday night. Once a commuting London architect, a small pencil on a very large drawing-board in the early days, he had soon become established in his own right. Constant travelling and London pressures began to get to him and he decided, wisely enough, to quit the city while still sound in mind and body. From then on he had acted foolishly, certainly as far as his marriage was concerned. He plumped for Oxford as his next move—visited, explored, leased a floor in a charming old house converted to office space. He even amassed a sheaf of very possible homes from local estate agents. Ella, when he eventually told her, admitted that she had nothing against Oxford as a place but a very strong objection to being presented with a *fait accompli*. True, communication had been poor of late, restricted in the main to good morning and goodnight, but that was no excuse. You've done it again, she shouted at him. David Caine, the great unilateral decision-maker. You can damn well find yourself another Ruth. I am not going—nor did she.

'Boys home yet?' he asked, kissing her frugally on the cheek.

'Tomorrow morning. Your first paternal duty for a long time, collecting them. Fingers crossed they catch the same train.'

It was strange seeing him sitting in his accustomed armchair for the first time in—how long? Two years at least. Familiar, yet someone she did not know. Half century clocked up, long, lean, ageing with infinite taste; white flashes at the temples, a slight salting to the otherwise luxurious brown, laughter lines deepened and extended around the eyes. David Caine, the ambitious young man she had loved so passionately twenty-four years ago. Where had the love gone? Philip could rest his uneasy mind, she felt no desire, no impulse to touch this man with whom she had been so intimate. Yet she was glad he was there. Twenty-four years. Silver wedding next. Should it be acknowledged? Ought she to send him a card?

'You've been decorating again.' He looked around the room he had created. 'It's good, I like it.'

'It's a super room,' she said. 'You gave it your best.'

'I know it's a bit late,' he said slowly, 'but I want to apologize for being so dictatorial in the past. About colours and furnishing, I mean. I thought I knew best.' He laughed. 'You hated the kitchen, didn't you?'

'Infinitely. It was the first room I tackled after you left.' She was curious. 'Why this sudden awareness?'

'Helen. She pointed out the error of my ways, said the woman should always have the final say.'

'Hooray for Helen. How is she, by the way?'

'Quite well, thank you. What about you? Found anyone for yourself?'

'Not on your life. Once bitten, five million times shy.'

'What a pity,' he said. 'You're much too good to be wasted.'

Was this a compliment? If so, was he feeling well? There had been very few in their years together and far too many criticisms.

'Whatever do you mean?'

'Exactly what I said. You are still an extremely attractive woman who looks at least ten years younger than she is.' And so she is and so she does, he thought, watching a smile begin in her eyes and spread to her mouth. What went wrong?

171

Was it my fault entirely? No. Two to make, two to break.

'Thank you, kind sir,' Ella said, wishing that he had voiced his opinion sooner. Fifteen or so years sooner. 'And thank you, Helen. She has changed you almost beyond recognition.'

The boys came home together and, in the resultant disorder that always followed, Ella felt the fluid that was now family begin to jell. 'Where am I sleeping, Mum? Oh God, not in the same room as *him*.' 'All right if I shower now? Which is my towel?' 'Could you *possibly* wash a *very* few things for me?' 'Ella, does this metamorphosed dog have a lead? I'll take him out for five minutes.' Head thumping, she sat at the kitchen table cherishing a feeling akin to joy. It won't last, I know that, God, but thank you for letting me relive how it sometimes was.

The bickering began on the way back from the Foresters'. They had walked down there for a lunch-time drink. An unusual sight causing many a Darrington head to turn. The Caines *en famille*. Was there something in the papers they had missed?

'We should have taken a car,' Andrew

172

grumbled. 'It's a long way when you're hungry.'

'You can't possibly be hungry,' Ella protested. 'You ate—'

'Don't itemize, Mum. I know what I ate. I also know I'm hungry.'

'Pity the pubs changed so much,' David said. 'Too many loud-mouthed bores for my liking.' There had been a fair sprinkling of Grots, guffawing mindlessly. 'I would have thought, Ella, with that crowd taking over you'd be only too eager to leave.'

'They are not my friends. I have very little to do with them.'

'A divided Darrington, eh? Not like the old days at all. Definitely time to move on, I would say.'

'I'm sure you would.' Her hackles were truly up. 'Especially when it's in your interests to pass such judgement.'

Dinner began well enough. She took time to look at her sons, enormous dark-haired young men. Good stock, strong and healthy appetites to match. Her efforts were applauded and appreciated. 'To the lady of the house,' David raised his glass, 'for doing us all so proud.' Mellowed by food and wine, he was a delightful companion. Pity I couldn't have kept him permanently stuffed, Ella thought. 'Another toast.' Glasses were recharged. 'To John, seafarer. May he have fair winds and a safe passage home.'

Noisily, Ella clattered dishes. 'Mother, please don't start.' The sailor had been quick to see bright tears.

'Start what, you silly boy?'

'You're going to blub, I know you are.'

'I am not. But I am sad. It's so far away, John and for such a long time.'

'Six months is nothing. When you were my age it would have been a three year commission. Six months is minutes.'

'You'll have to get used to it,' Andrew continued heartlessly. 'When I've taken my degree I'm off to the States for a couple of years.'

'Jolly good,' Ella said. 'Make sure you let me have your dirty washing in good time before you go.'

They skirted around the sale of the cottage interminably. Or so it seemed. Who was moving out of Darrington, who moving in. The exorbitant amounts asked, the astronomical prices paid. Ella could stand it no longer. 'Your father wants to sell,' she said to John, 'and Andrew agrees with him. How do you feel?'

'Give me a moment to think.' He was quite taken aback. She was surprised that Andrew had not primed him.

'Take as many as you like. *I* am going to clear up, wash up and feed Ben.' She waited for, 'We'll give you a hand,' or 'Need some help?' Predictably, neither was forthcoming. She went on her very audible way.

'I can understand how you feel.' John said later. 'It's a super house, I shall miss it myself.' (Note tense, decision taken.) 'The garden too, you've done wonders with it. But there are other houses and other gardens and it isn't fair to stop Dad having somewhere of his own.'

'Vote counted,' she said brightly, 'three to one. I lose.' She felt furiously angry. They were right, she was wrong and she knew it, but where had the memories gone? 'So where shall I go? Come on, let's find a map and stick a pin in it.'

'There's no immediate rush,' David said gently. 'We'll hang on a bit longer to get the best price possible. That way——'

'That's what the farmers are doing. Holding out against the developers for that extra million or two.' She gulped her brandy. 'I know your arguments are right, it's your lack of real caring that hurts. All our years together under this roof and not one of you gives a damn.'

'Oh God,' said Andrew, 'time for the violins.'

'Stop that!' David was sharp. 'Ella, we do care.'

'No, you don't.' She would not allow them to, not now. 'You're all utterly selfish, you think of no one but yourselves. You boys make me ashamed. You gorge on the food it took me hours to prepare but will either of you lift a finger to help me with the dishes? Not on your sweet life.'

'You never asked.'

'I shouldn't need to ask. And if I had, I know the answer by heart—in a minute, Mum. It always was. In a minute. You, too, David, you were just as bad. So rather than wait interminable minutes that stretched into hours, I did it all myself and I still do.' She felt marginally better for her outburst although no one looked suitably ashamed. Only uncomfortable. 'Some family,' she spat, determined to go out on a bang.

'You are quite right,' David said slowly, 'We are all selfish and that, my dear Ella, includes you. As for family, we've never really been one as such. Just four individuals going our own selfish ways.'

Andrew and John were sent down to Briar Cottage on Sunday morning to confirm that lunch was on. Lunch with the Caines. As in plural, as in all four.

'I can't remember whether I was positive or not,' Ella said. 'I know I *told* Jenni but I don't think I was absolutely sure at the time. That you would all be here. I must be going senile.'

Jenni was looking, John reported back, about sixteen. No glamour that sunny Sunday, no aura of earthy sex appeal. Jeans, trainers, a loose shirt and hair fastened into a pony-tail.

'Good-o,' she had said cheerily. 'That knocks hours off my stretch of hard labour.'

Stephen, stripped to the waist, was demolishing an unattractive path. He expected her total involvement. He always did.

Andrew took up the tale. If Jenni was looking stunning, Stephen was looking odd. And the twins as miserable as sin. How odd? Ella demanded, he's not heading for a, you know, is he? Not likely, Andrew said, not with all that concrete to smash. But his eyes were funny and he was whinnying a lot. He said he wanted the kids to help him and then he changed his mind. Just as well. There was dust, bits of debris, flying everywhere.

'But they're only three,' Ella protested.

'I know. That's what Jenni said. And *he* said three was old enough to start learning that life wasn't all playtime. Jenni made tea and he eased off for five minutes. Congratulated John on his appointment! Appointment, would you believe? And told him to pot as many Argies as possible, that's if there were any left.'

'God forbid,' Ella said fervently.

'Anyway, he seemed to be enjoying himself in his own peculiar way. Said destruction was satisfying, it took so little time, and that concrete should be kept for bunkers. He'd got tremendous strength. And stamina. Smash, smash, smash and never a pause. Only I had the feeling it wasn't just concrete he was smashing.'

'Oh Lord,' Ella said, 'I wish I knew how his mind works.'

★ ★ ★ ★

Stephen Templeton's mind was, in fact,

running riot. Here, there and everywhere. Lucky devil, young Caine, off to the Falklands. Mines, he had almost shouted when Jenni brought the kids out and the bits started flying. About the only thing the Argies were good at, laying mines. And dying. They did a lot of that as well. So what had happened to his MC? Why did Hetherington get one, and Manners, and not Templeton? Smash, smash, smash and why, why, why? He'd been as brave as the next one and he hadn't lost his temper, not once. He was sure on that one. Well, almost sure. No red mist, no uncontrollable rage, the way Jenni sometimes got to him. He had performed his duties in an exemplary manner. He had, hadn't he?

Stephen Templeton, Captain. He was sick of it. Too many years, far too many. The Old Man, the General, must be sick of it too, sitting small in his wheelchair, plaid rug over his knees. Nothing much left for him now, only medals and memories and the tasteful trappings of Templeton money. He could have helped if he'd had the mind, he could have pulled strings to help his son on his way to the top, but no. Merit only, that was his motto. But he must be disappointed. Sister Dorothy too, did she feel let down? He doubted it. Poor sad Dodo, in and out of homes and still no cure. Still the depressions clinging to her like a shroud. She wouldn't care, she probably didn't even know. Was there a weakness somewhere in the family line? On Mother's side? He ought to know. Just as he ought to know the reason why he was still Captain, so smash, smash, smash and why, why, why? He was senior enough, he'd had top seniority since Mafeking. No results this time and he'd kick up a stink. Just see if he didn't.

Back to the Falklands. Remember a time that was better, forget a future that might never be. Kill, kill, kill and more besides. Good comrades, lots of laughs. Disciplined men doing the job they had been taught. Men with dirty faces and sweaty feet. Men who joked to the bitter end and men who kept silence from morning till night. And in amongst them all that odd cross-section of non-combatants: correspondents, TV crews, reporters, probably a historian. *They* can't have enjoyed it much; *they* didn't join up to go to war. But no complaints from any of them, well, none to speak of. Remember the one who seemed everywhere at the same time? Small, no meat on him, rimless glasses? Far too old for that sort of caper but always a tight smile on his face. Wished you the time of day, remarked on the weather, then shut up like a clam. Not a good mixer, not sociable, probably wrote for *The Times*.

The small man with rimless glasses worked for neither newspaper nor television. He was, in fact, a medical man with specialist qualifications, an expert in observation and subsequent evaluation. A gentle man and a pacifist, he hated every minute of the campaign but he did the job for which he was being so generously paid. His written reports were clear and concise, if somewhat difficult to decipher. His assessments were fair. He worried words in an effort to sum up Captain Stephen Templeton. There must be no emotion, no exaggeration, no hypothetical allusions to what might happen unless...The final report was probably the briefest he was to write. Single words, 'Good', 'Fair', 'Excellent' beside the general headings. It was only in the conclusion that he damned beyond all redemption. His handwriting was bad, his wife and daughters were always complaining so he printed for clarity. FURTHER PROMOTION NOT RECOMMENDED. He afterwards under-lined the word 'not' so that there should be no mistake.

★ ★ ★ ★

Ella, putting finishing touches to the lunch table, had a sudden thought. 'If we can't park them all in the drive, someone tell them to drive onto the verge.'

'All? Surely the Templetons won't drive?'

'They might, just to be difficult.'

'Does this mean,' David asked, 'that we are in for a repeat performance of yesterday's old crocks' parade?'

'I'm afraid it does.'

'Then prime the estate agent, for heaven's sake. Viewing on weekdays only.'

'A little premature, aren't you?'

'Sorry. Yes, I probably am.'

The men in Ella Caine's life were behaving like angels (she excluded Philip, he was something apart). John and Andrew had skipped willingly down to Briar Cottage; David was being warm and accommodating. She had a gut feeling they would all be charming, attentive hosts throughout her lunch party—which

182

was, in a way, sickening. She still felt drained by the hostilities of the previous evening and was also committed to a deal of soul-searching. Was she really as selfish as those she had accused? Surely not. By common standards she had been a good wife and mother, always there when needed, always ready to listen. Not true. Always there but ready only to listen to what she wanted to hear. She had tried to mould them all according to her aspirations, her requirements. David was right. She was selfish. Oh wad some Pow'r the giftie gie us...

'Lovely party, dear,' Eve said, outstanding in two-tone reds that screamed at each other. In a whisper that must have reached Brunton she asked, 'How's it going?'

'All right. A few initial snarl-ups but today is all sweetness and light.'

'Philip's giving David some strange looks.'

'Is he? I can't imagine why.' Pack it in, you fool. If Eve's seen, Fran will too. If I can cope with family situations, why the hell can't you?

'Heavenly men in your life, darling.' Jenni, tarted up now, flitted through to

183

flirt with David. 'Why don't we see more of them?'

'Her party performances are becoming boring,' Eve said. 'Why doesn't she grow up?'

'You should have seen, and heard, her at the Foresters'. A night Darrington will remember.'

The Highcroft bangers began their Sunday lurch up the lane leaving trails of black smoke in their wake. David excused himself from Jenni. 'Can't something be done about them, Ella?'

'No. I asked Jonno Antony when he called about Bill and he said no.'

'We could organize something ourselves.' Stephen had been bending John's ears, briefing him on Falklands map references he would never see. 'Got any tacks or drawing-pins?'

'Not a good idea. The ghastlies would probably abandon their wrecks outside my garden. Besides, Jack Downing's not a man to cross.' And yet I am involving myself, sticking out my neck. I must be mad.

'Wonderful,' Eve chortled—'we've acquired a new breed. First the Grots, now the Ghastlies. What a fun place Darrington is becoming.'

There was little to do after the guests had gone, little to talk about. The boys packed their bags and decided on which train would make which connection. David, too, began removing all evidence of his brief return. 'I'll run them into Brunton, then head back if that's all right by you.'

'Perfectly all right. Thanks for playing taxis. It will save me.'

He was rummaging through dresser drawers, a habit that had irritated Ella in their past life. It still did. 'Another of your maps? Who's this one for?'

'Me,' she said. 'It's for me. For all of us. Lest we forget.'

'It's sad and I'm sorry,' he said, but sincerity was lacking. *You* don't live here any more, she shouted at him silently.

She managed a few more private words with John. 'Make sure you come again before you sail. Bring Mary. I'd like to meet her.'

'Honestly?' He seemed pleased. 'Then I will. You'll like her, Mum, she's great.'

'I'm sure I will.' Casually, so as not to embarrass him, she asked. 'What about sleeping arrangements?'

'Oh.' A deep flush began in his neck and spread over his face. 'Same room, please.

185

That's if you don't mind.'

'I don't mind at all.'

So that was that. It was all over. They had come and they had gone. The house seemed huge and empty and she pondered on her aloneness, envied David returning to Helen, John to Mary, Andrew to a gathering of kindred spirits. Which was all very silly. She was perfectly happy living alone, enjoyed her own company, was never bored. But stripping the beds, eliminating identities, was somehow too much for her. She lingered over John's, then held his pillow to her breast and face, breathing in his smells. And then she wept. Beside her, Ben whimpered sympathy but not understanding.

For Eve, it had been a good Sunday. No cooking, which made a real break, and super to see David again and young John. And the pickings still to be shared with Adam. Yes, a good day that was ending well.

'I don't believe for one moment,' she said, 'that Philip Russell did not ask how much the consortium was prepared to offer. Do you?'

'I find it surprising.' Adam limped to his chair. His walking-stick hooked itself over a high wing, a homing pigeon returning to roost in its accustomed groove. Carefully and painfully he lowered himself onto the leather.

'It's more than surprising, it's bloody peculiar. I've said it before, that man makes me feel uneasy at times. And did you notice how short he was with David?'

'No, Eve, I did not.'

'Well, he was. Very much so. I wish I knew why.' No input from Adam on that one so she settled to thinking. And remembering. Remember coming here ten years ago and how super everything was. Except the weather, of course. The Caine boys still at prep. school. Emma Russell non-existent and the Templetons not even heard of. The Courtneys at the Manor, the Harringtons, the Swaythlings, the Dykes all in their lovely old houses with glorious gardens. Tom Antony, a snip of a boy, sniffing the wind and prophesying changes. Lord, but he was right. Was he perhaps a little fey? She had often thought so. The Swan, just the other pub run by—? Run by whom? Cyril and Edna whoever, the long and the short of it. Edna beanpole and Cyril dumpling. She died, poor soul. Breast cancer. Such a mean trick to play on her, she had none to notice. And the Foresters', Harry Senior still very much in charge. Where was Harry Junior? She couldn't remember his being around. Christmas Eve at the Foresters' and Harry opening up the big room at the side, the one that was now permanently closed. Chintz-covered armchairs and sofas and a roaring log fire. And the tree in the corner thick with tinsel and decoration, the fairy lights winking and blinking. They all went. It was a ritual. And now the ritual was ended and most of them gone.

'Penny for them,' Adam said, opening tired eyes reluctantly. The snooze had been deep and pain-free.

'They're worth much more, I assure you. I was thinking about Christmas Eve at the Foresters'. Do you remember?'

'I do indeed. That wonderful warm happy room. What good times we shared.'

'That Catholic couple, the Smythes. Remember them? They used to get pissed as newts, then go on to Midnight Mass. And Harry. Harry Senior. What was it he said at closing time?'

Adam laughed. 'How could you forget? He said, "Only two truly great men have been born into this world and the other one died at thirty-three. Now bugger off, the lot of you!" '

'You're right, how could I forget? But I did.' She smiled at him. 'Going up now?'

'Yes. Will you be long?'

'Not very. A few more bones to rattle.'

She found her bone-rattling taking her back even further, back to the days when she and Adam had travelled the world. And further still. Back to Edward and his wondrous ways, the son in whom they could find so little fault no matter how hard they tried. She heaved herself up and went to the photograph. 'I'm trying to work things out, Edward. Trying to find reasons. Because for every event, every happening, there is a reason. I've asked you this before. Why did you leave us? Why?'

Adam in bed, dozing, drifting, flared suddenly to a new awakening. This monologue of grief must cease. He put on his robe and went, slowly and carefully, downstairs.

'Stop, stop!' he shouted even before the last stair had guided his feet. 'There has to be an end, Eve, so end it now.'

'End what?' She masked her face. 'What

on earth are you jabbering about? My poor darling, was it a bad dream?'

'It has been a bad dream for far too long. You and Edward. This sick pretend-sharing that has no foundation except in your imagination. He's dead, Eve. He has been dead for over twenty years. He is no longer the laughing boy you see in the photograph, he is dust in the wind, no more than a memory. And do you know what hurts me most of all? He is a memory you cannot, will not share. *Our* son, Eve, not yours alone.'

'I talk to him, yes, but only as I would to a sleeping dog or a teddy bear.'

She was hunched, white knuckles gripping the table. Defiance for her lies, hatred of his intrusion smoked from her broad back and enveloped him. 'Why such a song and dance? I bet you chat to the ledgers when the feeling takes you.'

'Look at me, Eve.'

'I don't think I want to. You've become very odd. I'd rather remember the old Adam Grayson, not the one who's suddenly taken to objecting to my sometimes eccentric behaviour.'

He turned her forcibly, searching her granite face for the smallest sign of emotion. 'Look at you. Eyes dry as a bone.' His own tears were falling fast. 'What have you done with all those unshed tears? Will they be released when *I* die?'

'They might.' She mouthed a ghastly smile.

'Do you love me?'

'Yes, Adam, I love you.'

'But not enough to share Edward with me.'

'Oh come now.' She broke his grasp and made for the stairs. 'There's a limit to everything. Even love.'

NINE

The real heat came at last. Brassy blue skies with the sun riding high and proud. Windows were opened wide and left that way throughout the still warm nights. Hosepipes uncoiled themselves from garden sheds and Eve Grayson sold five watering-cans in as many minutes. Butter melted the second it hit the air, stone paths burned children's feet and people remembered the sea with nostalgia as though it were the Promised Land. Sprinklers turned on browning Grot lawns, and one enterprising Grottle, no more than fifteen, topped up the family swimming-pool with ice cubes. It was a somnolent, indolent, wonderful time.

Ella was showering and washing her hair when the telephone rang. Eight o'clock on a bright morning, heat already shimmering above the lane. She let it ring. Important or not, whoever wanted her would ring again. But still the insistent tones cut through the splash of water. All right, hang on. She wrapped herself in a towel and went through to the bedroom to answer.

It was Jenni. 'Ella, please come.' Nothing more. Three quietly desperate words.

'Right. Five minutes.' Less than that really. A quick dry, a quick brush through. Underwear, shorts, top and sandals. God bless the summer, dressing was so easy. A reassuring word to Ben and over the fence, across the field. She reckoned she had done well.

Stephen Templeton met her at the front door. Red face, blue eyes unnaturally bright. Inside, the twins sobbed and Miriam screamed and she thought she could hear Jenni weeping.

'Go away, Ella,' he said politely. 'I don't want you here.'

'But Jenni does.' She made to push past him but he stepped aside. 'Where is she?'

'Upstairs.'

There seemed no damage as she sped through. Kitchen, dining-room, sitting-room all intact beyond open doors. Destruction met her on the landing. Toys everywhere, broken and bent. In the bathroom, limbless dolls drowned in a half-filled bath, sodden teddies sank, an upended musical lamp tried bravely to sing Brahm's *Lullaby*. Connie's room, door closed. The twins' room an indescribable mess—beds overturned, pictures off walls, more broken toys. Two small children clung to each other sobbing as though their hearts would break. She hardened hers. They were alive and she would come back for them. Miriam's room, strangely untouched but Miriam herself, purple-faced and clutching her cot bars, screaming blue murder. Jenni. Where was she? Only one room left. She heard Stephen on the stairs, heard him go to the baby and lift her, soothing and clucking, Father of the Year.

Jenni was sitting on the bed, rocking.

Endless tears rolled and intermittently she choked on huge sobs. The room was undamaged save for one thoroughly smashed telephone.

'Are you all right?'

'Yes. Thanks, Ella, thanks for coming.' A shaky smile. 'Your hair's wet,' and then, 'The children...?'

'Like you, all right. Very distressed but not hurt.'

'They didn't want to help him, you see. He's making a new path and he asked them to help him move stones. He said, will you help Daddy? And they said no, they didn't want to, so he went up to their room and started smashing things. Like soldiers, he said. They're only three, Ella, only three.'

'Hush,' Ella soothed, holding her close. 'Try not to upset yourself. What would you like me to do?'

'We would both like you to leave.' Stephen was in the doorway, Miriam in his arms. His colour had subsided but his eyes were terrifying. 'Please go. I'm becoming bored with your interference.'

'Brute! Bastard!' Jenni shouted, suddenly alive. She went for him, fists flailing, and he backed away. Ella, watching the colour flood his face, had only one thought.

'Give me the baby,' she commanded. 'Stephen, give me the baby.'

Amazingly, he did so. Calmly and precisely he placed Miriam in her arms. And then he hit his wife across the side of her head, an almighty blow. And then Jenni started screaming.

For a moment Ella froze, mind racing. Top priority, children out. 'Come on,' she said to the twins, 'we're going to see Ben. He asked me this morning, can Mark and Minette come and play? We'll take Miriam too, shall we? I think she's been crying because she knew *you* were going visiting and she wanted to come too.' Her chatter got them down the stairs and out of the door. Stephen did not follow.

'Miriam cry because Daddy naughty,' Minette said, lifting a woeful face.

'Daddy naughty,' echoed Mark, knuckling his eyes. 'Mine Thomas the Tank all smashed.'

'Never mind,' Ella chirruped. 'We'll buy you another Thomas the Tank, and lots of new dolls for Minette.' She hesitated at the gate. Home, or—? The Swan was nearer. 'I'll tell you what, before we go and see Ben, let's pop in and see Henry. You like

Henry, don't you?'

Henry was another Tom Antony only his pockets bulged with sweets and pennies. They nodded solemn agreement. Henry was better than Ben.

Giles opened the door to her knocking, irritation apparent. It was, after all, not yet eight-thirty. Very elegant he was in a black silk dressing-gown with silver motifs, and very taken aback when Ella thrust a damp baby into his arms. 'The phone,' she said—'I have to use it.'

'Ella! My dear, whatever's wrong?' Toby bustled through, anxious and pale. He was at least dressed.

'I need a doctor. Have you the number?'

They listened while she gave the details. No, not an ambulance, just immediate medical attention, someone in authority to control the situation. Yes, the children were fine, she had them with her. She turned and two were gone. Henry had been, seen and drawn them both into the safety of his kitchen.

'Thanks,' she said, relieving Giles of Miriam. 'Oh Lord, I *am* sorry.' The impeccable robe would never be quite the same.

'Nothing to worry about,' he said

196

bravely, dismissing her apology with a flicker of white hands. 'Gracious, is that the time? I must dress.' He was already out of the room. 'Toby will help you with anything else, won't you, Tobes?' She knew he could scarcely wait to strip, to shower, to be clean again. She was equally sure that the black silk would be off to the cleaner's that very day.

'Of course I'll help.' Toby was more than willing. Behind his glasses, brown eyes showed sympathy and concern. He pushed back a flop of hair. 'Is there anything I can do?'

'Well...' she hesitated. 'Do you feel up to taking Ben for a short walk? He must be bursting at the seams by now.'

'Oh,' and then, 'yes, all right. He's very engaging now, isn't he? Quite a dear.'

'Just five minutes,' she said. 'The back door's open and his lead's on a hook behind it. Toby, you're a pal. I'll just check on the twins and then I must go back.'

'Will you be—safe?' His concern was nervously apparent.

'Oh yes.' She was certain. 'I shall be safe.'

The twins sat side by side at Henry's

table drinking mugs of milk and munching home-made cookies. They looked as happy as she had ever seen them.

'Can you keep them a little longer, Henry? I have to go back.'

'Madam dear, I'd keep them for ever only kitchen knives and little chucky hens don't mix well. But we're okey-dokey for another hour, aren't we, lovies? We've had our hands and faces washed and when we've drunk our milk we're going to make pastry men, aren't we? And if we want we-wees we're going to tell Henry because we don't want any puddles on Henry's clean floor. Oh dear me, no. Giles would be cross about puddles, wouldn't he? He would go...' He pulled an extraordinary face and flapped his hands. 'How would he go?' The children laughed and did a fair imitation.

'Henry, you're marvellous with them. Thanks a million.' A thought occurred. 'If Captain Templeton comes for them, don't say anything, will you? He doesn't remember clearly what he does.'

'Then God save us from another war, Madam dear, that's all I can say.'

Stephen met her at the door and took Miriam from her. 'Lord, she pongs.' He

198

laughed. She saw from his eyes that he was back to normal. 'Where are the others?' She told him. 'Decent of him,' he said. 'I'll clean this one up and then I'll go for them.' Jenni, he said, was 'resting'.

Jenni lay silently on her back. She was white as the pillow, the only colour angry redness that had suffused one ear and was spreading from her hairline.

'The doctor's on his way,' Ella said.

'Good.' Not much more than a whisper. 'I hurt like hell.' Mayhem had not been part of her plans.

'Jenni—'

'Don't say it, Ella. Not now.'

The doctor was young and new to the practice. He was also very thorough. In the end he did no more than leave sedatives and pain-killers but he wrote detailed notes. 'I'll make an appointment for her in a few days. She needs to be properly checked over.' More curious than concerned he asked, 'Does this happen often?'

'Quite regularly,' Ella said.

Stephen thanked her profusely when she left. 'You *are* a brick, Ella, a real friend. Miriam's flat out so I'll nip down for the kids.'

'I will if you like.'

'No need. You've done enough. I won't be two minutes.' Again the crazy laugh. 'How was Henry entertaining them?'

'They were all set to make pastry men.'

'That sounds fun. I'm glad. They must have been disappointed.'

'Disappointed about what, Stephen?'

'They were going to help me clear up the garden but things went a bit haywire.'

The telephone was ringing again when Ella reached home. Isn't this where I came in? 'Hello?'

'Ella, Alex Jameson. You're rather elusive for an early summer's morning.' It was then nine-thirty.

'I'm sorry. There's been a—crisis.'

'At Highcroft?'

'No.' No, damn you, not at Highcroft. There is life other than Jack Downing and his intimates.

'Ella, there's something big on, we're sure of it. Could we ask you—'

'Not at the moment,' she said. 'Ring me later. Sorry.' Start again, shall we? Shower and hair wash and then poor old Ben out for a decent walk. She unplugged the telephone to make sure.

She had to speak to him, of course.

The other option was to disconnect the phone for the rest of her life. She listened to what he had to say, she asked some questions. Are you absolutely sure? Yes, I'll accept that, as sure as you can be. All right, I'll do it. What time and where? Thank you, but you need more luck than I do. She afterwards thought things through. Carefully. She even made notes. And then she rang Eve and told her. But not Fran.

'What I don't understand,' Eve said to Adam 'is why the Russells are being totally excluded, Fran especially.'

'In what respect?' Adam limped to the table with unaccustomed ease. The heat was helping. If not a new man, he felt decidedly different.

'In every respect. First the Highcroft business and then the Templetons. Fran came into the shop this morning and when I said there'd been quite a to-do yesterday by all accounts, she asked where. Ella hadn't said a word. Don't you think that odd?'

'Eve, you are allowing your vivid imagination to run away with you.'

'Adam, I am not. The drug scene, possibly safer to keep silence, but not Jenni. She and Stephen have concerned us all, and I mean all, since forever.'

Lunch-time. Another blistering day and no hint of any immediate change. Eve felt almost alive. She had shed her trousers and sweaters, her tights and her socks and was now happily perspiring in a cotton frock that had once been comfortable yet smart. Still comfortable and to hell with smart.

'I'm not happy about Ella,' Adam said, starting a frown.

'I'm more worried about Jenni. There could be permanent ear damage, you know. That bloody man. Ella said he was quite unaware of anything he had done.'

Curious, she asked, 'Why aren't you happy about her?'

'I think she's taking on too much. I know you said she hasn't enough to do but all of a sudden she has and I wonder how she will cope. David and the house, John and the Falklands, Jenni, and now this stake-out. The build-up has been too swift.'

'So why hasn't she talked to Fran? I am quite aware, Mr Grayson, that you and I are the best listeners and advisers in the world but Fran's a natural for confidences. They've been chums so long.'

But Adam's concern leant a different

way. 'What exactly is going to happen tomorrow?'

'Tomorrow? Oh, the surveillance. I'm not sure and neither is Ella. Apparently there's wind of a big consignment heading down to the West Country. The Elephant Fair, or something equally ridiculous, in Plymouth. Ella's pal thinks Jack Downing could be giving it a bed for the night.'

'Dear God,' Adam sounded despairing. 'I wish I lived on the moon.'

'Do you? It must be frightfully cold. I quite like it here at the moment.' She remembered something and laughed. 'I do wish I could have seen Giles with poo all over his dressing gown.'

'With—what?'

'Poo. You know, crap, shit, faeces, excrement. No, you wouldn't would you? *You* never—'

'Never what, Eve?' The break was nearer, he was sure of it. The night he cared not to remember had been ignored as though it had never happened, yet there were changes. And not for the better. Snide comments, sarcasm, insults even. But he knew she hated herself far more than she hated him for knowing so he said nothing. He just waited. 'I never what?'

'Nothing. It doesn't matter.'

They ate in silence. A bee that had flown in through the open window appeared unaware that it could go out the same way. Eve assisted with a newspaper. 'Silly buzzer.'

'I have a theory,' Adam said slowly, tormenting his nose, 'about Ella and her closeness with the Russells. Closeness from, not to. She has a big secret and she told us. It follows that she can now talk freely to us about related events. As with yesterday. Jenni rings, the detective rings. With Fran she would have to edit and she hasn't yet learned the art.'

'You're right,' Eve said. 'It could be just that.' She looked at him admiringly. 'You really are very wise, Pinocchio. I wonder yet again why you married me.'

'And I say yet again that love had a lot to do with it. Love on both sides.' Ponder on that, dear heart, and see what it does to your unquiet spirit.

If Eve had spirit problems, Fran was burning up. Inside and out. A glimpse of heaven for Adam, the soaring temperatures. For Fran pure hell. Her cotton shift clung wetly to every excessive fold and bulge but the heat had no direct association with the smoulder in her blue eyes.

'She hasn't said a word. she didn't ring me, didn't come round to tell the tale. I just don't understand.'

Philip was not interested in Fran's grievance. Who cared what happened to the Templetons? He had troubles enough, and now Ella was bloody furious with him.

'I shall call on Mrs Caine this afternoon and find out why I am being ostracized. Ella and I are friends, we've shared all sorts of secrets before. *Your* appalling behaviour shouldn't affect our friendship.'

'What do you mean by that?'

'You know damn well what I mean. You were downright rude to David.'

'I was not.'

'You were. Why?'

Philip thought hard. Why? Tell the truth for once. Because the atmosphere was so relaxed and happy and I was convinced that Ella had spent the night in his arms. A whole night. Interminable slow minutes of touching, rousing and entering her wonderful body. We've never had a night together, never more than an hour, and I was jealous.

'I was jealous if you must know. David has everything. Money, a successful career, a house that will fetch a vast sum and he's—'

'Free? That's it, isn't it? David Caine has no responsibilities, he can do as he likes and you hate him for it. Grow up, Philip. You can't run away.'

She heaved herself towards the kitchen door.

'Where are you going?'

'To ring Ella. To clear the air.'

Damn you, Fran. If only you knew how much I hate you for this. As much as I hate David for having Ella, literally having her. And Ella for betraying me and the developers for estimating me so low and the bloody farmers for not selling and the world for turning. Hate, hate. It is destroying me.

Fran trundled back into the kitchen. She seemed mollified. 'She apologized, said she was just about to ring. This afternoon it is.'

'Why not go tomorrow, give her a break?' And me the chance of a reconciliation. I *need* this other woman, Fran.

'Tomorrow, she said, is out. She's either going to the solicitor with Jenni or spring-cleaning the kitchen. Either way, she does not wish to be disturbed. She must be out of her mind—imagine any sort of cleaning in this weather. Apparently David hinted that it should be tarted up before the house goes on the market.'

Listlessly, she searched the crowded mantelpiece for a chocolate bar. 'Did I tell you, I've lost five pounds.'

'How sickening. Any idea where?'

'Pounds as in weight, you fool. Aren't you pleased?'

He forced a smile. 'Of course I am. Well done.' I could kill you, of course, then run to Ella before anyone found out. But I won't. For one thing I haven't the energy and for another, I don't relish the thought of years in prison while you fritter away my millions. I'll settle instead for hating you. You really would be surprised if you knew how much.

Ella collected two detective constables from a lay-by just outside Down Darrington at eight on another glorious morning. A man and a woman, both very young. The driver of the car that had brought them looked keenly at her as she pulled in. She wound down her window. 'Hello. Are you—?'

'Mrs Russell?' The man spoke.

'No, Mrs Caine. You know that.'

'Just checking.' He grinned before showing her his warrant card. 'Can we put this stuff in the boot?' This stuff was a square black suitcase and a shopping bag, the woman's, bulging with packages and a thermos flask. They both sat in the back. 'We'll have to duck going through the village, that's why.' Ella wanted to ask their ages; he seemed no older than Andrew and she was a mere slip of a girl. 'Peter Jones, that's me and WDC Noble here is Wendy. All right if we call you Ella?'

'Please do.' She waited until the police car, very new and very red, headed towards Brunton. 'A smart car. Isn't it rather conspicuous in rural areas?'

'A bit, but you tell that to the top brass. Rules and regs, you see. Keep up with the times.'

'What exactly is going to happen?'

'We're going to watch. The rest is up to our friend at Highcroft.'

'And you really expect some—action?'

'Yes, Ella, we really do.'

She drove the Street without incident. How many windows watching, how many curious minds? Wherever has Ella Caine been at this time of the morning? She had rehearsed the route a thousand times, waking in the night to worry at unexpected obstacles that Fate might throw in her path. But none occurred. Old Mother Hubbard did not have a heart attack under her wheels, no dog ran out, no child. Jenni did not coming running towards her, screaming and distraught, nor did Philip signal her to stop. She thought she saw Eve at her bedroom window as she passed the shop and she felt encouraged. At least someone was rooting for her. She turned into the lane. 'I think you should stay out of sight until I've opened up and had a look around. It seems quiet enough but I'd like to make sure.'

'We're in your hands, Ella.' DC Jones sounded muffled.

'Are you all right back there? It can't be very comfortable.'

The girl giggled. 'I'm sick of looking at Pete's awful shoes.'

'Right.' She switched off the engine. 'We're here. I'm going to close the gates and then I'll go in the back door. I'll shut Ben—my dog—in another room until you're inside. Leave your gear in the boot. I'll fetch it later.'

'Got it all worked out, haven't you?' Young Pete was admiring. 'Well done.'

'Save the compliments until you're safe.'

It all went according to plan. Upstairs, she scoured the lane and fields. No sign of anyone dog-walking, no hint of Tom Antony lurking behind the trees.

'OK,' she said, back at the car, 'get out of the left-hand door and go around the side of the house to the back. The hedge should screen you.'

They ran, doubled, as in the best TV movies. I don't believe this is happening, she thought.

The black case was heavy as she heaved it out and she was glad to put it down on the kitchen floor. 'Gold bullion?' she asked.

'The radio. Sorry you had to lug it.'

They followed her upstairs. 'I thought my room would be best. It's nearest Highcroft and there's a side window as well. There are chairs so you won't have to sit on the bed. Do either of you smoke? That may be a problem. The windows are open and everyone knows I don't.' They looked at her enquiringly. 'This is a small village. Anything unusual is thoroughly chewed over before being written into the annals of Darrington's history. Just remember, I live here alone, my children are not at home at present and I should find it difficult to flush the lavatory from outside in the garden.'

'Have you done this sort of thing before?'

She laughed. 'No. The first and, I hope, the last time. I thought it all out, though, and did some forward planning.'

She left them fixing the radio aerial to a wall light and went about her normal business. Ben out, then the shop. Pity she hadn't forward-planned more carefully and remembered yesterday she was out of several essentials. Eve raised interested eyebrows and she nodded confirmation and smiled. Doris Antony chatted about the boys, how tall and handsome they were and how proud she must be, and Alicia Hargreaves said to make sure she and Bertie were kept informed. The only disruption to smooth running was leaving and meeting Fran coming in.

'Hello. What's with the solicitor?'

'Not until next week would you believe. The wretched man is on holiday. And before you ask why I'm not scrubbing the kitchen walls, I've decided it's much too hot. I've a splitting headache and intend taking things very easy.' If only she could have added, don't tell Philip, will you?

She prayed he would respect her mythical headache and stay away.

Back at the homestead she made coffee and carried it upstairs. Crackles and a disembodied voice met her as she opened the bedroom door. 'Anything happening?' she asked after listening to car descriptions, references to targets and several, yes, yes, yesses. Whatever had become of 'Roger and out'?

'He's on his way driving a blue Ford van, registration—'

'That's new,' she interrupted. 'It's a green Range Rover nowadays.'

'Possibly to divert us. No activity at the farm yet. One bloke we know mooching around and talking to the horses.'

'How can you possibly know that?'

'We've a couple of lads up trees.'

'Honestly? What happens if they want to—'

'Tie a knot in it, that's what happens.' DC Jones grinned and lost several more years. 'See our chap in the village, did you? The one on the motor bike?'

'You mean a huge black shining monster, big as a bus? Everyone saw and everyone is now trying to work out who he was. If I may make so bold, I don't think

212

discretion is the better part of your surveillance.'

'We'll get a result this time. Wait and see.'

But by lunch-time their confidence was waning. Jack Downing had driven up in the blue van, grinning from ear to ear. Close in his wake followed the usual motley collection of weekend visitors. They were all having a great time, a tree man reported, and he was getting cramp.

'He's rumbled us,' Wendy said sourly. 'He's playing games just to show off.'

'Maybe, maybe not. I reckon it's gone up in one of those old jalopies. If nothing else, we'll get them for MOTs and dangerous vehicles.'

'Are you planning a raid?' Ella asked.

'Perhaps.' He shot her a quick look. 'You didn't hear that. OK?'

'OK,' she said and went back to the kitchen.

Time hung heavy as the heat. She could concentrate on nothing productive, not even reading a book. She wondered when and if something would actually happen, how long her guests would stay, whether she would be as successful on the outward run as she had been ferrying them in. A shadow darkened the open doorway and there, damn and blast him, was Philip. 'How's the headache?' he asked, advancing to kiss her.

'Still thumping.' She backed away from him, an impromptu dance without contact. 'I told Fran I didn't want to be disturbed.'

'But that didn't include me, did it?'

'It included you.'

'Look, Ella, I said I was sorry about David. Can't you forget it?'

'It's forgotten.' She tried a smile. 'Thanks for calling, Philip. I'll see you soon.'

'What's wrong with now? Can't we spend a sweet half hour together, just talking if you're not up to anything else?'

'No.'

'Why not?' The question was answered for her. The upstairs lavatory flushed, footsteps were heard, cheery whistling even. Her bedroom door closed and thereafter silence. 'You're cheating on me,' Philip snarled. 'You've got someone else up there.'

'If I have it's none of your business.'

'It bloody well is.' He was past her and up the stairs before she could stop him. White-faced and furious, she followed and

214

saw him fling wide the door. 'What the hell—?'

Peter Jones cut short his radio conversation and stood up. He looked at Ella for an explanation. 'Philip Russell, a local farmer,' she introduced. She could have said friend but he wasn't, not any more. 'He thought I had intruders.'

The warrant card was shown. 'DC Jones, Brunton Constabulary, sir.' Caution at last, no mention of the Drug Squad. 'I'd be obliged if you would go about your normal business, sir, and say nothing of what you have seen or heard. Not even to your wife.'

She showed him to the back door without a word. 'I apologize,' he said; 'I jumped to conclusions.' She said nothing. 'I don't know what's going on but you could have told me, a brief outline even. You could have trusted me.'

She saw that he could not look her straight in the face. The blue eyes that had undressed and ravished her so many times were assessing her kitchen, taking note of the brilliant day beyond the window. She saw his mouth, soft, petulant, the lower lip thrust forward like that of a thwarted child. In her mind she heard his voice, high and querulous, an old man demanding and complaining. She saw him at last as he really was. A devious man and a loser. Revulsion swept over her, and shame. Shame for her complicity in such a wanton worthless game. 'Goodbye, Philip,' she said steadily. 'And I mean goodbye. It's all over.'

In mid afternoon young Wendy came down and tapped on the sitting-room door. Ella and Ben were dozing. 'It's all off,' the detective said.

'Oh?'

'Just as I said, he rumbled us. He's had the time of his life making fools out of just about everyone. Shouting up at the boys in the trees and asking if they want pisspots, marshalling all the toe-rags in Brunton to give our cars the two fingers. One of his cronies even flagged down the motorbike and asked for details about joining the Force.' Wendy was bitter but she could also see the funny side. 'Bloody man. D'you know how he ended it? He rode his horse up to one of our plain-clothes men on the main road. No saddle, not even a rug, our chap said, looked more like a Mexican bandit than a drug dealer. Understand you're looking for me, he says, well here I am. Want to search me?'

'A plain-clothes man in a very new car?' Ella asked pointedly.

'That's right. It's as Pete said, the policy's all wrong.'

She got them out unobserved. There was quite a party going on at Highcroft, the radio said. The tree men weren't so lucky, they had to suffer a lot of wisecracks and ribald comment when they descended. Alex Jameson was waiting in the lay-by.

'An absolute fiasco, Ella,' he said. 'Egg all over our faces but thanks so much for being hospitable. Better luck next time, eh?' She hoped sincerely that next time was a long way off.

Just before seven that evening she watched several police cars and a white van spin up the lane. Two hours later, she watched them return. Alex Jameson rang her just as she was putting a sleepy Ben to bed. It was then eleven-thirty.

'We went in,' he said; 'you must have seen. Took the place apart but no sign of the goods. The parcel must have gone down by another route.' He brightened. 'Never mind. We nicked most of them. Cannabis, cars, defunct road tax, but not Jack. Clean as a whistle, damn him.

And he's a close one. No comment to everything. He didn't even bat an eyelid when I asked about the package your dog found in the straw.'

'You did—what?'

Silence. And then, apologetically, 'Sorry, Ella. I see what you mean.'

'No one knew about that. It went clean out of my mind until I met you.'

'Yes, but you *might* have told someone about it. In conversation, talking about Highcroft.'

'But I didn't.'

'*He* doesn't know that.'

'If *he's* clever enough to run rings around you all, *he'll* certainly wonder. Thank you, Mr Jameson. It's been a wonderful day. I hope you sleep better tonight than I will.'

TEN

It was Alicia Hargeaves who urged them to hold a public meeting. Speaking on behalf of Bertie, of course. It was as well Alicia had joined the committee instead of her skinny husband with the bleak eyes. He

218

had little to say for himself. Yet it was always Bertie's opinions she voiced, his views she reported back. 'Bertie thinks...', 'Bertie said...', 'Bertie was interested to hear...'

'What does Bertie do?' someone had asked.

'Something nebulous in the city. There's a lot of it about.'

'Alicia Hargreaves wants to speak to you,' Fran reported to the chairman, 'on the phone. She sounds frightfully—positive.'

'Her milk yields can't be plummeting the way mine are.'

Fran giggled. 'Did she ever yield, I wonder? I've heard no mention of any little Berties. Go on, Philip, find out what she wants.'

Without enthusiasm, Philip went. He had a good excuse for being morose and he was making the most of it. No one asked, What's up with Philip Russell? They all knew. The sun continued to blaze down and the grass had stopped growing. It was withering and dying before his very eyes. The hay crop had been good admittedly, sweet and succulent, but dairy cows need more than hay and the price of supplementary feed was out of this world.

It was always the same. Whatever the weather, whatever the season, the animal-feed companies laughed all the way to the bank. There was no way they could lose. Why, in God's name, had he ever wanted to be a farmer? Mastitis too was running around on knobbly, knotted feet. More vet's bills. More everything bills. One thing for sure, if Jack Downing slipped his horses through the wire once more he'd grab him by the short and curlies. Clever, the way he had done it, cutting the wire close to the posts, then hooking it into hoops driven into the wood. But not clever enough for Tom. He missed nothing. The only trouble with Tom was that he needed paying once in a blue moon and from the way he had started rattling the change in his pocket, the moon must be very blue, almost navy. Money. He was sick of worrying about it. Come back, Mr Smith in your polished shoes, I'll take whatever you offer.

Ella, too. Come back and I'll take whatever you offer. Only come back. No point in pursuing that misery, not at the moment. Later I will wallow in the depths of despair and Fran, not knowing, will pretend to exude sympathy and try to feed me chocolate.

He lifted the phone. 'Mrs Hargreaves —Alicia. What a pleasure. Is there something I can do?'

Bertie had heard, Alicia gushed, that the consortium plans were now open to public inspection at the council offices. Had Philip heard the same?

'I believe they are.' I know they are. I have already been down to look and make sure I'm still a public library.

In which case, Alicia continued, Bertie thinks we should hold a public meeting. After every single person in all the Darringtons has seen the plans, of course. We can organize lifts for those without transport, you know, the way they do at elections. And then, after the meeting, the landowners can give their opinions and make known their intentions. And we can all sleep easier, Bertie says, when we know for a fact there is solid opposition and no one is prepared to sell. What did Philip think?

'Excellent,' Philip said. This should be interesting. Thank God I'm chairman and therefore impartial. 'I think we should call a committee meeting and start organizing, don't you?'

Exactly what Alicia had been about to

suggest and she and Bertie would love to hold it under their humble roof. Now, when and at what time?

'Good idea,' Fran said when he reported back. 'We'll need leaflets first, won't we? Will funds stretch that far?'

'If they don't, Bertie will have to toddle around Grotland with his hat.'

Off you go, Fran. Start ringing around the committee with suggested dates. Check the hall bookings, find out the cost of posters and leaflets. You're in this as much as I am. Correction. More than I am. You are still honest and true and fully committed. I have sold out to mammon and I am also very miserable. How could she do this to me? You can't end such a fantastic relationship because of such a trivial mistake. True, he had reacted badly to the unknown quantity upstairs but it's natural to be jealous when you love someone, isn't it? There it was again, that indefinable word. It was becoming a nuisance, mucking up his plans. He wanted his millions but he wanted Ella as well. Perhaps, when they all moved, they could stay within spitting distance and he could still see her frequently. And for longer periods. Take her away on holidays, the Caribbean, the Bahamas, New York. With all that money he could manipulate anything and everything. Pack Fran off to a health farm, the kids to school and take himself off on some mythical business trip. With Ella. Only, if he was to believe her, she wouldn't come, not now. It's all over. Her exact words. Where are you, Ella, what are you doing? Are you thinking about me?

Ella was not. She and Jenni were on their way to Brunton, a solicitor's appointment at eleven. Yesterday had been the health centre and Jenni had gone alone. 'So what happened?'

'The usual examination, usual questions. Ears, eyes, balance, reflexes. Was I dizzy at all? Did I have tinnitus, that's ringing—'

'I know what tinnitus is,' Ella said. 'Do you have it?'

'No, it's gone. I feel all right, Ella, honestly. Anyway, they said to go back if I felt something was wrong.'

Jenni, for Jenni, was subdued. It had taken a deal of pressure to get her this far on the road towards taking legal advice. Everyone had said the same. The children next time, Jenni, and how will you live with yourself when it happens? That blow to your head, Jenni, imagine what it would to Mark or Minette? There's something radically wrong with him that he cannot, will not, recognize. You have to protect yourself and the kids, you have to get out.

'What's he like, this bloke of yours?'

'Mike Carter? He's pleasant and courteous and very sound. Don't try to vamp him, will you? He adores his wife, they were married only last year.'

'He's taken his time over your divorce.'

'Not at all. There was no rush. Neither of us has hurled knives or dirt at each other, we went for a straightforward breakdown of marriage. That's exactly what it is. The nisi hearing should be next month, I think, and the absolute a formality six weeks later unless—'

'You change your mind. Will you?'

'No, and neither will David. Why should he, with Helen in the offing?'

'So what do I go for, that's if I decide to go for anything?'

'Unreasonable behaviour should cover you pretty well.'

Michael Carter, solicitor, had been primed by Ella. He was therefore surprised to meet a young woman described as

224

stunning and vivacious and find her surly, unwilling to communicate. But only in the beginning. Under his questioning she began to expand, became animated. The floodgates opened and the history of her five year marriage to Stephen Templeton poured forth.

'A little slower, please, Mrs Templeton.' He smiled gravely. 'I have notes and I have to be accurate.'

'Ella has a list,' Jenni said, impatient at the interruption. 'We worked on it last night. Dates, places and what happened.'

'Thank you. If you will read through later and sign it as being a true statement, I can use it in conjunction with my notes. Now, this last incident occurred when?'

It was all over at last, all out of her system. There were tears in her eyes but she seemed relieved. Ella too, when he took the time to glance at her. 'Well?' Jenni demanded.

'The only factor that puzzles me, Mrs Templeton, is why you have waited so long before seeking legal advice.'

'Ah. That's another story.'

His eyes questioned her.

'I still love the bastard.' And I still think there's a slim chance of his taking me where I want to go. To the top.

'That's beside the point,' Ella said. It was the first time she had spoken since making the introductions. 'There are more than enough grounds for divorce, aren't there, Mike? What do you advise?'

'The same as you obviously do. A place of safety for Mrs Templeton and the children and a speedy divorce.'

'Oh, do stop calling me Mrs Templeton. It makes me feel as old as Ella.'

'Not possible,' Ella smiled. 'My children are always telling me nobody can be as old as I am. Well, Jenni?'

'I'll think about it. I can't say go ahead, I honestly can't. We're still living together, sharing our lives. What am I supposed to do when we make love? Do I tell him before or after? By the way, darling, I'm divorcing you.'

Mike Carter screwed the top on his pen. 'I'll have your statement typed up and put on file. Then when you decide—'

'If I decide.'

'No. I am confident that it will be when. Please don't wait until too late.' Showing them the door he asked, 'Has your husband sought medical advice at all?'

'No. Why should he? He isn't sick, he just has a bloody awful temper.'

They were half-way home to Darrington before Ella spoke. 'Why is it,' she thundered, slamming the steering wheel with one hand. 'that everyone else can see that Stephen is unbalanced at times and you persist in performing your ostrich act?'

'It's only temper brought on by frustration. I don't like insinuations about, you know. They're very much below the belt.'

'Not insinuations, fact. And if I'm hitting below the belt, phone someone else when he's hitting you above it.'

'Sorry,' Jenni said. 'Let's change the subject. Tell me about the police raid at Highcroft.'

'Nothing to tell. The cars went up and a couple of hours later they came back. That's all I know.'

'Any idea why?'

'I've just told you, I don't know. All the old crocks were up there. It could have been a clampdown on them: keep death off the road.'

'I wonder, does Jack Downing think you had anything to do with it?'

'Why should he, for God's sake?' A

sharp look at Jenni. 'What makes you say that?'

'I thought you saw him on the other side of the road when we left the solicitor's. He saw you. If looks could kill you'd be on your way to the mortuary by now.'

Which, that same evening, was the direction Jack Downing thought he was taking. He felt lousy. Temperature in the eighties and he'd been shivering all day, cold as charity. And now he was hot, sweat pouring off him like an orange being squeezed dry. Thirsty as hell too, and shaky. No strength in him. Lofty said he looked awful: black circles under his eyes and a pasty colour. He hadn't bothered to check in the mirror, he'd taken his word for it. Seeing wouldn't help how he felt. Must be flu or something like, but who gets flu in the summer? Colds, hay fever, but not flu. Aspirin and an early night, no doubt on that one. That's if Duggie would let him, that's if his thoughts would crawl away and die. And Jack the lad close after them, the way he felt.

Who had shopped him? Someone had from the questions the fuzz had asked. Which one of the boys was due for a knee-job? Not Ned for sure, Big Charlie neither. Lofty? Not likely. Why should he? His cut's the same as the other two. Or does he want to run the game, is that the angle? No chance. A do-as-you're-told-keep-your-mouth-shut bloke, Lofty. Not enough up top to think big. Cross him off, think further down the line. Some little squirt with ideas above his station, but who?

That stupid cow down the lane? Not her either, she knew nothing, only what she'd seen. Bit of shit-stirring there and he'd get her for it. Nothing too drastic, just a few things to upset her, make her think twice before she poked her nose in again. Interfering big mouth, running to the fuzz with her tales. Or did they run to her? Has she been snooping for them in other ways. I'll get her. And I'l get to bed soon as Duggie lets me know it's down there. Come on, Duggie, ring. Every bit of me aches, I want to die.

'Nothing yet?' Lofty asked. He was listless in the heat.

'Nope. Got any aspirin?'

'Might be some in the caravan.'

'Have a look, will you?'

The phone jangled. Duggie at last. 'Yes?...Thank Christ...Yeah, just as well

229

we had the tip-off and sent it down a day sooner. Place was swarming with filth the day after...Tell the boss. Someone grassed. Find him...When's the pay off?...See you then, if I'm still alive...Dunno. Some bug or other, I feel real bad.'

'All right?' Lofty asked, anxious for Jack, anxious for himself.

'Safe as houses. Think I should give Jameson a bell to set his mind at rest?' Twisting a smile took a real effort.

'Home to bed now then, Jack?'

'Not tonight. I'm sleeping here. Knackered, that's what I am. Done the horses yet, have you?'

'Not yet.'

'Jesus, Lofty, not the Horseguards, is it? 'Tis Highcroft. Two horses, two bales of hay, two buckets of water. Not much to ask. Don't like the horses, do you? Don't like my little room neither.'

'It's like a cell, Jack. Them bars on the window give me the creeps.'

'Bad memories, eh? Nice little room, full of dreams. Where's the aspirin and the lamp? And water, gallons of it.'

Safe now, the stairs, and still light enough to see his way, but Christ, the effort it took. Along the passage right to

230

the very end, then into his den, his safety, his retreat. Smashing it looked now; white walls, white ceiling and the floor stained dark; bed along one wall, dressing chest, chair, po under the bed. Curtain on the rod across the corner. Only the window-seat still to come and the red cushions. Light the lamp, turn it low and onto the hook with it. Good old hook, still firm into the beam. Good old room, quiet, peaceful, holding him still with tight arms. Aspirins, a good long drink and sleep. Never so weary before, never so sick, but it'll pass. Right as rain tomorrow, you'll see.

So what was this in his hand along with the aspirins? Paper. Paper that had been stuffed through the door. Something like in the caravan too, only he'd never bothered to look. What now then, as if he cared? Jumble sale, village hop? Printed words, lot of 'em. Bedtime reading seeing as how there were no Bible by his bed. Let's see, then. Only the words ran away from him as if they had legs. Try again, Jack. Development...plans...meeting...and at the bottom in capitals so 'twas easy...GO AND SEE FOR YOURSELF. See what? The plans, that's what, go and see the plans. Not friggin' likely. Wouldn't affect him. Spoil the view from the back mebbe so put up a fence high as a house, that's what he'd do. Or plant trees, fast growers. But no land to sell, not now. Shouldn't have done it, Dad, should've held on. Worth a fortune now. Who'll be the first lucky bugger to tumble? Farmer Russell, betcha, he'll be first.

The posters went up in all three Darringtons a week before the public meeting.

'If it's still as hot as this I'm going in a bikini,' Fran said. Everyone laughed. The idea of Fran in a bikini was enough to make a cat laugh. The occasion was a last-minute informal meeting of all involved in the organization of the meeting, the venue Highcroft Cottage. The lady of the house appeared preoccupied. There had been two dead rats on her path that morning and she was still wondering why.

'The vicar has asked, nay demanded, that he be on the platform,' the chairman informed.

'That should guarantee a good turn-out.' Adam Grayson's turn to comment. 'We all want to see what he looks like.'

'So we have the vicar, Hugh Courtney and myself in the chair. That's the platform. Agreed?' Agreed by all but

Alicia Hargreaves who looked a little peeved. Hastily Philip continued. 'We want our best guns in the congregation, so to speak, firing the ammo. Chaps like Bertie Hargreaves will do it splendidly in that respect.' Joke, but Alicia wouldn't see it. A quick glance assured him she was content. 'And Percy Pigg has volunteered to speak from the floor.'

'Who?' squeaked Alicia, disbelieving.

'Two Gs, dear,' Caroline Courtney boomed, 'two Gs in Pigg. A Northumbrian name. Sir Percival Pigg, to give him his correct title. An unfortunate choice of Christian name but some parents don't think ahead, do they? Percy's all right, oodles of land and oodles of money.' She asked Philip, 'He's come out into the open, has he? A firm stand against?'

'Yes, but if I remember correctly the plans Reg Powell brought, the consortium won't worry too much. He's on the extreme end of the proposed development and they only want about twenty-six acres from him. It won't break their hearts to cut out one new estate.'

'Not everyone knows that,' Caroline said. 'Outspoken opposition will sound good. And let's hope many others do the same. Have you canvassed, Philip? One hundred per cent support, I've no doubt.'

'They all *know*.' Philip bent to pick up conveniently dropped papers. Lying to Caroline wasn't easy. 'Farmers are funny chaps. They don't like committing themselves. There might be an outbreak of foot-and-mouth or a cyclone. Know what I mean?'

Adam stayed on after the meeting had dispersed. Something was wrong with Ella, she had hardly spoken a word. 'Trouble, my dear?' he asked kindly.

'I'm not sure. I found two revolting dead rats outside the back door this morning. They didn't have labels but my feeling is they were a present from Highcroft.'

'Ah.' Adam did not disagree. 'That man Jameson should be shot. I've never heard of such incompetence. From what you told us, the operation was a farce from beginning to end.'

'I know, and I took such care planning my end of it. It makes me sick. Should I say or do anything about the rats?'

'You've no proof. If there are further love tokens, or any form of unpleasantness, we, and I mean we, will go to the police.'

'It won't come to that, will it?'

'I'm sure it won't. Don't worry.' But he was far from confident.

'I forsee bad times ahead for Ella,' he told Eve later. 'Jack Downing is not a man to cross. Thank God she has us.'

'He can't do anything too ghastly,' Eve reasoned. 'He'd be number one suspect if he did. How was everything else?'

'Nicely sorted. I'm quite looking forward to the occasion.' He hesitated. 'Another thing. There's an atmosphere between Ella and Philip. He was too charming, too effusive and she, when she bothered to speak, cuttingly cool.'

'You're doing a me,' Eve chortled. 'You're speculating.'

'I am not. I am simply relating fact. And don't think you have the monopoly on observation and speculation, Mrs Grayson. You just shout louder and longer.'

The public meeting took place on a Wednesday afternoon which allowed for the attendance of small shop-keepers in all three Darringtons. It was timed to begin at three so that village publicans could shut their doors and hurry along. The whole operation had, in fact, been well thought out. The local Drug Squad

235

could learn a few lessons from us, Ella thought bitterly.

Turn-out was exceptional for Darrington. True, numbers were swelled by a sizeable input from the other Ds and true, a hot sultry afternoon threatening thunder offers little alternative entertainment. All uncomfortable chairs were soon occupied and more had to be brought from behind the stage. There was a fair cross-section of Antonys and Hubbards, a goodly gathering of Grots. Giles came, but not with Toby. That caused some whispered comment. Who was the willowy youth with the angelic face? Surely not...? 'I'll bet Toby's having hysterics,' Eve Grayson muttered.

Neither Templeton bothered to attend. 'Connie's day off,' Jenni had apologized, 'and Stephen's on duty.' But it was common knowledge that they didn't care one way or the other.

Nor did Jack Downing put in an appearance. 'He looked ghastly when I saw him this morning,' Fran said when they had all remarked on his absence. 'Just getting over flu, he said. I told him he ought to be home in bed.' Or in gaol, Ella added silently.

Ten minutes after three and the platform

party took their place. Philip, Hugh Courtney. Nothing unusual there, familiar well-respected faces. It was the vicar who caused the greatest stir. 'Look, it's the vicar,' Mother Hubbard screeched to her kith and kin. 'What's he doing up there? Haven't seen him since our Florrie's Brian was christened and that were three year ago.'

The chairman opened the meeting. He welcomed everybody and outlined briefly the hopes and fears of the Darringtons. Hugh Courtney's speech was longer and much more interesting. He delivered a potted history of the area since the Norman Conquest in mellifluous tones. Amusing, concise, the audience applauded warmly and someone at the back shouted 'More!' The vicar did not speak. He contented himself with smiling agreeably into space. 'Useless prat,' Eve murmured and those nearest her sniggered agreement.

'Percy Pigg is going to start the ball rolling,' Philip said. No titter was heard but Alicia Hargreaves was seen to dig Bertie with a sharp elbow. 'Percy, as you all know, farms six hundred acres in Upper Darrington as did his father and grandfather before him. But will his sons?

Ladies and gentlemen, Sir Percival Pigg.'

'Well now,' Percy said, turning from his seat in the front row to face the chairs behind, 'we all know what's going on, don't we? My fellow landowners will agree with me...' He looked around. His fellow landowners were conspicuous by their absence.

'Only you and me, Percy,' the chairman called in light tenor tones. 'Makes you think, doesn't it?'

'It certainly does, Philip, it makes you think.' The wind was out of his sails but he put on a brave show. He hadn't dolled himself up in his plus-fours and deer-stalker to say nothing. Shame on those who valued money above land, he thundered. If everyone refused to sell there could be no development. He was hanging on to every last inch of his and he had told them so.

Lukewarm applause, nothing to ring the rafters. 'Everyone knows Percy owns breweries and betting shops as a sideline,' Adam said. 'Money means nothing to him.'

'It does to Philip and he isn't selling,' Fran said.

'We all know that but he's in the chair.

Where are the others, for God's sake? I can't believe they're not interested.'

'They're interested all right,' Eve said grimly, 'but not in the same things that we are.'

And that, more or less, was that. There were a few questions and several accusations, there were demands for compensation and threats of sabotage. But all very half-hearted. The public meeting had been a failure, an abysmal flop. As much of a fiasco, Ella thought, as the Drug Squad stake-out.'

'Bloody Philip,' Fran complained bitterly to Ella as they were leaving, 'it's all his fault. Why didn't he make sure there was a full turn-out?'

'It may be as he said at the committee meeting. Farming's an unpredictable profession.' And why am I defending him I simply do not know.

'Crap,' Fran spat. 'He's useless. Other things on his mind, that's Philip's current weakness. To be precise, one other thing.'

We all have, Fran. Other things on our minds. I am trying to concentrate on the good things, I am looking forward to seeing my son again.

John Caine brought his Mary home at

239

the end of his leave. 'We're driving,' he informed his mother over the phone. 'Should be with you around mid morning.' Ella had not known that he owned a car.

There were more dead rats, three this time, on her side of the gate when she and Ben set off for their morning walk. She was staring at them, summoning courage to go for the garden spade and remove them when Tom Antony appeared. 'What you got there, Mis' Caine? Something nasty by the look of it.'

'Rats, Tom, dead ones. Do you think I have an infestation?'

Tom, splendid Tom, was preparing to remove the offence. A stout stick under the first disgusting corpse and a closer examination. 'Nothing like that, Mis' Caine. This varmint's been peppered with shot. You stand well back now. I'll soon shift 'em.' The deed done he looked keenly at her. 'Not the first time, Mis' Caine, by the look on your face.'

'No, Tom. There were two by the back door the morning before the meeting.'

'That right? Any idea where they come from?'

'A very strong idea but I can't prove it.'

He nodded in the Highcroft direction and she did the same in agreement.

'That's Jack,' he said. 'Wouldn't put anything past him. Let me know, Mis' Caine, if there's more I can do.'

She was so grateful she wanted to tell him the whole story, to beg for his protection. She wanted the entire world on her side. She watched Tom Antony striding over the field and wondered what he would say if he knew. Which he did. Jonno had told the tale because Jonno too had needed to talk, and talking to Tom was safer than telling the priest. And now Tom had something to tell Jonno and, with luck, a big burly copper would come along and lean heavily on Jack Downing. Someone had to, her being all on her own.

Only until elevenish on that particular day. A deal of horn-tooting and John was leading the way up the garden path. Behind him was Mary. Ella held her breath, not knowing what to expect. The Wrens, people said, was not the same service. Hard, brassy girls notching up sexual conquests around their money belts. Was Mary one such?

'Hi, Mum,' John hugged her hard; 'we

made good time. This,' he said, standing aside, 'is Mary.'

For what seemed hours, Ella could only stare. Never before had she seen a girl so lovely. Black curls around a pansy face, enormous blue eyes searching hers for signs of welcome and approval. A tiny creature, pale-skinned but with pink blushes in her cheeks and a shy sweet smile. Still Ella could say nothing. She simply held out both hands and Mary grasped them, laughing with relief.

'Not bad, is she?' John, so happy, so proud, ready to explode. 'I'm not sure yet but I think I'll keep her.'

Later, Ben and the pair of them out for a long walk, Ella telephoned Eve. 'She is quite the loveliest child in the world. A chatterbox once she gets going and they obviously adore each other. I couldn't be more delighted.'

'Then don't keep her to yourself, meanie. Adam and I need some joy in our barren lives. Drinks tomorrow about six?'

Saturday morning found both gates, garage and house, totally blocked on the outside by well-distributed mounds of straw and horse manure. The accumulation of several weeks mucking out, Ella reckoned.

'Did you order this?' John asked.

'Don't be ridiculous and if I had, I certainly wouldn't have asked that it be dumped there.'

'It must be the chap at Highcroft, his idea of a joke. Who else has horses? I'll go and have a strong word with him.'

'Don't,' Ella snapped and Mary widened her blue eyes. 'Just move it, please. We'll analyse afterwards.'

'Move it where?'

'The verge on the other side, as far away as you can manage. It stinks to high heaven. I'll ask Philip to cart it away.' No I won't. I'll ask Fran to ask Philip.

'Why don't you ask the chap who dumped it? That makes more sense.'

'Please do as I ask.' She would say nothing more on the subject.

The itinerant dung-heap raised its smelly head at the Graysons that evening. Ella had known that it would but there was no way she could instruct John to say nothing. 'Anything else?' Adam asked quietly, worrying his nose to death. (Eve, enchanted by Mary, had taken her upstairs to show off the gen-u-ine priest's hole.)

'Three more dead rats yesterday. Tom Antony removed them.'

'I think you should tell John. He has a right to know.'

'No. There's nothing he can do and he would only worry. He sails in a couple of days.'

'Tell John what and why would he worry?' He had returned from the cloak-room sooner than expected.

Adam and Ella looked at each other. 'I will,' Adam volunteered.

'You have to do something, you can't let him get away with it.' Her son's verdict was delivered in impassioned tones. 'It's harassment, Mother, and that's an offence. Why are you holding back?'

'Because nothing could be proved and more bad feeling would be generated. His dung, yes, but unless someone actually saw him, why should he admit to dumping it? I shall just have to bide my time.'

'Until when? Until he fires the house? I'm totally in favour of Dad's idea of selling the place. Get out. The sooner the better as far as I'm concerned.'

'And what do I tell the prospective purchasers when they ask why I am leaving such an ideal home? That my neighbour is a drug dealer who objects strongly to the slightest interference in his lifestyle? That

244

their weekends will be hell on earth? Or do I lie through my teeth, say he's a sweetie and that Darrington is peace and tranquillity and destined to remain so?'

'You tell the truth. You say the time has come to dispose of the family home and you tell them why.'

'I suppose you're right.'

'I know I am.' And Adam agreed.

ELEVEN

'Where was Tom going at the crack of dawn with the tractor and trailer?' Breakfast-time at Dowsett's, a chaos of children and crockery and clamour. Fran asking the questions.

'To return something to its rightful owner, he said. He wasn't gone long, no more than half an hour.'

'Have you paid him yet?'

'A bit on account.' Careful, Philip, you could trip up over that lower lip. 'Don't glare at me, Fran. I know it isn't cricket but neither is this damned weather. That thunderstorm did as much good as the bloody meeting to Darrington's morale.' Change the subject, stir another pot of discontent. 'I hear John Caine brought his girlfriend home for the weekend. Lovely little thing by all accounts.'

'I heard too.' And that was that. She had no intention of rising to the bait, on wasting time on argument and conjecture. She had something more positive in her mind.

John and Mary had been gone no more than minutes when the Russell's old car turned into the lane. Philip? Please God, no. Not Philip, Fran. Was this better or worse?

'You've just missed John,' Ella said. 'Still hot, isn't it? Come on.'

'A good weekend?' Fran asked pointedly.

'Very good. I enjoyed meeting Mary.'

'So did the Graysons.'

'Yes, well, we only popped in for a quick drink.' Lord, this was awkward, and Fran so red in the face she looked ready to explode. Which she did.

'All right, Ella, out with it. What have we done to upset you? Why is our company suddenly so undesirable? And don't give me any of that I-don't-know-what-you-mean baloney. I want the truth.'

'Oh dear,' Ella took coffee to the table and sat opposite her irate accuser. The morning post had arrived. There was something from David and she was dying to open it but Fran demanded precedence. 'I've been trying too hard to be careful.'

And then the whole Highcroft story, but only after secrecy had been solemnly sworn. It was amusing in a way, watching Fran's face change expression as the tale unfolded. Anger and resentment were replaced by interest and, finally, concern.

'But why the Graysons and not us?' One hurt remained to rankle.

'I suppose because they are older and wiser and less of a family. No children to overhear. I remember what the boys were like. They always heard what they were supposed not to. Like John the other evening at the Graysons.' That part too had been related.

'Yes, I can see that,' Fran said, satisfied at last. 'Oh Ella, what a mess, and I promise I won't say a word, not even to Philip. He thinks the same as everyone else, that it was something to do with the old bangers.'

'Tom knows there's something amiss but he probably thinks the attention I'm

247

getting is no more than perverted humour on Jack Downing's part. He moved the dung before we were up and about this morning, bless his noble heart, but I don't know where.'

'Back to Highcroft. What a joke. I wonder who signed for it? Ella, much as I hate to think of your going, it might be wise to put the house on the market now. It's what David wants and he's justified, and it's what John wants as well. It would set his mind at rest while he's away if he knew you were on the move.'

'You're right. I'll ring the estate agent later and have the place valued. What a rotten state of affairs. Driven out by a drug dealer.'

Not absolutely true, she thought later. Just prodded by Jack Downing into getting her skates on and doing what she had to. And Fran was right, John would be much happier when she wrote and told him. He had worried the subject like Ben would an old slipper ever since learning the truth.

Mary must think she's involved herself with a very peculiar family. What a darling the girl was, and wise too, like an ageless fairy. 'Don't worry,' she had whispered before leaving. 'He'll be back before we know it. May I come and stay with you sometimes when he's away? I really would like that.' As if there was need to ask. She was more than welcome any time; they would share John and their missing him and look forward to the future. Had David met her yet, she wondered? David. Where was his letter? Why write when he could have phoned?

She found the envelope. It felt as though it held a card or a photograph. Yes, a card. Oxford, seat of learning, guardian of great names. Why put a postcard in an envelope unless you don't want the world to read your message? It was simple and to the point. 'Helen moving on. Delay selling the house.'

So where do we go from here? Just when she was reconciled—more or less—to selling the cottage, moving away, another die had fallen and shunted her back to Go. She wanted desperately to stay but could she do so with Jack Downing as a neighbour? Please, please let something happen to send him packing—a Grot or a developer become passionately interested in acquiring Highcroft and offer him tens of millions. He'd move then, wouldn't he? Please, please. Should she ring Fran and tell her the news? No panic on that score. They would meet again soon enough. Now that the atmosphere was easier they were bound to.

They did, on another flawless day. And in different states of mind. Fran, trudging the track from Dowsett's on her way to the shop, worried relentlessly at the latest development in her unsatisfactory life. Why was Philip suddenly so damned cheerful? Days, weeks even, of gloom and misery, hardly a civil word, and then, overnight almost, incessant whistling and oh what a beautiful morning. The weather forecasts gave no suitable explanation. Little change. So why one so dramatic in such an ardent fan? Had "she" been away somewhere (misery) and had "she" come back (joy)? Was there, in fact, a she? Be honest, Fran told herself, how much do you care one way or the other? Not a lot. Hurt pride maybe, but no feeling of betrayal, no agony of love lost. Because love went ages ago and the awful thing was, liking and respect were following fast on its heels. How on earth would she cope when she didn't like him any more, when the sight of that petulant lower lip drove her to a frenzy, not just irritation? God knows she had tried hard enough. Sympathizing, encouraging, assuming interest, but the concentration and energy required was too high a price to pay. If there was any justice in life she should be as thin as a rake, all the effort she had put into pretence. Time to face facts. She and Philip were not designed to totter, hand in hand, into the sunset. Was there an alternative? She would have to find one. The future, as now viewed, was too frightful to contemplate. Bleak penny-pinching years, the children gone, hope gone. It simply was not acceptable.

Ella, approaching from a different direction, was feeling light-hearted and optimistic. There had been no Highcroft disruption for several days. She dared to hope that her punishment—or persecution—was over. Poor David. He must feel rotten about Helen. Should she ring him and sympathize? No, wait until the hurt had eased. Intrusion now might seem like crowing. You've lost, I've won, so there. But how good it felt to be resettled, to look forward to continuance of *status quo*. Even if Darrington changed beyond all recognition, her little corner would remain unspoiled. Unless, of course, they built on the field opposite. Who owned it?

She must find out, and she must also ring Mike Carter and ask behind which legal botch-up her decree nisi was lurking. What a glorious day. She ought to want rain as much as Philip did, the garden was becoming a desert. Philip? Who was he? Just someone she had once known.

The shop was empty save for the postmaster and his lady wife. She, indescribable in baggy cotton trousers and a shirt that had seen better days, was bubbling to the boil. 'Permission to take a coffee break, sir?'

'Off with you, gossipmonger,' Adam indulged, grey eyes twinkling. 'And since when have you required permission to do anything?'

It was, Eve told her audience, all happening. Item. Maggie Hubbard was engaged to be married. That set them buzzing. Shrieks of delight and disbelief and a stream of questions. Who told you? Have you met him? What's he like? I don't believe it. Are you sure?

'I am sure and believe it you must. Maggie herself told me, introduced me to her fiancé and, quite honestly, he is absolutely awful. And we all know why she's marrying him, don't we? Altogether now...'

'He has a car.' A united chorus. It was well documented that Maggie Hubbard had sworn she would marry the first man who had a car. Provided, of course, he asked her. And this one had. Forget the fact, Eve said, that he looks like a weasel and has a distinct squint in one bleary eye. Forget also that he reaches no higher than her shoulder and exudes a powerful combination of halitosis and BO. Maggie has got her man. She is about to become respectable.

'What about her business?' Fran asked, giggling. 'Will she continue working?'

'My dear, how could I possibly ask that? I wanted to quite desperately but good taste forbade. Now, aren't you glad you came in this morning? Tit-bits of tittle-tattle to titillate. Oh, another item, supposition and not yet fact. Toby could be heading for a nervous breakdown.'

Toby had obviously been distressed when Eve served him that morning. Tears behind the eyes and nervous mannerisms twitching at his hands. Giles was being beastly, so difficult to please. None of the girls who had applied for the vacancy had been remotely suitable. Or so Giles said. Toby had been hoping against hope that someone wonderful would appear and that—that Keith person would go away. Yes, he knew Giles had said it was only a temporary arrangement but it didn't look like that now, did it? He, Toby, quite enjoyed working in the restaurant but not on a permanent basis. He wanted to work with Giles. Eve understood that, didn't she? She wouldn't like it, would she, if she and Adam were separated after such a long and happy time together. And that—that Keith was taking more and more on himself, becoming quite bossy, even daring to try too teach Toby his job. It was all sad and horrid and he hated it. For two pins, he said, he would run away.

'Poor old Toby,' Ella said, 'it is sad. Sad that life has afflicted him, made him different, and sadder still that he can't find happiness amongst his own kind.' She and Fran left as they had come, together. 'How's Philip?'

'Better,' Fran said. 'He's been miserable as sin for ages but yesterday he cheered up. I can't think why.'

'Do you still think he has someone else?' God, I am so brave. It must be the respite from Jack Downing's intrusions.

'I'm not sure.' Philip's wife looked hard

at Ella. 'Do you know, that's the first time you've mentioned the subject since I told you.'

'I didn't want to pry,' Ella lied. 'I reckoned on your telling me without prompting.'

'Fair enough and thanks. You're a good friend. Speaking of friends, has Jenni made a move?'

'No, I'm inclined to wash my hands of her but I won't. I never do.'

She walked home slowly, enjoying the heat and the burning blue sky. Not a cloud to be seen. Was that a good omen? Hardly reliable, it had been cloudless on the Downing deposit days. Why was Philip so cheerful—had he found someone else? If so, he can't have thought much of me. I don't care a jot one way or the other. I am free, I am me and it feels absolutely wonderful. Now, should I ring Jenni, give her a push in the right direction? No. She can motivate herself. All the same, I wonder what she's up to.

Tom Antony knew. He had taken to patrolling the Dip at least once a day. Even though Jonno had sworn it would never happen again, even when he was doing duty in Brunton, Tom had to make sure. A nasty sight that had been, two bare bums rollicking around in the moonlight and not much covering the top halves either. Not nasty to begin with, funny really, wondering who. Not Philip and Mrs Caine, that was over and done with. Don't ask him how but Tom knew. And that pair had always kept cover, never gone public. Not Maggie Hubbard either. He'd seen her bum more times than most, fat and flabby, nothing like the shapely darling down there in the Dip. So who? And then the voices and the laugh. He'd know that laugh anywhere, had heard it enough times at the Foresters' in between so-called singing. A gurgle more than a laugh, naughty, leading menfolk on. 'Jonno darling, this is such fun.' That's what she had said, as though the pair of them were having a picnic or dabbling their toes in the sea. He'd wanted to go down there, to send her packing back to her husband and children, to knock Jonno's head clean off his shoulders. He'd gone back home instead and sat by the window until he saw Jonno in the Street, watched him make for his own front door. And then he'd grabbed him. 'You come in here, young fellow m'lad. You and me's got some straight talking to do.'

So here he was again, just making sure. Late afternoon, well gone four and the heat only now beginning to ease a little. No point in checking fences; they were all good because he'd done them himself, and hanging around Dowsett's for other work was a waste of time. Only made young Philip embarrassed, seeing him there. Can't be that short, can he? Didn't matter much, he and Doris could manage fine. And here too was that Mrs Crown from the Manor. Lord, what a sight. Hair cropped short like a boy, legs even more like a sparrows now they were burnt brown by the sun. Stick almost as big as herself, a staff more like—what was that for? Like someone out of the Bible she was, striding forth. Moses leading his people out of the wilderness if she sported a beard and a flowing robe. And those blessed dogs padding along behind like followers. Morning and afternoon, regular as clockwork, never a murmur out of them. They must know these paths better than any rabbit.

'Afternoon, Mis' Crown. Still keeping hot.'

'Good afternoon, Mr Antony. We shall

certainly be relieved when it becomes cooler, shall we not?'

The squeal of brakes, like pigs in mortal fear, carried clearly through the still, hot air. The Honourable Alexandra and Tom Antony looked at each other.

'Sounds like Dowsett's.' Tom said.

'Some madman,' Mrs Crown said, 'intent on destruction no matter whose. I mourn the days...'

Then the screaming started, one young voice, shrill and terrified. It would be hard to judge who ran faster at first, Tom Antony or Alexandra Crown. She, forty years his junior, brown legs twinkling through the long brown grass. He, fit as a fiddle and a stride from here to next week, but time against him. And pointless for both, such exertion, when you considered. Darrington Street, houses either side. Others would get there first, others would stop that terrible noise.

Others had. Quite a crowd had gathered around Emma Russell, lying silent in the dusty Street. Her bicycle, rear wheel still turning but otherwise almost unrecognizable, had been carried several yards, then dropped. Quite a crowd around that too. But no one seemed interested in sister

Lizzie, leant against a tree, her mouth a permanent open scream. No one until Fran came running and Lord knows where she found the speed. Red as a peony and screaming herself. 'Stop it, Liz! Do you hear me? Shut up!'

And then the miracle. Little Emma rolled over and tried to sit up. Blood everywhere and dust, but no tears. 'It was a green car, mummy. And the man had a beard.'

The police came, then an ambulance and finally Philip, but at no great pace. Puttering up the Street in his dreadful old car, waving at folk, grinning like a fool. But the grin went when he saw the scene.

'What happened?' He elbowed his way through, took in the stretcher and Emma, Liz, sobbing now, and his tight-faced wife. 'Are they all right?'

Like an animal, Fran turned on him. 'Where the hell have you been? Couldn't you leave her? Hadn't you finished copulating?'

That, Tom told Doris and the Graysons, was the worst part of the whole sorry business. Fran, wet with sweat, taunting and accusing and Philip protesting his innocence. Tom had gone straight to the shop when everything was over. He had remembered his promise to help Doris with the groceries, her back being bad. Adam had taken one look at the weary walk and tight face and declared that Tom was going nowhere except to a chair and a mug of strong sweet tea. He locked the shop door and hung a "closed for stock-taking" sign. 'That's exactly what we're doing, taking stock.' Eve nodded approval and Doris went to make tea.

'I saw the bastard,' Eve said. 'Emma's right about colour. A green flash, that's all I saw.'

'They'll get him,' Adam assured. 'He must have come from somewhere, been visiting. The Swan perhaps.'

'At four in the afternoon? Giles has more sense. How are you feeling now, Tom?'

'Better, Mis' Grayson, and thank you kindly for the interest shown. 'Twere a fair run and it being so hot, that's what done it.'

'He'll rest tonight,' Doris promised, 'and then we'll see what tomorrow brings.'

'Bossy boots,' Tom muttered but he did not argue.

Evening came, and the Graysons were still mulling over the day, concentrating now more on Fran and Philip than the children. 'I'm not altogether surprised,' Eve said, 'but it's still hard to believe. I asked Tom what he thought and he said yes, but not any more. That man must know more about Darrington than the good Lord Himself.'

'But who?'

'Exactly. Who? I wonder if Ella knows.'

'Knows the other woman?'

'No. About the accident. I haven't seen her all day. Fran would be frightfully hurt if there was no concern from that direction.'

Ella did not know. She had spent the afternoon in Brunton waiting impatiently for a gap in Mike Carter's diary. There had been a letter second post from Jack Downing's solicitor. The chestnut tree on her boundary onto Mr Downing's lane, it said, would have to be felled. It was impeding the free passage of vehicles to and from Highcroft.

'It's been there for centuries and no one's ever complained.' She was hot and thoroughly agitated.

'But the lane was barely used until recently,' her solicitor pointed out, 'and vehicles have become bulkier over the years. His complaint may be valid.'

'It isn't, he's just doing it to spite me. Oh Lord, I suppose I'll have to tell you the whole story.'

Mike Carter listened impassively throughout. 'Very unpleasant,' he said. 'I'm glad I know all the facts in case—'

'In case what?'

'Let's walk before we run, shall we? Now, despite all you have told me, this man may still be in the right. He must think he is or why the expense of a solicitor's letter? Not a good letter, I admit, and the spelling, oh dear me, but a letter nevertheless. On the other hand he may, as you suggest, be simply intent on worrying and frightening you.'

'So what do we do?'

'We acknowledge receipt and say that the matter of obstruction is being looked into. Then I come and see your tree and take some measurements, but only after I have initiated enquiries into whether Mr Downing does or does not have legal claim to the lane. Does that make you feel any better?'

'A little. That wretched man. And there I was thinking the other day that all my troubles were over.'

She passed a police car and an ambulance on her way home but thought nothing of them. It was not until Eve telephoned that she knew what had happened and that Fran had accused in no uncertain terms. 'I suggested as much ages ago, didn't I?' Eve said. 'Did you know he had a fancy woman?'

Fancy woman. Is that what I was? 'Fran said some weeks back that she thought there might be someone else, but I put it down to hyperactive imagination.'

'Not according to Tom.'

Yes, and if Tom knows, he must also know who. And yet he had never changed towards her in any respect. Dear Tom. Not his business to pass judgement, that's what he probably thought.

'I'll ring Fran now. No, I won't. I'll go and see her. Dear God, what an utterly dreadful day. I'll be glad when it's over.'

Fran was calm enough, the girls sleeping, she said. Cuts and bruises for Emma, nothing serious, and a hell of a shock for Liz.

'And where were you when I needed you?' she demanded.

Ella told her.

'Someone up there doesn't like us.' She

managed a trembling smile.

'My someone will never get up there,' Ella retorted. 'He's heading for the fiery furnaces. Where's Philip, by the way?' She had steeled herself to meeting him, was prepared to be pleasant.

'I don't know and I don't care. Probably telling "her" it's all off because wifey knows and so, by now, does the whole of Darrington.'

'Fran, you still can't be sure. You were distressed and turned on the person closest to you because, like me, he wasn't there when you needed him.'

'You have a legitimate excuse. He hasn't even bothered to make up anything plausible. Something about the milking parlour, asked how the girls were and said he was going out. Wouldn't you think he might have stayed with me after what happened? A show of concern would not have gone amiss.'

'I have to agree with you there,' Ella said. You are a bastard, Philip Russell. I wish I'd found out sooner.

Oblivious to all condemnation, Philip was walking his fields. Getting it out of his system, said all who saw him striding towards the setting sun. Could have been curtains for the little'un, must have been a shock for them both. Not true. There was nothing Philip wanted out of his system, he was supremely content. Nasty for the girls, of course, especially little Em, but they'd soon get over it. He'd make sure that they did, now that he could afford to. The deed was done, the ink dry on his signature. What a good thing Fran had not been astute enough when they bought Dowsett's to insist on joint ownership. She could still kick up a fuss if she wanted to, delay matters with a legal wrangle, but she wouldn't. Not if he told her he was prepared to walk out and leave her to run the farm if she didn't see sense. Two and a half million, that's what he was getting. Worth it, Mr Smith said, to start the ball rolling. (Eric Norton must have developed cold feet.) Once the others knew they would all follow suit. Don't start spending yet, he had warned with a dry smile, there were still some formalities to be gone through. How long? Not more than a month, which would give Mr Russell time to sort out his own affairs, the disposition of the dairy herd, so on and so forth. Yes, he could assist with an advance of sorts, were finances really so embarrassing? He would send a copy of the signed agreement to Mr Russell's bank. That should be collateral enough to ensure a further loan. By the way, how did Mrs Russell feel about the transaction? Very excited, he had no doubt. Philip had told him. She doesn't know yet, he had said. There had been a certain satisfaction in being honest for the first time in months. So there it was, or nearly was. Two and a half million pounds. No matter if they drummed him out of Darrington, he didn't care. And the best thing was he didn't care about Ella either. The yearning had dissolved the minute he signed that wonderful piece of paper. He'd soon find someone else to compensate for Fran's limitations and with all that money he could afford to be choosy. Yes, indeed, a great day. He felt like dancing, like singing at the top of his voice but that would cause comment in view of what had happened earlier. Try to remember, Philip, what *did* happen earlier?

The rains came, preceded by a gigantic thunderstorm. Ella awoke at first light to the noise of heavy downpour. Was it the rain that had so disturbed her or Ben, grumbling and growling with a yelp thrown in for good measure? 'Shut up,' she said, 'Silly dog. Go back to sleep. Andrew won't be here for hours yet.' She sat up with a start what seemed only five minutes later but the clock and the sky told her an hour had passed. A car was pulling away from outside the cottage. Andrew. It must be, he had hitched a lift. She waited for footsteps, for the sound of his key in the lock, but none came. Mystified, she went to the window. Oh God, no. What had happened to her garden?

In Wellington boots and an old raincoat of David's she inspected the damage. It was unbelievable and deliberate and her tears streamed faster than the rain beating into her face. Shrubs hacked and broken, second bloom roses snapped from their stems, flowers torn up by their roots and trampled on. Something heavy and sharp had been dragged across the lawns, cutting them to shreds of mud and mutilated grass. She went inside and telephoned the police.

Tom Antony came before they did. Grotesque in a sou'wester and heavy cape, his eyes showed sympathy far more than words could say. ''Tis terrible, Mis' Caine, terrible. But weather's in our favour, we'll save the lot, you'll see.'

'Not yet, Tom,' she said wearily, bringing him into the kitchen. 'not until after the police have been. This time I'm fighting back.'

The police came. They looked, they pulled long faces and made copious notes. 'Any idea who could have done this?' one of them asked.

'I know who did it,' she said, 'but I'll bet he has an alibi for every minute of last night. A message to Detective Sergeant Jameson of the Drug Squad, if you please. Tell him his careless talk has cost hundreds of lives. Tell him also that if he does not put this man behind bars very soon, there will be no requirement. I will have killed him.'

'Now, Madam, calm down. I can understand how you feel, but—'

'You,' she said icily, 'do not know the whole story. Remember the names. Jameson and Downing. They go well together.'

She laboured with Tom in the rain until it was time to collect Andrew from the station. She left reluctantly. There was still so much more to do and it was grossly unfair to leave Tom to do it alone.

'I'll never be able to thank you enough,' she said.

'No thanks needed, Mis' Caine. You go and fetch that boy of yours. Best thing for you, having him home.'

Andrew did not appear unduly surprised when she told him. A long letter from John had put him fully in the picture and he had to admit to wondering why things had gone so quiet. This was also the reason for changing his holiday plans and coming home for a couple of weeks. No, he wouldn't be bored, that's if she let him use the car occasionally. 'You've called the police in this time, I hope? It's not funny any more.'

It never really was, dear boy, except perhaps Tom taking all the muck back to source. And I'm so glad you're here. All those years protecting and caring for you both and now the roles are reversed. It makes me feel rather more than my age but I'll accept being geriatric and remain grateful that you're here.

They forced Tom at gun-point into the kitchen and made him sit down to tea and toast and slices of buttered fruit cake.

'Not much left to do, Mis' Caine. A few bedding plants still to go back in and whether they'll perk up again's not certain. Grass'll be a sorry sight for weeks yet. I've heeled in as best I can and when it dries up a bit we'll roller over it a few times. Can't do no more than that.'

Ella went back to the garden. The rain had eased to a fine drizzle and she worked hard and fast, trying neither to think nor see, just work. Tom and Andrew seemed deep in conversation each time she straightened her back and looked through the window. In the sitting-room now, and Andrew had something in his hand. She opened the door to the ominous words, 'I think she ought to be told. She should know exactly what she's up against.'

'Go on,' she said, sinking into a chair, 'tell me.'

'This is blood on Bill's collar,' Andrew said, showing the small leather band, 'And Tom's just told me why.'

Alex Jameson rang late in the afternoon. Andrew spoke to him first. She had not realized his command of words was so fluent and extensive, but then there were so many things she had never realized.

'Phew! That was some pasting I took.' The DS was still attempting to make light of the matter. 'Ella, I'm very very sorry and

270

if any of what's happened is my fault, I'm sorrier still.'

'You can't be blamed for my dog,' she said stiffly, 'but you knew about him and should have acted accordingly. As for the rest, yes, I do blame you and I intend taking matters further. What, if anything, have you done about today's vandalism?'

He had been to see Jack, he said. No admissions of course, just stony silence. And was the man sick or something? He looked it. Anyway, he had laid down the law and warned that a close watch was being kept on all his movements and that if he dared so much as say good-morning to Ella, they'd have him. 'I was also able to tell him something he didn't know. The Devon boys grabbed the parcel before it was even opened and all those waiting to untie the string. Makes us look even stupider, I admit, but the gloom on Jack's face took the edge off that.'

The day finally ended. 'Poor little Bill,' Ella said. 'What a horrible end to his life. Do you know, Andrew, I've never actively wished harm on anyone but I do now.' The stream of invective that followed surprised and shocked her son.

It was hard to believe that she knew such words, never mind uttering them. They were certainly all getting to know each other. Not before time.

TWELVE

A Saturday morning in August. The English summer is back on form; grey, wet drizzle but still, thank God, relatively warm. Saturday morning, and four people are making deliberate decisions to visit Highcroft that afternoon. Not in conjunction with each other. For their own reasons. A fifth will also go there but not through choice. He will simply find that Highcroft is where he must go. It is beginning.

Down at the Swan, Toby was through in the kitchen talking to Henry. He was spending a lot of time with Henry these days. Giles was still the same, that's when he could prise him away from the interloper, but Keith hated Toby. That was the one source of satisfaction in Toby's bleak life. If Keith hated him, Giles had not been unfaithful. But for how much longer?

'My roses are looking very sad,' he said.

'You'd be looking sad too, sweetheart, if you'd been stood out in the rain for days on end.'

'No, I wouldn't. I'd be perking up. That's if I were a rose. I think I ought to feed them properly. Ella told me ages ago she had found some lovely manure at Highcroft.'

'Odd things turn people on, don't they? Me, I'm into offal more than manure. I like the feel, all slippery and slimy. Now why the face? I didn't go sour when you started drooling about horse shit.'

'Henry, you're awful and it isn't just, you know. It's wonderful rich mature stuff that's been rotting for years, long before that dreadful man moved here. Ella said it was full of worms and maggots and very nutritious.'

'Tried some, did she? I'll know what to serve her next time she dines out. *Specialité de la maison*, Madame. Dung salade avec les worms et maggots.'

'You're impossible,' Toby said, pushing back his hair, but he had cheered up. Henry was infuriating but he always made you smile. Time to go back to the restaurant,

273

time to start on chores he had grown
to hate.

'I don't know why you bother about
roses,' Henry shouted after him. 'There
are plenty of pansies around.'

'What was all that about?' Giles asked
as Toby passed by, trying to ignore the
fact that Giles was not alone.

'My roses. I've decided to go up to
Highcroft this afternoon and ask Mr
Downing for some of the old manure
that's been there since his grandfather
died. Just a little to try. He won't mind,
will he?'

Keith, without turning from the spirit
bottles, laughed nastily. 'My, my, we are
brave today. Better take an armed escort,
Tobes, he'll eat you alive.'

'Don't call me Tobes.'

'Giles does.'

'Giles is different. Giles is my friend and
companion.'

'And I'm not? That suits me very well.
I don't like you either.'

'Stop it, you two.' Giles adjusted the dark
thrill of his voice to an appropriate tone and
managed to sound exasperated. But he was
not. It was quite fun being fought over. It
boosted the ego and made one feel utterly

desirable. Not fair on poor old Tobes, of course. He was looking haggard these days and twitching constantly like a mechanical doll. Fiddling with his hair, smoothing it, raking it with trembling hands. Fingering his glasses, pushing them back, taking them off and polishing them as though his life depended on clear vision. And sad, sad brown eyes with tears never far away. He, Giles, must stop being so cruel and do something about finding a replacement waitress. A pity in a way because Keith was fun and very sweet. He liked having him around. But Tobes came first even though he could be very silly at times. Their arrangement was, after all, business as well as personal and any rift would be catastrophic for the Swan. 'You do that, Tobes. I can't see why Jack should object. Mind you, he might charge you by the pound.'

'He wouldn't would he?' Too late Toby saw the joke. 'You're becoming as bad as Henry, always pulling my leg.'

'I wish that horrible man would go away.' If Keith hated Toby, he hated Henry even more. 'He's rude and coarse and doesn't fit in here at all. I don't even think he's a very good chef.'

Foolish boy, Keith. To unite Giles and Toby, all you have to do is criticize Henry. They think their grizzle-haired, dough-skinned chef is wonderful and his cooking and presentation superb. They don't mind the jokes at their expense because they know there is no malice in them. Henry makes them laugh and he is also their strength. What you do not know, Keith, is that Henry is also a partner in the Black Swan enterprise, that he put in his savings at the very beginning and is only now reaping the rewards. That made Giles and Toby very proud, Henry's having faith in them—a chef who could find employment anywhere, and straight, chancing his luck with a couple of gays. You would do well, Keith, not to say anything against Henry, not if you still want to lure Giles into your bed.

'I think a change of scenery would do you good, Keith,' Giles said pleasantly enough without a smile. His eyes were narrowed and cold. 'Why don't you try laying the restaurant tables? You've watched Toby often enough.'

Wisely, Toby held his tongue.

'Help me finish up here, Tobes, there's a dear. We'll be done in a flash, you're an expert at everything. And then we'll go upstairs and have a chat. I've some new ideas about special evenings. I really would value your opinion.'

O happy day! The roses were looking better already but only because he was seeing them with bright clear eyes. He must neither forget nor neglect them. He would put on his wellies and walk up to Highcroft as soon as the restaurant was closed.

★ ★ ★ ★

Briar Cottage around the same time. A wet morning without but inside the temperature rapidly rising.

'I still can't understand why you let her go.' Stephen Templeton's colour was darkening and Jenni was watching the signs warily.

'I had no option. Her mother is in hospital. I shall complain, of course. I shall say, how dare your mother fall under a bus when Captain Templeton and I had made plans for the evening.'

'Don't be facetious, Jenni.'

'Then don't you be so stupidly unreasonable. What would you have done under the same circumstances? Answer me that.'

'I suppose you're right.' Grudging, but the colour was ebbing. 'So what do we do now? They're definitely coming. Major Tom said so yesterday.'

'There is doubtless an Antony or Hubbard who will sit in with the kids.'

'Not on your life. I wouldn't trust any of that lot sitting for my pet parrot.'

It's worth a try, there's still a slim chance. Major Tom has stacks of influence and in the right places. A gentle hack through the North Hampshire countryside, that's what I promised him, and dinner afterwards. He seemed keen. So if the day goes well, and Sundays usually do, he may put some pressure on the bastards, the ones who have passed me over for the umpteenth time and never shown the courtesy to tell me why.

'Ella?' Jenni suggested.

'No. Definitely not. I'm not asking *her*.'

Careful, Jenni told herself. If he's off Ella, he's heading in the usual direction. But caution and Jenni had little in common these days. Different, yes, before she had broken the barrier to a Better Life, but why hold back when she was so arrogantly established.

'It's a mad idea, anyway. From which hat are you going to conjure up two horses? And even if you did, it wouldn't make any difference to your promotion. You're not getting it this time either, are you?'

'I can't be sure. The final lists aren't out. And no problem with gee-gees. Jack Downing has a couple.'

'You're not serious...?'

'Why not? They look decent enough beasts.'

'They've gone, Stephen. He got rid of them.'

'Don't talk utter rubbish. I saw him only the other day. Riding one, leading the other.' Red again, red mist starting behind the eyes, 'What's the matter? Does Missus and her classy background make you feel inadequate?'

Unlike Stephen to make such a jibe, one she would neither forgive nor forget.

'I saw them leaving. Horse boxes mean only one thing. Horses. It was ages ago.'

'I don't believe you. You're only saying so because you want to ruin the day, ruin my chances.'

'All right,' Jenni said, clipping her beautifully enunciated words, 'ask.'

'I will. I'll go up to Highcroft after lunch

and ask Jack if we can hire his nags for tomorrow afternoon.'

Go look for your ghosts, Jenni said, but not in words. Knock seven bells out of Jack Downing when he tells you the horses have gone and see what he does to you. A fair fight for a change, that should be worth a paragraph in the local press. You frighten me now, Stephen, and fear never featured in any of my plans. Ella's right, they all are. It's time to go. There *is* a sickness inside your head, I've known that for ages, but I thought it would get better once we shot into orbit. But *you're* not spiralling anywhere, are you? Your orders are to march on the spot for the rest of your bloody life. Leave me out. Jenni's fed up with marking time, she's destined for the heights, wait and see. Four years of my life sacrificed in planning and practising to reach them. Four precious years, maybe the best ones, living like a nun. Mind and body, a nun. You never knew that, did you? You fell for the finished product, the glossy gift-wrapped package just as I fell for the handsome officer who was going to take me where I wanted to go. The top. I didn't know then about dotty Dodo, in and out of the nut-house. I didn't know then you had been expelled from four schools for beating and bullying, nor that your father washed his hands of you the minute you took the Queen's shilling and were no longer his responsibility. I wanted to be the Colonel's lady. I told Ella, didn't I? Someone else will give me that plum, or the equivalent, or better. Not you, Stephen. I'm sorry. Part of me hates doing this because we've had a lot of fun, in and out of bed. But the other part has made up its mind. No more stagnation, no more false hopes and promises. No more dreary village and dreary friends. I can get any man I want, I've proved that a hundred times. Experience has taught me to do my homework more carefully. Next time, I'll make sure I collar the right one.

★ ★ ★ ★

For Ella, that morning, there was a letter from her solicitor. A brief one introducing the copy of another sent to Mr Downing and expressing the hope that she had now seen the end of the matter. She read eagerly. Appropriate searches have been made, it said, and it has been established that the lane leading to Highcroft Farm from Darrington Street is, in fact, owned by Brunton District Council and has never been part of the land pertaining to your property. Although Highcroft Cottage was once part of your estate, this property and the half acre of land in which it is situated were purchased from Mrs Ruth Downing by Mr and Mrs David Caine in 1966. Moreover all land surrounding the cottage as far as the boundary to the south-west, Darrington Street to the north-east and the land of Mr Joseph Turtle to the south-east is common land and you have no just cause or right to prevent passage over this land. The land on the north-west side of the lane known as Highcroft Lane is also common land. (Yippee! No builder's lorries in that direction either.) The chestnut tree, the letter continued, which you claim impedes the passage of vehicles to and from your property has been examined. This is an ancient tree and the branches, although overhanging the lane, are of a height to cause no inconvenience to any vehicle other than, perhaps, a combine harvester. In view of the use to which your property is now put and the delineation of other surrounding land, it is unlikely that such a vehicle would have reason to use the lane as access. The circumference of the tree is approximately ten feet (120 inches), the diameter being therefore approximately 38.2 inches. Fifteen inches only of this diameter protrude onto the verge on the Highcroft Cottage side of the lane.

There was a final paragraph warning against threats and any form of bodily contact, the latter mention causing Ella to smile. She passed Andrew the letter.

'Great,' he said. 'Now we can all relax. May I have the car this afternoon to celebrate?'

'As long as celebrating doesn't mean pub-crawling. Yes, of course you may.'

'Did Mike Carter really measure the tree? I wish I could have seen.'

'It was,' Ella admitted, 'a rather lovely sight. He was not dressed for the occasion and my tape measure's nowhere near long enough. We had to improvise with string.' She sighed happily. 'It was worth it. What a thorough fellow he is.'

David also had written. He thanked Ella for her kind note and appreciated her understanding. Just one of those things, he said—how right the old song was. He was happy in Oxford and the firm was doing well. His flat was comfortable and not lacking in character. Ella must visit sometime. Renting was throwing money down the drain, of course; he would probably start looking around for somewhere to buy but Ella could rest easy as far as selling the cottage was concerned. He would have no difficulty in getting a mortgage. How were the boys? He was sure she heard from both of them more frequently than he did, and Mary sounded delightful; he was looking forward immensely to meeting her. He ended by hoping she had enjoyed the summer, preferring for his own part that it had lasted longer. A nice letter, Ella thought, putting it away. A nice letter from a nice old friend. Odd that they should now be so courteous and kind to each other. Older and wiser, perhaps, or simply grown apart?

Andrew went off on his travels after an early lunch. He promised to be careful and not too late home. Ella felt somewhat at a loose end. There was nothing to do in the garden. It was still resettling and she felt she should leave it in peace. What should she do with the rest of this most excellent day?

She read again the solicitor's letter. Jack Downing must have received his by the same post. She wondered as to his reaction, whether he was spitting bullets or simply laughing because it had all been a joke anyway. Some joke, when she looked at the garden and thought about Bill. And now that he no longer had a leg to stand on, would he accept that it was all over? She wanted to know. She wanted his assurance that he understood. She decided to confront him. Andrew away was as good a time as any because Andrew would quite definitely disapprove. She felt extraordinarily brave. The police on her side, the strong weight of legal interpretation in her favour, she had nothing to lose. No second thoughts, decision firmly and positively made. As soon as she tidied up the lunch dishes she would take Mike Carter's letter up to Highcroft and tackle the evil beast in his den.

Philip too was finding time difficult to fill. It seemed pointless doing anything that required effort or money, not with the finalized agreement so close to his hot sticky hand. Yet he must occupy himself or Fran would become even more suspicious. He still had not told her. He really must. Any form of conversation with Fran was fraught with danger these days. She remained prickly and defensive and lost no chance to dig at him, to accuse and condemn. So here he was on a grey drizzly afternoon, sawing wood for a winter that would find them all far away from Darrington, he had not yet decided where. If they were going as a family he would need Fran's opinion but how could he seek that when she had no inkling of his intention to sell? No longer intention, the wheels were turning. The bank manager was full of smiles and congratulations—and how much money did Mr Russell require as an advance on his most profitable sale? None at the moment, thank you, even though I am itching to kick that old car of mine into Darrington pond. How can I spend money when Fran believes we are up to our necks in red ink? Or type, or whatever they use nowadays. It's all too ridiculous. I shall tell her tonight. Get a few drinks into her first and then sweet-talk and persuade until she sees it's for the best. Damn it, now the chainsaw's packed up. No point in trying to fix it, might as well chuck the antique away. And what shall I do with myself now?

'The chainsaw's broken,' he told Fran, 'and just when I was getting stuck in. I think I'll nip over to Highcroft and ask Jack Downing to lend me his.'

'Is that what she's called: "chainsaw"? Not a very pretty name. And she lives at Highcroft? Where? In one of the stables?'

'Give it a rest please, Fran. How many times do I have to tell you there is no other woman in my life?'

'And how many times must I tell you I don't believe you? You may have cooled things off for a time in an attempt to make me think I was wrong but I am neither fooled nor persuaded. Some little bitch somewhere is waiting for you to rip off her pants the minute you walk through the door. Well, she can bloody well wait. I'm watching you like a hawk from now on, Philip Russell. Not a recipe for a happy marriage, I have to admit, but when was our marriage last happy?'

'Fran, I have to talk to you.' Look at me, damn you. Can't you see the excitement I'm generating?

'About her? Don't tell me, I know already. You love her so much you simply cannot live without her. QED, you have been forced into the decision of leaving me and the children in order to start a new life. Am I right? What a joke. On which particular peanut will you start your new life? A wife and three children to support and a chain of debts that makes you sound like Marley's ghost. Think on these things before you disappear.'

'Forget it. It doesn't matter,' Philip said, surly now. God, that woman was capable of taking the pleasure out of everything once she got going. 'We'll talk this evening if you can discipline yourself into a better mood. Please try.'

'My moods are dependent on you and your behaviour.' Of a sudden she lost interest in taunting him. She was sick of churning, sick of being angry and suspicious. 'Go on. See if you can borrow the Laird of Highcroft's saw. I'll bet he makes you pay a hire charge.'

'After the grass his horses have consumed? He wouldn't dare try.' That was better. She was sounding much more reasonable. Finish the wood when I get back, regale her with the Highcroft gossip and then down to business. I can draft my speech as I go. Very careful with this one, no opening punchline. Lead in with fact,

288

follow on with reluctance to make the inevitable decision and then—sock it to her. Two and a half million pounds. No woman in her right mind would turn her nose up at that. So that's settled. Right then, Jack Downing, you conniving rogue, here I come.

Highcroft Farm on a damp summer's afternoon. Not somewhere you would take the family for an outing, not somewhere you would take anyone unless forced. As much mess and rubbish as there ever had been, probably more with all the gutting and stripping that had been going on. A different dung-heap, a new generation of rats but no change for the better. The caravan empty now that Lofty had moved out, the stables too. No weekend visitors, no friends, no old crocks in the yard save the two dead ones and the engine of a third. Rusty now and still seeping oil.

And the Master of Highcroft, the Laird, as Fran Russell had called him, where was he? Coming now from the house but slowly. He had taken up residence at last. Jack Downing was home. Not that the house was finished, far from it. He had his room, a lavatory that sometimes worked and he had the two-ring stove in the caravan. That took care of his needs. What more does a man want when he is dying?

Dying, dying. He said the word in time to the tired plod of his feet. Time for a brew-up, time for a think of sorts, then back to bed. 'Twould save a deal of energy if he moved his bed to the caravan, but no. That little room, waiting all those years for him, that's where the end would come. Hospital, the doctor had said, and quick. Blood transfusions, injections, some sort of transplant and he might make it. Hospitals. He hated them. The smell, the glossy floors, the busy feet and the stink of death. People moaning, flowers and grapes and relatives with nothing to say until they were outside again. He would die if he went in there and he would die if he did not. Face up to it, Jack, it's a two-headed coin. Whichever way you flip, you lose.

Think, Jack. Put things in order before the day's over. Too late tomorrow, too late by far. The business then. No need to fret. Ned running it now but not from an address. Back in the old routine was Ned. Pub handovers, pick-ups in lay-bys, never the same one. Good luck to him. Worked hard, had Ned, been loyal. Liked that, liked the red cushions on the window seat only they never came back.

Pity about most things. Pity the Devon drop went wrong and Jameson smug and pleased as if he took all the credit. Stupid sod, couldn't pee without someone to hold it up. Ran rings around him that day. What a laugh, but no more laughs to come. No more horses. Flash and Royal, Peter and—? Forgotten that one, and why Peter? Stupid name for a horse, Peter.

Old Reub, was he laughing now? Someone had to, Jack couldn't. Old Reub, did he remember Jack the lad shinning down from his little room? Would he be there waiting, ready to scold and cuff? Ruthie too, and Sammy, all laughing because Jack had lost his dreams. Bella as well. All her fault and he knew that now. All her fault and he'd get her for it. But how? Couldn't take the gun where he was going.

What to do with Highcroft? Burn it? Someone might but not Jack. No strength to cart petrol and throw it, no strength to strike that match. His now but afterwards who gets it? Her by rights, her up there in the Midlands and the two kids. Still married, wasn't he? That's right, married to her. She'd sell but who would buy? No one left mad enough, no one with dreams like Jack.

'Burn it,' he said aloud. Strange now, his voice, as if the sound was gone. My place, burn it. Paper somewhere, a scrap will do? What's this now, a letter? Yes, and for him. Not the hospital—he'd had that one already. Please report to...No bloody chance. Please report to hell more like. Oh God, all that writing to read and him so tired. Try, Jack, might be a laugh in it. And there was. Measured the chestnut, did they? Should have seen that. Sorry about her garden, sorry about her dog but she'll not know. Silly cow, shouldn't have stuck her nose in.

So here was paper, where was pen? Come on, someone, show me. Good on you, no trouble to reach. Date. Must put the date, what was it. Date of letter, that would do. No, day after, that made more sense. Now what? Nothing much, just what I want. Burn Highcroft. There, that was done, now sign. J.M Downing. That was done too.

Tack-room next. Find the gun and cartridges. Left it there last time we shot rats. Ned five, Big Charlie two and Jack three. Rats. He hated them. Rats and Bella, that's what he hated most. Find the gun, then into the front room. Sit a little, think some more. Then up the stairs, slowly. Along the passage to the very end and into his little room. Glad it was raining, glad the place was such a mess. 'Twould be hard to go with the sun shining and the horses leaning their great heads out to see. Flash and Royal, Peter and—? No good, that one was gone. Stupid name for a horse, Peter.

★ ★ ★ ★

Not far distant from Highcroft, that's if you trudged cross country, Tom Antony reached over and switched off the television. Nothing worth seeing nowadays, not even sport. Blah-blah-blah voices telling you what you could see for yourself, given half an eye. Changes, always changes, and never for the better. Time was when 'Lijah Hubbard drove his horse and cart along the Street, emptying bins. Open the gate, around the path to the back and up onto the shoulder with the bin. Empty it careful like, no spill on the ground, then back up

293

the path, lid on firmly and out the gate, taking care to close it fast. Not now. Dratted yellow contraptions and men grabbing black plastic bags as if their days were numbered. One torn, and they left the mess. One box or old pram, they left that too. Same with the milk. Clip-clop down the track from Dowsett's, clip-clop along the Street, the old mare stopping without being told. Churns at first, then bottles with yellow heads as long as your thumb. Now it was taters and fruit juice, frozen birds and sliced rubber they called bread. And wishy-washy white stuff, milk with all the goodness gone, milk that had left the cow weeks since. Same with sport. The days were when he would cycle to Upper Darrington to watch a match on the Green. Cricket, nothing better on a summer's afternoon. Slow, lazy, the smack of a ball on bat, the clapping gentle as pigeons rising. Now it was crash helmets and balls so fast you never saw, and hugging and kissing and the Green gone anyway. Tennis courts and a public lavatory now. What sort of games went on in there? Tom wondered.

He went to the door. The weather too, but no need to start on that. Folks talked more on the weather than any subject under the sun. Talked as if they remembered better days. Tom remembered because he had lived them. Rubbish now like everything else. He sniffed the air like an old gun-dog and felt the hair on the back of his neck stiffen and rise. Trouble.

'Something wrong, Dad?' Doris was at his side, her hands white from the pastry she was rolling.

'Dunno, Doris. Might be. On the other hand, might not. Think I'll take a walk.'

'Where to?'

'Dunno that either, Doris. Wherever the wind tells me. Take the gun along in case I see a rabbit, shall I? Rabbit pie, does the idea suit, you at the pastry board and the oven hot?'

'So long as you skin it. And the rest.'

'I'll do that all right.'

He was down the path and off towards the Dip before Doris remembered. There were no cartridges in his pocket, she'd emptied them that morning searching for handkerchieves for the wash. Dad would know that though, wouldn't he? There was nothing on earth that Dad didn't know.

THIRTEEN

They were converging on Highcroft, independent pieces in a game of chance. Ella was almost there, her hand on the yard gate. Toby was five minutes behind her, stepping lightly, trowel in one jacket pocket, bin bag in another. If he had delayed a few minutes longer and if Stephen had found the boots he was still looking for, they would have walked together. That is, if they had liked each other. Philip was on his way across the fields at the back of Highcroft and Tom Antony was hurrying now, lengthening his stride. He had left the Dip just beyond the school and crossed the Street. Now he was cutting up diagonally through the wet grass, broken shotgun over one arm. Highcroft, that's where trouble was. He might have known.

Ella suppressed a shudder as she looked around. In a rapidly changing world, was this the one spot on earth destined to remain the same? There was no sign of

Jack Downing. The caravan perhaps? She peeked inside the open door but saw only a cheerless box. A mug half filled with cold milkless tea was on the doll's-house table alongside an opened letter. The twin to the one she carried in her pocket, she had no doubt. That was good. There would be no need to explain or refer, he knew the facts already.

He must be working inside the house. She had hoped never to go inside again, but it seemed she must. Unless he came when she knocked on the door, open and swinging on squeaky hinges as the wind caught it. She knocked. No movement of any kind. She knocked again, calling this time. 'Mr Downing! Jack! Are you in there?'

He answered from the direction of the room known as front. Not a shout, not a whisper, but something in between.

She made her way through carefully, stepping over rubble and patches of damp earth where the stone tiles had been torn up. What an indescribable mess; it was worse than before they started. The tack-room to the left looked more inviting than the kitchen. At least it had a floor. She noted a modern sink-unit propped against one damp kitchen wall and lengths of copper pipe. Electric cable snaked down from the bare rafters and there were light switches in sealed packets beside the new sink. The intention was there, but for this century or the next? She went on. Dining-room to the left, if she remembered right. The door was closed as was the one opposite. Ahead the front room and door ajar. There was no noise from within. Was he waiting to pounce on her, to frighten her with a leap from a dark corner? She rehearsed her carefully prepared speech and tapped on the peeling wood. 'Mr Downing?'

All antagonistic intent left her the minute she stepped inside. Anger, recrimination, hostility, all flew out through the broken window-panes and she was left with a feeling of unutterable pity. She tried thinking of Bill and of her ruined garden but the only thought in her head was that never in her life had she seen anyone look so ill. Jack Downing sat on the one piece of furniture the miserable room contained, a hard straight-backed chair. He resembled a shrunken rag-doll. His pallor was grey rather than white, his eyes drawn far back into his head and black bruises beneath them. Fine rain outside but cold it was not, yet he shivered beneath two thick sweaters. Shivered while the sweat lay thick on his brow.

'Come about the letter, have you?' The words were slurred, each one an effort.

'Yes, but—Jack, you look very ill. Have you seen a doctor?'

A slow nod. 'Flu a while back. Pulling up takes time.' He was leaning, she saw, more on the reversed shotgun beside him than the chair back. She looked at it enquiringly. 'Rats,' he said. 'Take a pot later.'

'Yes, rats.' She tried to cancel her concern with a stern approach. 'Rats and dung and my chestnut tree.' I cannot speak of the rest. Thinking of Bill and seeing you as you are, I might cry.

'Chestnut tree here back along.' He turned a weary head towards the window. 'Big chap, tall as the house. Leaves like plates.'

'You wouldn't have felled my tree, would you? You were just being spiteful.'

A twisted smile. 'Tit for tat.'

'And it's all over now?'

'All over.'

She turned to go.

'Sorry,' he said—'the little dog and the garden, sorry.'

Don't do this to me, she shouted silently. Apologies are not in your line of business. Don't make me feel as though somehow I am in the wrong. 'And the rats?' she asked lightly.

At last came the smile that melted mountains, although it must have been hard to summon. 'Plenty here. Like sharing, don't I?' Again she made to leave. 'Ella. Take a turn in the garden before you go. Find where the tree was. Show me through windows.'

'All right,' she said, 'I will.'

She found Toby outside in the yard which was good, considering the confusion of her emotions. 'Hello,' she called. 'What are you up to?'

'Ella, I'm so pleased you're here. You can show me where the manure is. You remember, you told me about it when we were talking roses ages ago.' He looked fearfully at the steaming pile outside the stables. 'It isn't like that, is it? It doesn't—smell?'

'Heavens, no. Come on, I'll show you, that's if it's still there. You'll have to pull out the weeds first and dig down but it's well worth it.'

'Oh, it's absolutely scrumptious, isn't it?' They were looking down at a patch of what a layman would have called black soil. 'I'm quite excited. My poor roses, I don't think they liked the sun.'

'Go and ask Mr Downing—Jack—if it's all right to take some and I'll give you a hand.'

'Will you really? You are kind, Ella. I don't want to be too long. Giles told me to go hours before we closed and I must hurry back.' He blushed a delicate pink. 'We're going to have a siesta this afternoon.'

Dear Toby, so naïve, so embarrassingly outspoken at times. What do you say to such an announcement? Have fun, lucky you, or do you just try and keep a straight face? She was spared the effort of conjuring up an appropriate comment.

'Hello there,' Philip called, swinging long legs over the wire fence. 'What's this then, Highcroft Open Day?'

Stephen Templeton was marching though the yard to join them.

'A small errand on my part,' Ella said. 'And Toby's after a dollop of this. The roses, not the restaurant,' she added. It

301

was easy enough to look into the face that had once lain on her pillow. Easy and quite unemotional. A good-looking man, she had to admit, but only when smiling as he was now. A bit like an advert for country life: wellies, cords, green waterproof jacket and the smiling face of a successful farmer. Only he wasn't, was he, so why did he look so cocky? He was different. There was a confidence about him she had never seen, not even when he had raped her with his eyes. Golden brown face, long lashes bedewed with raindrops, blond hair darkened into wet curls, and that smile making the whole into something from a glossy magazine. He was unreal and she wondered again at her involvement. A diversion, that's what he had been, a convenient diversion.

'What's your excuse for being here?'

'The blasted chainsaw went sick on me. gathering winter fu-oo-el, you know. I'm after borrowing Jack's. How about you, Stephen?'

'Horses.' A neighing laugh to cover irritation. His rubber boots were missing; someone had stolen them. He had been forced to wear civilian shoes as his combat boots were also AWOL. A written report on his desk by the time he returned, that's what he had told Jenni. 'We've some friends coming over tomorrow, promised them a hack.'

'Horses?' They looked at him as though he were mad. 'They've gone.'

'I know that.' Damn you, Jenni why didn't you tell me? What sort of fool must I look? 'But Jenni thought they were on their way back.' He questioned Ella with blinding blue eyes. 'Where is Downing?'

Don't try anything here, she warned. Toby may be effete but Philip is not. Physically, that is. 'Straight through in the front room. Don't shout at him, Stephen. He isn't well.' She watched them go. 'I'll wait for you, Toby,' she called. 'If I'm not in the yard, I'm looking for the remains of a chestnut tree.'

She went around to the front of the house into what must have once been a dream of an English country garden. There were still tangles of marigolds and Canterbury bells, lavender, and lupins reverted mauve through the passage of time. She began searching for where the chestnut had been, pausing to look down the hill into the Dip beyond. What a view, much better than her own. And blow me down, wasn't that Tom crossing the fields? A veritable gathering of the clans. She waved and he waved back, only his acknowledgement was strange. A sort of one direction get out-of-it instruction that she did not understand. She returned to shuffling through the long grass, feeling with her feet. Here it was, overgrown with creepers and swarming with scurrying ants. What a shame. It must have been enormous, much bigger than hers. She bent to touch the wood sawn smooth, to try to count the rings, and then she stood on the trunk and shouted. 'It's here, Jack.' The light was against her, she could not tell whether or not she had been seen or heard. She went to the window. 'I've found the chestnut,' she said through a hole in the glass.

They were gathered around him and he, still as a wax model, seemed not to have stirred an inch since she left him. Philip was on his haunches leant against the wall opposite, Toby standing beside him. Stephen had withdrawn to the fireplace corner, red-faced, seemingly intent on examining his wet shoes. 'You what?' Jack asked without interest.

'Your chestnut tree. I've found all that's left of it. It must have been beautiful.'

''Twas.'

'I'll go and stand on it,' she said, 'And then you can see.'

'You do that. Thanks, Ella.'

She went back to the tree and stood and waved. He saw her through the soft rain and he thought, you were wrong on that one, Jack. Could have had a friend there, a real one, the first. As for these others, why don't they go? He'd said yes to everything 'cept the horses and that Captain must be daft thinking them still here. So why don't they all piss off and leave him alone. Talking over and around him, they were. Never a what do you think, Jack, or that's right, isn't it? And laughing. Laughing at him? Gloating perhaps because Jack was on the way out. Look at them. Healthy fresh faces, colour and strength. Nothing left for Jack now—they had it all. Black rage filled him, bringing back strength. Rage at God, if there was one, for dealing him short. Rage at Bella for arranging things and rage at the men who laughed and talked and lived when he was dying. He had his gun at waist level before he knew it. He pulled the trigger and fired.

Philip died instantly, the blast cutting across his chest. Toby, turning to run for the door, was holed like a colander in the backside. He fell to the floor screaming. Stephen Templeton, back in his corner, was unhurt. For an instant he froze and then the mist came red behind his eyes. Red, red and kill, kill. Jack Downing had thrown his gun from him in a final gesture of disgust but still Stephen Templeton leapt. Hands around the throat and kill, kill.

'Leave it, sir!' A voice from nowhere, a command. Still he pressed, driving out breath, ending life. And then blows to his head and the red mist clearing. Another man and another gun. Tom Antony had climbed through the window and was looking down on him with contempt. 'He had no gun and I had him covered. You were aiming to kill a defenceless man.'

Stephen went back to his corner. He crouched down and hid his head in his hands. And then he wept. Not for what he had nearly done but because he saw the truth at last. He knew why he had not been promoted, he knew he never would.

And now Ella was at the door, hammering, trying to open it but Toby had fallen across. 'What's happened? Let me in, someone let me in.'

306

Tom pulled him away by his legs. He was wailing now, howling like a dog.

'Thank God you're here, Mis' Caine. Don't think I could cope on my own.'

She stood for what seemed hours taking in the scene that was to remain in her head for the rest of her life. Photographing it in dreadful colour. Jack limp on the floor. Was he dead too? Philip had died laughing and his face had frozen into a terrible grimace. She watched Tom take off his jacket and cover the grin and the bloody chest and she listened to the sobs and wails. Not human, witches mourning the passage of night.

'Shut up!' she yelled at Stephen, pulling at his hands. 'Shut up and stand up. You're with the Paras, not the Brownies. Pull yourself together, soldier.'

She was more gentle with Toby but just as firm. 'That's enough, Toby. You're hurt but not seriously. If you don't stop that noise I shall have to stuff a hanky in your mouth.' Hardly Florence Nightingale but it did the trick. The wailing subsided to gentle moans.

'What about Jack?' she asked Tom.

'Half dead, but he was already, poor bugger.' Tom, so careful with words, normally so courteous in female company. 'I'll take him up and put him on the bed.'

'Without a guard?' Stephen was on his feet now. Drained of all colour, eyes shifty and ashamed, trying to assert the authority he once had. 'Out of the question. The man's a maniac.'

'Bars on the window, sir, and lock on the door. He won't escape. Look at him.'

'It may be a bluff,' Stephen blustered. 'I've seen it before. The Argies were—'

'Go and find the phone, Stephen,' Ella said. 'It's somewhere, probably the tack-room. Ambulance and police and then Giles. Tell him not to come yet, we'll let him know.' She looked at Tom. 'What do we do about Fran?'

'Dunno, Mis' Caine. She ought to know but don't let her come.'

'I'll go if you like,' Stephen volunteered. 'I've done that sort of thing before.' I've done lots of things before. Do any of them count?

'Will you? Thanks, but I think we should all wait here for the police.' She sat on the floor beside Toby. 'Cheer up, old son. It's not the end of the world although you probably feel it is. They'll take you to

308

hospital, dig out the pellets and you'll be back with Giles in no time. Pity about the roses. Never mind, I'll come and look at them.' She stroked his hair. Soft fine hair like the boys' when they were babies. She found the glasses, miraculously unbroken, that had shot from his nose as he fell, and placed them, folded, beside him. Better that he should not see. How old was he? Thirty or thereabouts? The face filled with swimming brown eyes, the face he kept trying to lift and turn to her, was that of Mark or Minette. Frightened, bewildered, throat lumpily sad.

'Oh Ella, what will become of me now?' They were alone. Tom was half carrying, half dragging Jack upstairs and Stephen through in the back. 'Why couldn't it have been my legs or my back?'

'Your legs and you might have been crippled, your back and you would have been dead. Like Philip is.'

'Is Philip dead? Oh God, I didn't know. What will Fran do, and the children? That dreadful man. I wish I hadn't come here, I wish...Ella, will Giles come soon?'

Tom Antony laid Jack gently on his bed. Sweet Lord, he'd never seen a man look so ghastly and the eyes open, intensely bright,

309

trying to speak almost.

'A drink, is it?' He poured water from a jug on the small chest but it was waved away. 'What then? Tell me, lad. There's not much time.' Two words only, words he barely heard and certainly did not understand. 'Aye, I will. Rest easy now.' And I would if I knew what you meant.

So here he was in his little room, just as intended. Only the gun was gone. Not much time, Tom said, and he was right. Put him in hospital, they would, make him live when he wanted to die, and then prison. Fifteen years, less if he was lucky. He hadn't meant to kill. Hospital and prison. Not for Jack, not if he could find the strength to do things his way. That little hook on the beam, that would hold him. Good little hook and good strong beam. Sheet or belt? Sheet. Belt was fastened, that took time and trouble. Chair in place and one last look through the window. Jesus, he was tired, just wanted to sleep for ever and ever. Do that soon, that's if Bella would let him. Raining still and the horses gone. Star. He'd remembered it. Flash and Royal, Star and Peter and he still said Peter's a daft name for a horse. Will Tom do it? He said so. A man of his word is Tom. Right then, Jack lad, let's get it done. Wish the window seat had been there, wish I'd seen the red cushions, wish a lot of things. Good dreams but all gone. Watch out Bella, you're in for it now. Jack's on his way, Jack's coming.

If Tom heard the chair crash he made no sign and to Ella it was just another Highcroft noise. Stephen was outside in the yard, pacing, trying to put his thoughts in order. He was there to greet the police and lead them inside.

'He's upstairs, officers.' Stephen Templeton, Captain, assuming command of the situation. 'Be careful. He's a dangerous man.' They were down in a minute. Sober faces and no prisoner. 'Well? Where is he?'

'Gone, sir.'

'Gone? Gone where? There were bars on the window, I saw them.' Angrily to Tom, 'You fool! You utter idiot! I told you—'

'By gone, sir, I mean dead. Jack Downing hanged himself.'

Tom stayed on long after the others had departed. Philip and Jack to the mortuary,

311

Toby to hospital, Stephen back home to continue pacing and stun Jenni into silence with his own. Sightseers had all been sent packing, folk Tom had never seen in his life. Bad news travels fast. But the police had let Andrew Caine through when he came searching for his mother. 'Take her home now,' they said. 'There may be more questions later.'

'Not today.' Andrew had been fiercely protective.

'No, not today. Got a car, have you?'

'I'm perfectly capable of walking,' Ella said. 'And it's only just down the lane. Tom, will you be all right?'

'Right as ninepence, Mis' Caine, you'll see. You take care now, and thanks. There's one thing young Andrew could do for me. Nip down and let our Doris know Dad's still in one piece. And tell her to turn the oven off. No rabbit pie tonight.'

'Is that why you had your gun, sir?' The police were now few and far between. Making inventories, looking for keys to lock doors. Joke, that was. Lock doors and the windows all broken. 'After rabbits, were you?'

'I'd not have bagged any,' Tom said. He

312

slapped his pockets. 'No cartridges. Must be old age. The memory's going.'

'You can go too, Mr Antony. There's no need to hang around. You've been a great help and we're grateful.'

'Just take a last turn around the old place if that's all right with you. Knew it a long time back when it was all smiling and happy, if you follow.' What was he looking for? Burn it, Jack had said, but what? Papers, drugs, some sort of evidence? He'd been through the house and found nothing. The tack-room was too cluttered to search properly and the police were in there now, using the telephone and comparing notes. There was only the caravan left, and the yard. Please God it's not the yard. Casually, as though lacking all purpose, he sauntered over to the caravan. Nothing there either as far as he could see. Just a letter and a mug of cold tea on an envelope. Wait now, the envelope, there was writing on it and a pen beside. 'Burn Highcroft', he read before stuffing the last will and testament of John Michael Downing into his pocket. And just in time.

'What's that you have there, sir?' Another bobby, senior this one. A crown on the shoulders and a smart cap.

'Must be the letter Mis' Caine spoke of.' He handed it over. 'And tea, stone cold. Going to analyse it, are you?'

A pleasant smile. 'I don't think so.'

'Just come over to shut the door,' Tom said, further explanation obviously expected. 'Blowing in the wind, it was.'

'What a dreadful place this is.' The officer was inclined towards conversation. 'I cannot imagine anyone wanting to live here, not even Jack Downing.'

'Not local, are you? Never knew what it was like before, never heard? You walk along with me for five minutes and I'll change the picture for you. To begin with, 'twas always sunny in them days. Old Reub was a mean sod, begging your pardon, but he liked a happy ship. Over here now, ponies...' I'll do it, Jack, but not today. Not until all the fuss has died down. All the snoopers and reporters gone, all the photographs taken and I'll burn Highcroft for you. Best thing for it. Clear the air.

'So why did it change? What happened?'

'That's something the likes of you will never understand,' Tom said slowly. 'Bella. That's what happened.'

314

FOURTEEN

'Dad's coming tonight,' Andrew said. It was early evening. Ella had been sitting still as a statue for the last hour.

'Who did you say was coming?'

'Dad.'

'Oh. That's nice but he needn't have bothered. The funeral won't be for a few days.'

'I expect he's coming to be with you.'

'I don't need anyone else. You're here and that's enough.' She wrinkled her brow, trying to recall a lost thought. 'There was something I was going to say. I know. Will you take a note around to Fran? I ought to go to her but I can't. Not today.'

'Eve's with her. She rang earlier to tell you.'

'Did she? You never said.'

'I did, Mother, I asked you if you wanted to speak to her but you said no. Look, I'm going to ring the doctor. You're in shock and he'll give you something to bring you out of it.'

'No, Andrew, don't. I'm numb at the moment. I don't feel anything. I'd much rather stay that way.' I shall have to weep sometime, I shall have to cleanse myself, but I don't know what to think of to get me going. Fancy David dropping everything and coming so quickly. All that way. What do I mean, all that way? Oxford to Darrington, it won't take him more than a couple of hours. I must have been thinking of John. It would be wonderful if he came but quite out of the question. Eight thousand miles. Oxford to Darrington was what, fifty or so? It will take David two hours, probably less. On that basis it would take John—? I can work this out if I try. A hundred miles equals fours hours, therefore...

John did not come. Mary came in his place, tumbling into the room like an anxious Tinker Bell and hugging Ella close. 'Andrew rang me. I've got a week's compassionate leave. Ella darling, it's me. Mary. You remember me, don't you?'

'Of course I do. How lovely to see you.' Heavens, Andrew had been a busy boy. The next phone bill would show just how busy. 'The navy's very kind these days. I'm surprised they gave you leave just to be with me.'

'John and I are engaged. Unofficially, but that was good enough for First Officer.' She dimpled a smile. 'You don't mind about us, do you?'

'I am absolutely delighted. It's wonderful news.' And so it was. She wished she could be more enthusiastic, she wished she could be filled with happiness for them both.

'Andrew, did you hear that? That's the best news today, isn't it?'

Well, it wasn't too hard to find something better in the news, not on today's showing. How far away was Portsmouth and how long had it taken Mary to drive? She must ask her and then she could work out exactly how long it would take John. Why do I keep going back to that one? Because I want to cry and thinking of John so far away should help me. Only it doesn't.

David came, serious and obviously upset. she introduced him to Mary. 'Hello, Mary,' he said. 'Thank you for coming to be with my wife.'

Wife. She still was. 'My decree nisi came through a few days ago,' she said. 'Have you had yours?'

'Yes, I have.' He looked at her curiously. 'What an odd thing to come out with.'

'Is it? We've never avoided the subject before. Why should today be different?' Because today is different and they want me to sit sobbing, pouring out all I saw and did so that they can share the horror with me.

She wrote her note to Fran. 'Forgive me for not being with you but I am thinking of you'—which was absolutely untrue. She wasn't thinking of Fran at all, she wasn't really thinking of anything. Just sitting. Sometimes I sits and thinks, sometimes I just sits. That's me.

'You might pop down and see how Tom is while you're out,' she said to Andrew. 'He was quite amazing today,' she explained conversationally to David. 'A veritable tower of strength. But that's just like Tom, isn't it? He helped me so much with all the nasties—the rats and the dung and the garden.' All of which matter not one iota. Not even poor little Bill.

She seemed to remember afterwards that she and David sat in silence until Andrew and Mary returned. Mary had been pleased to go. She was probably feeling superfluous, no comforting needed and a stony woman for a future mother-in-law.

'Did you see Fran?' Ella asked.

'No. Emma came to the door. Very red-eyed, poor kid. We saw Eve, though.'

'Did you? How is she? She had a rotten cold starting this morning.' This morning or yesterday or when?'

'Eve's fine. She sends you her love and Adam's and says she'll see you tomorrow. She said Fran was being very brave.' Brave, my Aunt Fanny. Numb, like me. 'And Tom was fine too. He didn't send his love but he asked kindly after you.' An attempt at light relief. 'Why don't you marry him, Mum? You obviously think the world of each other.'

'What a good idea. I might just do that.' The small smile that turned her lips was light years away from her eyes.

David poured drinks and she took one. She wasn't sure that she should on an empty stomach but they told her she had eaten supper. She was quite surprised. She had no idea when or what. Still no tears, but emotion beginning to churn and rage beneath the surface. 'That poor wretched man,' she shouted almost.

'I know,' David said. 'But we have to think more of those he has left. Fran will need—'

'Not Philip,' she said, amazed that he had not understood. 'Not Philip. I was talking about Jack.'

'You're not serious,' Andrew said. 'You can't be. After all he did you should be glad to have him off your back.'

'Don't you dare say that,' she shouted. 'Don't you dare say anything like that again. What do you know about him? What do you know about anything?' They sat around her, uncomfortable and embarrassed. 'I'll tell you what he said to me today, shall I? He said sorry and he said thanks.'

'Big deal,' Andrew muttered. She could have killed him only there had been more than enough of that for one day.

'Sorry and thanks. Two small words that we spit out umpteen times a day.' She was pacing now, doing a Stephen, surprised and relieved to find that she still had legs and they worked. 'And you know why we say them, don't you? Because politeness and the social graces have been drummed into us since the womb. We know all the right things to say and we do so without thinking, without meaning half of them. Please and thank you, excuse me and I beg your pardon, sorry, very sorry, extremely sorry, *ad infinitum*. Because of our ability to be so trite we are socially acceptable. Jack Downing was not. He had little in his favour and he made no attempt to change what he had become. But when he said sorry and he said thanks, he meant it. And I mourn him. He never had a chance.'

She looked at the three of them. In one ear and out the other and not the vestige of understanding of how she felt, what she meant. Tomorrow she might be as they were, conventional and conformist, agreeing that Jack was a dreadful man and had received his just reward. But tonight she mourned him. With anger, not with tears.

'I,' she said, 'am going to my room. Please continue living as though I were not here. And I'm taking this with me.' This was the whisky bottle. 'There's another in the kitchen somewhere if you want to raise a glass to Philip. I may even do so myself. I am perfectly all right and I do not wish to be disturbed. Good night.'

There was no way she could make herself weep. It was only fair on the others that she be released, yet she sat on the bed, dry-eyed, reliving the day minute by minute. The whisky did not help. It raised her to the ceiling and she hung there, suspended, looking down on Highcroft with the eye of a kestrel, seeing through the unfinished roof as though she were God. She remembered and she saw in vivid detail. Philip dying, although she had not been there. Jack hanging from the hook on the beam. Thank God they had all been spared that sight. And yet it was all the more horrible because she had not seen and her imagination was putting thoughts and feelings into the dead. Toby, how was he, and Stephen? She should have asked after them too. She would tomorrow. Only tomorrow she would probably be sitting where she was now, still hammering away at names and faces and blood and rain and a chestnut tree that had once been beautiful.

Someone tapped on her door. David. 'I know what you said but talking helps. Tell me about it. If you go through it again you might be able to cry.'

'What do you think I've been doing, saying my prayers? I've been over and over it all but nothing helps. I see and I hear, but an old picture-show would move me more. I keep trying to think of little things that might start me off. A bird somewhere, a clump of flowers that had somehow survived. Jack's mug of tea in that beastly caravan—that haunts me but it doesn't make me weep. I am dry, I am barren, I am without hope. It's always the little things that get you, isn't it, but I can't think of any? Do you remember, were you still around when they showed a science fiction film on the TV? Don't ask me what it was called, I've no idea. The earth as we know it had exploded and there was this spacecraft up in the atmosphere going around for ever with all the plants and trees that had been saved before we blew up. There were three men, I think, and some little robots to do the hard work. I can't remember exactly what happened. There were arguments and one of the men got rid of the other two and was left with the robots and this huge glass sphere with all these plants that had to have simulated sun and be watered. Then he had enough and jettisoned himself into space and something had happened to the other robots and there was only one left. And there he was, only a little chap, caring for the plants for all eternity. Watering them with an old-fashioned metal watering-can and—it had a dent in it.'

'It had what?' David asked gently.

'A dent in it. His little watering-can had a dent in it.' Tears at last, wonderful, healing, cleansing tears. She sobbed as though her heart would break and David held her close, soothing and comforting.

While Ella wept, the Graysons exchanged reports on their travels. They were sat, each with a large brandy, in front of the fire. It was still raining. Strangely passive, like Darby and Joan. No nose pulling, no finger gnawing tonight, hands quiescent in quiet laps. The day had left its mark, had shocked both faces white and opened eyes wide. For Eve, a radical change. Piggy, she called her eyes. Now they were almost too big for her haggard face. Adam and Eve, too stunned to think of sleep but retaining the energy for words. They had flicked words at each other over thirty-two years, exchanged news and views after each sunset. Tonight, though dreadfully different, was no exception.

'You first,' Adam said.

'What do I say? She's controlled and tight as a drum. Brave, but not really so. It hasn't hit her yet. Dan is being splendid. Fran's more worried about the girls than anything. How do you keep that sort of thing from the kids? Someone will tell them if they don't know now. Your Dad was shot, will he get a medal? Children don't comprehend.'

'Did you leave her on her own?'

'Of course not. The mamas came, hers and Philip's.'

'I didn't know Fran had one.'

'We all had, even ugly old me.' Eve looked at the fire through the glow in her glass. 'We're being flip, aren't we? We always are when bad things happen and today's happenings are almost the worst we've known.'

'Almost,' Adam agreed. 'So what about the mums? Will they cope?'

'Philip's mother was extremely distressed but holding back. Straight as a die and rather severe, but everything bubbling underneath. I didn't go much on Fran's maternal origin. Spineless, I thought, like a piece of celery, and banging on about irrelevancies. If only Frances lost some weight she might feel better. How's that for comfort and assurance that the agony will pass?'

'Anything else?'

'Andrew came with that lovely little Mary. He had a note from Ella, an

325

apology for not being supportive. As if it was expected that she should be. She has her own hells to live out. He said David was down but that Ella was behaving strangley. Normal, yet vague, and quite unemotional. No tears. She'll have to howl, won't she, or she'll never get any better?'

Listen to your words, Eve. Remember the writing on the Oracle at Delphi—Know Thyself.

'I did Tom, the Swan and the Templetons in that order,' Adam said. 'Tom was composed but sad. Sad for all the unfortunates and that included Jack. He said Ella was marvellous, very calm and collected, and Stephen apparently behaved appallingly. Not at all the officer and gentleman.'

'That follows.' A sudden random thought. 'What about the milking, for heaven's sake? Those poor cows. What's happened about them?'

'Darren Hubbard is carrying on as usual and Tom arranged for two chaps from Upper D. to come over and help out until a relief milker is organized.'

'Thank God for Tom. How was the Swan?'

'A bit chaotic. Restaurant closed, Giles at the hospital and Henry helping that willowy creature behind the bar. It was strange seeing him properly dressed. I didn't know he possessed a shirt and tie. There's no doubt he was very upset, far more so than—Keith, is it? I had the distinct impression he was gloating.'

'We all know what he's after, don't we? So how was Toby, had they heard?'

'As comfortable as could be expected, Henry said. He also said, and I quote, why couldn't it have been his belly and not his bum?'

'Not a preferable alternative,' Eve said, 'but I know what he means. Fate played a rotten trick there.'

'Jenni,' Adam continued, 'was very peculiar. Cold and remote and wouldn't let me inside the door. Stephen was resting, she said. Unusual for him, don't you think? She did ask after Fran and Ella but only after I had prompted her.'

'Selfish little bitch. I shall cross her off my Christmas card list.'

'So that's it,' Adam said: 'another piece of Darrington history written up for posterity.'

'And much more to come, my love. The inquest—there's bound to be one—and the funeral and then the repercussions. I don't like to hazard a guess as to what those will be.'

Ella slept most of the day following the Highcroft tragedies. She wished she could sleep for the rest of her life. The ghost of Jack Downing had faded a little but another spectre was haunting her. Philip was everywhere in the house. Her bedroom, the bathroom, the kitchen, on the stairs. Philip, following her wherever she went, and always the ghastly dead grin. She could hear his tenor voice, his light laugh, both somehow insincere. She could smell him but the scent was no longer hot and sweet, it stank of death and decay. The eyes that had blatantly coaxed and invited her were sightless, the soft weak mouth finally firmed into a permanent twisted smile. She hated his presence with a passion far greater than any they had shared.

'I'm not sure that I want to stay on here,' she told David later that evening. Andrew had taken Mary down to the Foresters' to show her off and the Graysons were dropping by to spend a quiet half hour. 'Too many horrible things have happened. I'll never be able to rid my mind of them.'

'It's early days yet,' he said. 'See how you feel in a couple of months. I'm quite happy to sell if you're sure that's what you want. Where would you go, have you thought?'

Where am I going? I don't know. What does it matter where people go? Down to the wood where the bluebells grow—anywhere, anywhere, *I* don't know. 'I'm not fussy. Just away from here.'

'I forsee a lot of consortium hand-rubbing.' Adam said later. He and Eve had brought a huge spray of glorious roses. Our love to a brave girl, the card read, and that triggered a fresh flow of tears. Now that she had started it seemed she could not stop.

'Fran will have to sell eventually even though I'm sure she will hang on for as long as possible. For Philip's sake. He worked so hard to keep the developer's out.'

'What about the Templetons, will they stay?'

'I don't see how they are in any way affected. Life should be back to normal

329

already, that is as normal as it has ever been.'

'I'm not even going to see Jenni,' Ella said. 'She hasn't bothered to come here, not even a phone call. A deranged husband, that's her only problem, and she can damn well sort him out for herself.' She wandered the room, restless now after her long sleep. 'But I have to go and see Fran. I must. And I can't tell you how much I don't want to. Will she ask me how he looked, do you think, will she probe for details? Did he say anything or did he die instantly? Was there a sheet to cover him or did nobody think of that? I've been through it all too many times. The police, the family, my own thoughts. And the inquest still to come. I wish I could put off seeing her but it has to be done. Tomorrow.'

There was still evidence of Philip inside Dowsett's when she went there. Jackets and caps on hooks outside the kitchen, socks and shirts on the floor in the utility room. How long does it take to erase the fact that a person once lived? But at least there were no ghosts. The dead man she was growing to fear had stayed behind at the cottage. She was certain she would find him waiting for her when she returned, probably on her bed.

'Come through,' Fran said. 'Kitchen as usual but you're used to that. How are you?'

'A bit shattered but coming out of it. More to the point, how are you?'

'Same as you. Shattered but coming out of it. Tom says you did well.'

'I kept my head which is more than Stephen did.'

'So I heard. Pretty bad show. Have you seen either of them?'

'No. Have you?'

'Not even a fleeting glimpse. Sit down, Ella. I'll make some tea. Or would you prefer coffee?'

This is ridiculous, Ella thought. We'll be talking about the weather next and what's on TV. Fran seemed strangely composed, no puffy eyes, no tendency towards tears. People react differently towards death, she had not known what to expect, but certainly not this glib mundane patter. 'Where is everyone?'

'In Brunton. Glad rags for the funeral. No, there isn't a date yet, it's the inquest first, isn't it? Will you go? I suppose you'll have to, and Tom and Stephen. And what about poor old Toby? Rotten luck, don't you think? It will be months before he can, you know.'

She brought the tray and placed it carelessly, slopping milk into the sugar bowl. 'You should have seen Ma's face when she measured me this morning. I can't be bothered to go and look for anything so they're doing it for me. She suggested a black tent but that's an old joke, isn't it? Jenni wore that one out ages ago. Tent, I mean, not necessarily black. Sugar? I can never remember.'

She passed Ella her cup with an unsteady hand. There were two bright spots of colour where her cheekbones should have been and her eyes were darting everywhere, taking an inventory almost, but never once looking at Ella.

'It was you, wasn't it?' Casual conversation between friends. 'It suddenly clicked after Philip went over to Highcroft. And when I found out you had been there too, I knew I was right. You were the chainsaw just as you were the trips to Brunton, digging ditches, going to see Tom. Jack Downing didn't kill Philip, you did.'

'That is not true. How could it be? Stephen was there and Toby and Tom—'

'I don't mean you were going to stay

there. Not a comfortable place for screwing, it wouldn't turn me on. Even Maggie Hubbard found herself a dry barn after they flattened the churchyard. Or so I've heard. No, you were simply meeting up and going on some place. With the chainsaw, of course. Philip needed that evidence to fool me.'

'That's not true. Believe me, it is not true.' Tears, stupid tears, because the accusation was so false.

'I'll believe you if you can prove otherwise. And turn off the waterworks, for God's sake. If I can stay buttoned up, so can you.'

'All right,' Ella said. 'I'll tell you.' Looking back, she was never able to remember how she felt in those moments. Numb again, that was probably the best description. 'There was, there had been, a relationship of sorts between Philip and myself but it finished weeks ago.'

'I'll accept that. He was as miserable as sin for a time. And then he cheered up again, was positively euphoric. That's when you started up again.'

'No.'

'You're just trying to let yourself off the hook, to salve your conscience for having

333

lured him to his death.'

Ella found strength in anger. 'For Christ's sake, Fran, stop being so melo-dramatic. Nobody lured Philip anywhere. He went to Highcroft to borrow Jack's chainsaw. Ask Toby, ask Stephen. They were there when he came, and I was waiting for Toby.'

'For Toby? Why? To do what?'

'To dig bloody manure for his bloody roses, that's what.'

Silence. A bird chirped somewhere and the kitchen clock ticked. 'I believe you,' Fran said at last. 'I believe that you and he had packed it in. He must have found someone else after you but I don't care. Not now. I'll never forgive you, Ella.'

'I can understand that you won't and I'm sorry. It was breaking the rules, I know that only too well. But we weren't in love or anything like. Just—'

'Just what?'

'Lovers. A physical relationship, some sort of chemistry, but no love. He filled several gaps in my life, excited me for a time. I don't know what I did for him.'

'Made him feel important, I expect,' Fran said. 'He needed that.' She was relaxed now, almost amused. 'I *am*

334

surprised. I found him a bore in bed almost from the word go. So why did you break up? Was it because I was breathing down your necks?'

'Partly. I felt terribly guilty, I think I always had. And when you told me that you suspected I knew it had to end. Besides...'

'Besides what?'

'I hate to speak ill of the dead but I didn't like him anymore.'

'That's funny,' Fran said. 'Neither did I.'

She was back home before the others, who had all been out and about doing useful things. She sat in the sitting-room in solitary splendour, trying to work out how she felt. Relieved more than anything. Relieved that it was out in the open. 'Hello,' David said, 'you look pretty drained. Was it awful?'

'Come in, all of you. There's something I have to tell you.'

David was not surprised. He had always thought it would happen, had felt it in the air even before he left. Andrew muttered something about playing a bit close to home and went out to the kitchen to start supper. Mary followed after saying that she could understand now why Ella was so upset.

'She's got it all wrong,' Ella said. 'Of course I'm upset but not because the love of my life has been killed. As I told Fran, I didn't really like him any more. Perhaps that's why he's haunting me, a sort of revenge for turning against him. He is, you know. I see him everywhere in the house. Not as he used to be, as he was when he died. Where are you going, David?'

'I'll tell you in a minute.' He was back in no more than three. 'Valuation tomorrow,' he said, 'and on the market by the end of the week. Does that suit you?'

'Yes, it does. Thanks. Eve said there would be repercussions, didn't she? I'm the first rat to desert. I wonder who will be next?'

FIFTEEN

It was Jenni who came to see Ella. Not, as it turned out, to offer support and express concern. More of a fact-finding mission to suit her own purposes. And dressed for the occasion. The earthy, sexy Jenni had been transformed into a sophisticated young woman. A dark blue cloth suit, a snow-white blouse with lace tumbling at the neck and showing beneath the cuffs. Shoes, gloves, handbag, all perfectly matched, and hair dressed backwards and up in a style reminiscent of the royals. Lessons from Alicia Hargreaves, perhaps? No one seemed interested enough to find out. David let her in, then disappeared. So did Andrew and Mary, so too did Ben. Not the most popular girl in Darrington, except perhaps where Jonno Antony was concerned.

'Sorry I haven't been sooner but what with one thing and another—'

'I quite understand,' Ella said. 'We all do. Philip's funeral is next Wednesday, the

337

day after the inquest. Is there a remote possibility that you and Stephen might attend? No, don't tell me, it's Connie's day off.'

'It is as a matter of fact but I expect we could change it. I'll try and come but Stephen won't be there.' The voice was louder, penetrating, more undeniably upper class.

'Oh?'

'He's away at the moment. On a course.'

'What sort of a course, R and R?'

'Do stop being so bitchy, Ella. It isn't like you.' A very bright smile that should have dazzled but had more of a nauseating effect. 'I'll tell you why I've really come. You had the house valued, didn't you? May I ask how much you were quoted?'

You may but I'm not sure I want to tell you. A show of sympathy for Fran and I might feel more inclined, although that's all it would be. A show. And a few caring questions as to my well-being. God knows we've spent more than enough time worrying about yours.

The house had indeed been valued and they were all still reeling a little from the shock. The estate agent had evinced unqualified approval of all he

338

saw. A beautiful house and in first-class condition. Lovely situation, secluded yet central. Yes, a pity about the garden, what a dreadful thing to happen, but gardens grow again, don't they, and the lawns were knitting together well. He was a keen gardener himself, nothing on this scale, just a patch back and front, but he knew how Nature helped recovery as no one else could. No trouble in selling—Highcroft Cottage, was it?—none at all. He had a strong feeling it would be snatched up overnight. They really should see the lists back at the office, lists of people begging for Darrington properties and money no object whatsoever. So how much were Mr and Mrs Caine hoping to obtain from the sale? He had his own ideas but would be interested to hear theirs.

Mr and Mrs Caine had not the faintest idea but they refrained from so saying. At the back of both minds was the sum of three thousand pounds, the amount they had paid Ruth Downing back in 1966. They wanted a lot more than that, taking into account the improvements made and escalating house prices, but neither could hazard an accurate guess. You, David reminded the man from Mather and

Bateson, are the expert, tell us what you think. A few calculations on a pad and the answer came pat. 'About two hundred plus. Is that what you had in mind?'

For a ridiculous moment Ella felt a huge surge of disappointment before reality took control. It must have showed. 'Mrs Caine, two hundred thousand, not just pounds, and the plus could be quite a big one.' What a joke that had been. He couldn't wait to get back to the office and set them all rolling on the floor. 'Two hundred pounds wouldn't buy one of your gates, not nowadays.'

And now here was Jenni wanting to know in advance what would soon be common knowledge. Measurements had been made, photographs taken, the inclusion of carpets and curtains agreed or refused. The draft property sale sheets would soon arrive for approval or alteration and they would sign their agreement to the proposed asking price and the speedy sale of their home. It would all be very exciting if it wasn't so unbearably sad.

'Two hundred thousand at least,' Ella said. 'Why are you so interested?' Jenni was positively alert. You could almost see the antennae sprouting from her ears. 'You aren't thinking of selling, are you?' You as in plural, the answer as in singular.

'Yes, I am, and as soon as possible.'

'*You* are? Has Stephen no say in the matter?'

'Not any more.' A play of varied emotions across the lovely face: stubborn defiance, reluctance to divulge, apprehension as to reaction. 'You may as well know. Stephen's resigned his commission.'

'Has he now? That might be a good move—hang on, I thought you said he was away on a course?'

'He is. A sort of introduction to Civvy Street, assessment of job potential. And he's not coming back. That's why I've been so busy, packing his things. I'm divorcing him, of course.'

'Why of course? You said often enough that his—temper—was caused only by frustration. He might be a changed man once he's out of the Army. You should at least give him a chance.'

'Don't be ridiculous, Ella. Can you see me living in some awful little box, frittering away capital while he tries to find some decent, well-paid job? I'm divorcing him and he's made the house over to me.'

'But what will he do? You can't leave

him with nothing.'

'There'll be something from the army and there's masses of Templeton money around. He'll do all right there. I shall expect a large settlement on the children, that's only fair, but he can keep the rest. I shall also insist on maintenance for the children and myself until I remarry. Apart from that, Stephen is free to do as he likes. But he really will have to pull his finger out and find lucrative work soon. I told him so and he quite understands.'

'Have you anyone in mind?' Ella asked weakly. She was floored by such calculated selfishness, such monumental conceit. 'In the marriage market, I mean. I know you're simply devastating but you may find three small children an encumbrance. Why don't you pack them off with Stephen?'

'Ella, how could you? The children are my life. By the way, I think I should say that I hold you partially responsible for Stephen's resignation. You taunted him when he was utterly shattered by his friend's cruel death.'

'I did? In what way?'

'You told him he should have joined the brownies, not the Army. Even strong men weep, Ella, when they suffer the loss of someone for whom they care deeply.'

'Rubbish!' Ella shouted. 'Absolute rubbish! Stephen was no closer to Philip than he is to the milkman and he was bawling because Tom clouted him and stopped him throttling Jack. I know. I heard the statements to the police.'

'Oh.' Some swift evaluation, an expression of cold disdain. 'What a pity he didn't succeed. Jack Downing was a little shit.'

Ella hit her then, twice, one stinging blow to each cheek. The elaborate hairstyle quivered a little from shock. 'Out!' she said. 'Go, and take your delusions with you.'

'Well done,' David said after the door had slammed shut. He had, he confessed, been listening in the hall. 'I've been longing to do that for years.'

'I'm losing friends faster than autumn leaves,' Ella said ruefully. 'I do hope I haven't done anything to upset Eve. And speaking of friends, will you pop down and see Toby later? I need to know if he's any—happier.'

Toby was coming along nicely. Or so the doctor said. Soon have you sitting down again, he promised, and laughed at what he considered a huge joke. Soon have you up and about, that's what we usually say, but with you it's soon have you sitting down. Funny, yes? Toby always managed to force the expected smile but it took some doing. The joke was a poor one and wearing extremely thin.

He had to admit, even to himself, that he was improving. Slowly and painfully he was getting there. Some bathroom functions remained agonizing and the very thought of lying on his back brought tears to his eyes, but he was moving around the bedroom now, reading cards, touching flowers and breathing in their scent. Everyone had been so wonderfully kind and sympathetic, cards by the sackful and florists' vans delivering daily. And visitors. Regular customers just popping upstairs to have a quick word, friends from the village. The Graysons, the Caines, even Fran Russell. He thought that was frightfully good and brave of her and he had told her so, tears running into the carnations she had thrust in his arms. Poor dear Philip. She did understand, didn't she, that he wouldn't be able to attend the funeral? But Giles would be there, and Henry. They were closing the Swan for the whole day as a gesture of respect. The Foresters' too? That was nice to know. Dear oh dear, Darrington would be a very dry village on that day, people would have to stock up well in advance.

Giles, of course, was being perfectly sweet. Up and down the stairs a hundred times a day, enquiring after needs, relaying scraps of gossip. And Henry. Henry had been his rock. Henry had surpassed himself. Dainty tempting meals, always a rose on the tray, and irreverent words to lift the spirits.

'I'm sure the Queen herself has no better attendance,' Toby had said.

'That's what you are, my heart. A queen. Queen of all the friggin' fairies. Now, don't laugh when you're sucking soup. You'll be throwing up all over my bit of fillet and there's no extra garnishing needed. How do you feel?'

'Better, but it's going to be ages before I'm back to normal.'

'Normal?' Henry shouted a laugh. 'That's something you'll never be. Queer as a pig flying, that's you, bless your poor little sore bum.'

Never, Toby thought, had he been so loved and cared for. Only Keith had stayed away, not even a nose around the

345

door. That suited Toby very well. To see his rival flaunting his perfect unblemished body would have been hard to bear. He wished he knew what was going on; he wished he could be certain that Giles was resisting temptation.

'Tom's here.' Giles blew in, dark, handsome, exquisitely groomed, the speed of entry in no way disturbing a single immaculate hair. A hero in any romance, a god to worship in Toby's. Elegant white hands moved a card here, straightened a flower there as he crossed the room. 'He's brought an enormous load of the manure you coveted and he's going to dig it in for you.'

'Really? Oh Giles, I don't know whether I want it now, not after—'

'Now do stop twitching, there's a dear. You've been so much better lately. It distresses me when you fidget. There, you see? Your silly old hair's flopping again and you're starting to punish your glasses. I think they deserve care and consideration, don't you, after the nasty tumble they took? Tom said to tell you the manure was there long before the bad times and it's lovely stuff.'

'Did he say that? He is good, isn't he? So

thoughtful and considerate. Everyone is. It takes something awful like, you know, to show how much people care.' Tears again. They came so easily these days.

'And that's enough of that,' Giles said briskly, sandpapering the deep thrill of his voice to appropriate asperity. 'Come on, I'll help you up. You can stand at the window and watch Tom working. Would you like that?'

'Yes, Giles, I would.'

'I expect to have a surprise for you later, Tobes. A surprise that will please you.'

'Oh, do tell me. Or give me a hint.'

'It wouldn't be a surprise if I did.' A surprise for Keith too, Giles thought, and not a nice one. He hadn't told him yet. The thought of the sulks and scenes that would result was enough to deter telling him at all. It was Henry who had arranged things, Henry who had delivered the ultimatum. In language quite unrepeatable, Henry had laid it on the line. Giles had been drawn unwillingly into the kitchen and forced to listen to a tirade of threats and promises. A meat cleaver had even been waved under his nose. If he so much as thought about taking Keith to his bed while Toby was indisposed,

Henry would do him a severe injury and serve him the severed member on a plate for supper. With a suitable sauce. Not only that, Henry would break his contract with the Swan and leave for pastures new. Better pastures at that, they wouldn't be hard to find. Added to which he would take Toby with him and where would Giles be then? In the proverbial, Henry had said but in more colourful terms. Up to his neck in it and struggling for air. It seemed also that Henry had a niece into her thirties and very presentable. Highly experienced, professionally trained. His brother had written that Sarah was out of a job for the time being, a restaurant fire in the Smoke. Henry had telephoned his niece and she was on her way, complete with references as long as her arm. So that was that, Henry said. Get rid of that creepy ponce and let's get back to a happy working relationship. Or else.

Sad in a way, Giles thought, waggling two fingers at Keith as he passed by. It would have been a beautiful experience. But lucky too in a way that it had never transpired. He knew Keith well enough by now. One slip, and he would have been blackmailed into other transgressions. That possibility was too awful to contemplate, Henry was right, they were a good team. He must do his part and keep it that way. What time did Sarah arrive at Brunton? He must remember to leave in good time to pick her up. He hoped she was as good as Henry said. He would have to leave her in charge on—oh dear, when was it? The unpleasant necessity he had promised to attend on Toby's behalf, the day before Philip's funeral, yes, that was when it was.

The inquest into the deaths of Philip James Russell and John Michael Downing was scheduled to begin at ten-thirty in Darrington Village Hall. At nine o'clock on the morning of the same day, David Caine asked his then wife if she had ever considered the possibility of their getting together again.

'No,' she said, 'I have not.'

'Then think about it now.'

Dutifully, Ella thought. 'No, David. Not a chance. We've got on extremely well over the past ten days or so but these have been exceptional circumstances. I shall always be grateful to you for your support but that doesn't mean I want to stay married to you.'

'I wasn't suggesting stopping the divorce. I thought perhaps we could try living together under the same roof as companions and friends. Two individuals, yet closely bound because of our related pasts.'

'It sounds feasible,' Ella said slowly, 'but probably only in theory. Who says I want to live in Oxford, and who says you would be prepared to uproot yourself yet again if I did not? And David, what a silly time to bring up the subject. Today of all days, and the funeral tomorrow.'

'I'm worried about you, that's why. The sale's going through. Another month, six weeks at the most and you'll be without a home. You haven't got the vaguest idea of where you will go or what you will do. It would please and relieve me if we—you—could decide on something now, even as a temporary measure. What do you say to putting everything into store and coming to stay with me in Oxford until you decide? Separate rooms, separate lives, but someone to listen when you talk through ideas. Ben would love it. There are some wonderful walks for you both.'

'It's a possibility,' Ella said. 'And a good one. I'll let you know. And David, thanks.'

Darrington turned out in full force to learn of the true facts. Tom, being Tom, had said little. Captain Templeton had disappeared (not that they had much time for him) and poor old Toby was out of circulation. To question either lady involved would have been indelicate, the height of bad manners, so let's see what the coroner has to say.

Date, time, place. Names. John Michael Downing. Ella Louise Caine. Philip James Russell. Stephen Templeton. Toby Pennington-Smythe. Thomas William Antony. Times of arrival at Highcroft Farm and reasons for so doing. The weather even, was that significant? Police statements, statements from witnesses. Stephen Templeton, reappeared and in civilian clothes, mumbled into his shoes and had to be asked several times to speak clearly. Mr Pennington-Smythe, the Coroner said, was unable to attend the hearing. He had reaffirmed his statement made at Brunton District Hospital and he, the coroner, was sure everyone present wished him a speedy recovery from his unfortunate injuries.

A doctor took the stand. John Michael Downing, he said, had been suffering from a rare blood disease. Immediate hospitalization had been imperative when the condition was diagnosed some ten days prior to the incidents at Highcroft Farm but Mr Downing had not been admitted to any hospital at any time. The rapid progression of the disease would ensure that Mr Downing had reached the terminal stages by the time of the shooting. He would be adversely affected both mentally and physically. Extreme fatigue, slurred speech, incoherent thought, deep depression. It was his opinion that the purpose of the shotgun had been to take his own life, not that of others, and that the killing of Mr Russell and the wounding of Mr Pennington-Smythe had been the unpremeditated act of a dying man. Silence thereafter. Tom Antony nodded his head in agreement and Ella Caine made no attempt to stem her flow of tears.

The coroner summed up. A tragedy, he said, but one that could have been very much worse. He commended Mrs Caine and Mr Antony for their actions throughout and expressed surprise that Captain Templeton had not behaved in a more exemplary manner. The verdicts were given. Unlawful killing and suicide, and the bodies released for Christian burial.

There were solemn faces in Darrington that night. Poor old Jack. Nobody had liked him but poor old Jack all the same. Wouldn't wish something like that on your worst enemy. Poor old Philip too, in the wrong place at the wrong time. Let's hope that's an end to it, they said, but what about Highcroft? No takers for that place, not now. Even a nutter would think twice when he knew.

Philip was buried the following day in Darrington churchyard. Family and friends, a goodly gathering. The whereabouts of the remains of Jack Downing was a mystery never to be solved and this distressed Ella. She had wanted to send something, if only a card.

'Don't come back to the house,' Fran said to the Graysons and the Caines. 'You'll die of boredom.' Unfortunate words under the circumstances but a widow, even a tearless one, can be forgiven. 'Come round for a drink tomorrow night. We can catch up on all the news.'

'I wonder if the invitation includes me,' Ella said.

'Of course it does. I'm not going on my own.' Andrew was leaving the next day. Mary had already gone. David too had planned to return to Oxford until the weekend. 'I'll stay on till Sunday if that's all right by you. We can start organizing the packing.'

They were surprised to arrive at Dowsett's and find no other cars outside. 'A final informal committee meeting,' that had been Eve's opinion. 'The Courtneys and the Hargreaves as well as ourselves, and Harry Junior. Reg Powell to even up the numbers, you never know.' Only the numbers would not have been even. The chairman was always away on other business.

'Come in,' Fran invited.

She was, they all thought, a changed person. Not sylph-like, but taut and determined. The flesh was still far too much but it no longer sagged, it had tightened, become elastic. Her walk too. Where was the trundle? Fran held her head high and skipped almost on very high heels. She was wearing a new frock, blatantly expensive, and cunningly cut and folded to conceal all but the most obvious. She led the way through to the sitting-room, unrecognizable through its tidiness and abundance of flowers. Champagne was in an ice bucket, four glasses on a table beside. There were several plates of tiny smoked-salmon sandwiches, dishes of savoury biscuits and an extensive cheese board. Nobody said a word, not one eyebrow was raised.

'Sorry about the salmon, Eve. It isn't yours but I was pressed for time. Sit down, all of you.'

She went back to her place. A bottle of low-calorie fruit juice was beside her glass and a child's drawing book on the table. Neither biscuit nor chocolate bar was to be seen.

'I've just been designing Philip's headstone. What do you think?' she held up the page. Across the top in bold print, the name. Judas Russell. Underneath, two lines of doggerel.

Here he lies, a tragic end,
Died before a chance to spend.

'Stop buggering about, Fran.' Eve, never one to mince words. 'What's happened?'

'This.' A larger than normal cheque was withdrawn from a sideboard drawer. 'Look closely and tell me. Have you ever seen so many noughts in one small space?'

'When did you get this?'

'Today. It would have been sooner but

they had to alter the name of the payee. It was made out to Philip, you see. I think they also held back because of the circumstances and the funeral, but that's only supposition on my part.'

'I don't believe it.' Adam was almost shattered. 'I simply do not believe it.'

'Ella does, don't you, Ella?'

'Yes, I'm afraid I do.'

'And you knew nothing? He gave no indication?'

'He was suddenly very cheerful but I put it down to—something else. He was working up to telling me, I know that. Before he went over to Highcroft for the jolly old chainsaw he said he wanted to talk to me that evening. But the sale had all been prearranged, I know that too. The herd goes tomorrow. Some man from way beyond Brunton rang to say they would begin shipping out after first milking. And his—my—new car arrives in the afternoon. The latest model of Volvo, would you believe? Not my first choice—I'll look like a minnow in an aquarium, but who cares? I can always change it.'

'Tell me,' Eve said carefully, 'what would you have said had he been open and told you his intentions?'

'I would have agreed, but only eventually. The farm's in very poor shape as you know and the bank manager was into poison pen letters. Lordy, you should have seen him today when I called. A positive Uriah Heep, slipping about in the charm he oozed. Oh yes, I would have agreed to sell, but not to be the first to fall. We should have made a stand to the end. He owed that to Darrington. Do you remember, Ella, the day you and I persuaded Alicia Hargreaves to join forces? That was also the day Mr Smith approached Philip. Remember? Remember the version we were given—no price quoted, sent away with a flea in his ear? I met Mr Smith today. He said Philip had asked for and been told the offer and the impression gained was that he was more than interested. That I will never forgive. All those weeks of lies, of false encouragement to others, of waving the anti-development flag. He had every reason to sell but he should have been honest and said so. He was a liar and a coward and I shall despise him until the day I die.'

'Shall I open the champagne now,' David asked, 'or are there further revelations?'

It turned out to be quite a jolly evening.

Even Adam made jokes about the way he had been duped.

Fran called Ella back as the foursome was leaving. 'I'm sorry I didn't believe you. It ended when you said it did. No hard feelings?'

'None at all. And I'm sorry for—cheating on you. You've had a raw deal all round.'

'Not any more.' Fran held out her hand. 'We'll keep in touch, won't we?'

'We certainly will.' They shook hands on the promise both knew neither would keep.

Highcroft Farm burned to the ground in the early hours of the Sunday following Philip's funeral. No one raised the alarm. The occupants of a police car patrolling between the Darringtons saw the flames lighting the sky and went to investigate. Isolated as Highcroft was, there was little fear of damage to other property and no sign of humans in the vicinity. Brunton men both and aware of recent history, they were inclined to forget what they had seen. But rules are rules. They radioed back to base that the property of the late Jack Downing had somehow caught alight and it might be an idea to let the fire brigade in on the secret.

The arsonist had prepared his bonfire well in advance. By the time the two fire engines arrived, one from Brunton, the other manned by local lads from Upper D, everything was burning nicely. The house, the stables, the barns, the caravan, the two dead cars. The dung-heap even. The firemen did little more than ensure that the conflagration did not spread. Their hoses dribbled water. A bloke could have done better after a night on the beer. It was afterwards reported, but unofficially, that the chief had been heard to issue instructions contrary to the book. Any sign of the fire going out, make sure you get the bloody thing going again.

The police came later in the day. There was little to investigate. Highcroft had been razed to the ground. They poked around perfunctorily in the ashes, shifted lumps of charcoal and kicked several rat corpses aside as they went. They returned to Brunton and wrote their reports. The file on Jack Downing and Highcroft Farm was finally closed and no one was sorry.

It was the same everywhere. Darrington learnt the news with delight and very few bothered to visit the grave. It was, after all, Sunday. A day of rest or a day of more pleasurable pursuits. The news filtered through to estate agents as they set off for golf or a visit to Mum or a drink at the local. All sighed with relief. There had been no instructions as yet but when they came Highcroft would not have been easy to sell. Too much publicity in national newspapers, too much coverage of past events in line with those more recent. Hardly a desirable residence. It would be much easier now. A valuable plot of land with potential for a large dwelling house and surrounding garden. Ample space for garages, greenhouses, swimming-pools. No renovations, alterations, modernization required, only a straightforward new beginning. Who would get in first, the developers or private buyers? They could hardly wait for the working week to begin. Speculation would be rife.

If Darrington questioned the identity of the person who had performed such a public service, it did so silently and with gratitude. But when Tom Antony took Doris down to the Foresters' that evening there were pints lined up on the bar. Several more in the pipe, Harry Junior said. It was weeks before Tom put his hand in his pocket which was something of a relief.

'Nasty bramble scratch,' he said to all who looked at the dressing but did not ask. 'Gone all pussy. Too many darned chemicals these days.'

Doris had spread salve over the angry burn that reached past his elbow without a word. She had bandaged lightly, then taken his stinking clothes to the bin in a plastic bag. Trousers, shirt, vest, the lot.

'Could have done it resting on the stove,' Tom said. 'Thinking the rings was off.'

'Could have done, Dad. That's if you were a contortionist.'

David and Ella Caine had been wakened by the fire engines rumbling past. Ella first. She had called David and they had watched from the side window in her room, watched Highcroft burn. 'Thank God for that,' Ella said, and then softly, 'Well done, Tom.'

'You can't be positive,' David said.

'Oh yes I can. That man was put on earth for a specific purpose.' They stood in silence while the flames of the huge funeral pyre leapt and crackled, finally to sink and die. 'I'll tell you something else.

361

The soul of Jack Downing can now rest in peace.'

It was much later in the day that she recalled that David's arm had been around her as they stood. And she had not moved away.

★ ★ ★ ★

'I never looked at the names above the door of the pub, did you?' Eve said. 'Fancy Toby being Pennington-Smythe. I shall never get over that. Do you think Giles is similarly afflicted?'

'Probably plain Smith or Jones. One has to retain balance.'

Bedtime for the Graysons. Adam already in there, propped against his pillows. Younger somehow without his heavy-framed glasses, long nose less accentuated. Grey hair tousled, grey eyes blinking and growing sleepy. Eve, resplendent in voluminous mauve, sat opposite. The basket chair sagged beneath cushions and her weight. Outside, summer drifting towards autumn. A nip in the air and mist lying heavy over the morning fields. Fruit picked, leaves turning, winter ready with his bags packed, ready to move in.

'All things considered, it's been a pretty bloody summer. The worst ever.'

Adam agreed. 'Not the worst time but certainly the worst summer. And certainly the bloodiest.'

'So when and where do we go? We can now, can't we? Everything's sorted more or less. Would Christmas be a good time? I had been looking forward to merry get-togethers and then I remembered there was no one left to together get.'

'So the exodus has really begun?'

'I suppose it began when Stephen went. I never thought I would say this but I feel sorry for him. He had a thoroughly rotten deal. And wasn't Jenni livid at having to sell a hundred thousand less than the Caines? Serves her right. It's still more than she deserves. I'll bet she fritters it away in no time and then starts touching up her ex for subs.'

Adam was pondering along other lines. 'Christmas, you think? The stocks ordered. We ought to be here to dispense the goodies.'

'Whoever buys can do that.'

'Provided, of course, the shop and post office continue as such. The next buyer might simply want a home.'

'Lord, I never thought of that. How ghastly. What would all the old biddies do? Buses to Brunton once a fortnight and not a mobile shop in sight. And Doris? She and Tom rely on her money. They'd lose all life's little luxuries. A trip to the Foresters' one night a year and in front of the telly for the other three hundred plus. It just isn't on.'

'Eve darling, we cannot allow our lives to be governed by others. Not any more. Time is running out.'

She looked at him steadily. 'It is, isn't it? It ran out for Philip in a single blast. All right. After Christmas. The new year, but everything signed and sealed before. How much do you think we'll get?'

'More than the Caines but I don't suppose they'll worry. When are they off, by the way?'

'Next week. Everything into store and a frightful plebeian cruise around the Bahamas and the Caribbean. Not my idea of fun. Yes to the area but thumbs down to the floating Butlin's. David's idea, Ella said. They might both meet someone, but that's a whopper on his part. He fancies her like anything, it's as plain as the nose

364

on your face and God knows that's plain enough. I don't blame him. She's very fanciable, still incredibly young-looking. Of course, she insists he has no ulterior motive. Why should he, she says? The absolute's through and they're travelling as friends. Single cabins even and won't that cost a bomb? It might do the trick though, you never know. I'd like to see those two together again.'

'And Fran gone already.' Adam smiled as he remembered. 'She was right, she did look like a minnow in an aquarium. But a very happy minnow and, given a few months, a very merry widow.'

'Months be blowed.' Eve heaved herself from the chair and crossed to close the curtains against an intrusive draught. 'She's that already. Get rid of that weight, which she firmly intends, pack the children off to school and there'll be no holding her. I'll wager she won't even remember where Philip is buried.'

'That's rather unkind,' Adam reproved.

'The truth often is. I wonder if *she* was at the funeral.'

'Which she?'

'*The* she. The other woman. Did you notice anyone lurking mysteriously in the shadows? Or dropping surreptitious flowers and tears into the grave?'

'I did not.'

'Neither did I. A figment of Fran's imagination, do you think? Tom said not and Tom knows everything. Added to which, Tom never tells. How infuriating. We'll never know, will we?' She smiled. For Eve, a very shaky smile. 'Adam, I shall miss them all horribly. The end of another road and who knows where the next will lead. I'm frightened.'

'You? Frightened? I don't believe it.'

'I am. The worst happened and we thought we'd had our share. Nothing could touch us again. But this has touched us more, it's come from so many directions.'

Adam was sitting transfixed. The un-believable was happening. Two fat tears rolled liked glycerine down Eve's cheeks and two more were gathered, ready to follow. 'That poor bastard, Jack Downing. I could have howled for him at the inquest, especially after all Ella said. And everything before and leading up. The rats and her garden and Bill, Stephen and Jenni, Emma's accident, Philip's death and Philip's duplicity. Friends gone and a new hierarchy to lead Darrington into an appalling cheek-by-jowl existence and—I'm crying!'

'I know you are. It's wonderful. Don't stop.'

'I don't think I can. There are so many tears that have gathered over the years, they have to spill. I can't send them back.' Still they rolled, faster and faster. 'I shall be soaked soon and I don't care. Oh Adam, if only you knew how it feels. Like shedding armour, like breaking down some rusty prison gate. I was too proud and too strong and much too selfish. Forgive me?'

'Come to bed, my love. There's nothing to forgive.'

'Not on your life, not yet. I don't fancy changing wet sheets at midnight.' A very watery smile. 'We would have been grandparents now, have you ever thought of that? Beautiful children, just like Edward. I wonder what they would have done. Something splendid, of course, because he was. He was, wasn't he? Our son was beautiful and splendid and we miss him still. We ache for him, we long to hold him, to touch his cheeks and his hair. Don't we, Adam, don't we?'

'We do, Eve. We always will.' Tears now

from Adam but more in sympathy for Eve. His mourning had already been dispensed. 'Come to bed now.'

'I will in a minute. I need more time.' Silence, while the stiff upper lip trembled. Silence, while twenty years spilled over and were washed away.

'You're free now, Eve,' Adam said gently.

'I know. I'm glad and I'm grateful. But tell me, O wise one, why does being free hurt so much?'